More Praise for *Perfect*

"Breezy, addictive...Kick is a delightful protagonist: utterly indulgent and yet self-disciplined, needing only herself to get through life, but loving her husband for the fun of it. Kellogg's burnished prose deftly immerses readers in a deeply pleasurable world of shameless wealth."

—*Kirkus Reviews*

"Delightful and charming."   —*Midwest Book Review*

"The world of...Kick Keswick is a nice place to linger."
—*Kansas City Star*

"Will transport readers to a world where caviar and champagne are as common as a glass of ice water."
—*The Roanoke Times* (Virginia)

"An arch tone and a terrific sense of humor...airy, light, and delicious."   —*Rocky Mountain News*

"This is just what you need for those last glorious days at the beach."   —*The Seattle Times*

PERFECT

PERFECT

MARNE DAVIS KELLOGG

ST. MARTIN'S GRIFFIN
NEW YORK

www.stmartins.com

Library of Congress Cataloging-in-Publication Data

Kellog, Marne Davis.
    Perfect / Marne Davis Kellogg.
        p. cm.
    ISBN-13: 978-0-312-33733-9
    ISBN-10: 0-312-33733-7
    1. Keswick, Kick (Fictitious character)—Fiction. 2. Women private investigators—Europe—Fiction. 3. Queens—Crimes against—Fiction. 4. Americans—Europe—Fiction. 5. Europe—Fiction. I. Title.

PS3561.E39253P47 2005
813'.54—dc22
                                                                2005042778

First St. Martin's Griffin Edition: February 2007

10 9 8 7 6 5 4 3 2 1

For Peter,

my beloved husband of twenty-five years,

who just keeps opening door after door

ACKNOWLEDGMENTS

There is something about writing the adventures of Kick Keswick that transports me—and more importantly, my readers—into believing we've become Superwomen, Wonder Women, super-rich, super-action heroines, so it's always startling to me, when I've finished writing for the day, or finished a book altogether, to realize that I don't actually have secret caches of diamonds, or unlimited amounts of Euros in various Swiss banks, or a farm in Provence. But I do have other, equally fine, compensations.

All this luscious knowledge of *la dolce vita* requires serious and meticulous research and I'm grateful mostly to Peter, who takes us regularly to Kick Keswick's favorite haunts. I thank also Bob Gibson at Raymond C. Yard, Inc., in New York; Brien Foster at Foster & Son in Denver; and Cartier and Van Cleef & Arpels in Paris, for their ongoing assistance and expertise in the world of magnificent gems and jewelry. I'm also grateful to Leslie Field for her extraordinary book, *The Queen's Jewels,* which has been an important resource in the writing of this novel.

The food in *Perfect* runs the gamut from lamb ragout to chocolate soufflé to devil's food cake, which Susan Coe made sure was workable. I thank my dearest darling for our twenty-fifth anniversary trip to London and Paris and the dinners at Carré de Feuillants, Chez George, and most particularly, our anniversary celebration at L'Espadon, where the table was covered with rose petals. I have no idea what we ate, but I do remember that it was the best, most memorable, and most romantic dinner I've ever had.

Blair and Suzanne Taylor at the Barolo Grill in Denver helped with the wines, and some are even affordable! If you can find them. Kick Keswick has a very refined, sophisticated palate.

Thanks also to Leslie Carlson, general manager of the Garden of the Gods Club. Leslie and her staff took beautiful care of me and the dog during my writing sojourn there.

As always, any mistakes are mine.

The more I write, the more I appreciate what it takes to make a book succeed at every level—the actual storytelling and writing are just the first steps. I am extremely blessed to have such a superb team of professionals dedicated to the same goal: making each novel the best it possibly can be. In particular, I thank Sally Richardson, publisher, St. Martin's Press, and Jennifer Enderlin, associate publisher and executive editor. Working with Jennifer is rich and rewarding—her vision, creative input, and knowledge are amazing and energizing. In fact, sometimes I think she actually *is* Kick Keswick. I also thank her assistant Kimberly Cardascia, who is surrounded by artistes but remains responsive, organized, and unflappable; John Karle, publicist extraordinaire, for his energy and innovation; and finally, copy editor Deborah Miller, whose knowledge and attention to detail not only almost gave me a nervous breakdown, but also brought me to a whole new level of appreciation and gratitude for the profession of copyediting.

My agent Robert Gottlieb, president and CEO, Trident Media Group, and Kimberly Whalen, vice president and managing director of foreign rights, are always available, interested, and thinking. I am very, very fortunate to be represented by such an outstanding, committed team.

I thank God every day for my family and friends—for their loyalty, steadfastness, and enthusiasm for my writing. My love and undying thanks to: Mary and Richard, who invite me over and take my calls even when they might just like to catch up with each other—they are also my opera experts; Mary Lou and Randy, who had a little bit too exciting of a year, and we thank God that you are still with us M.L., and appreciate that you continue, so selflessly, to do all that grueling shopping and restaurant research in Paris; Marcy and Bruce seem to know everyone and I am very grateful that they do, because they have opened many, many doors for me, in addition to throwing another beautiful launch party; Pam and Bill offer us wonderful, solid friendship that we treasure, particularly during this period while Hunter is in Iraq; Margaret and Mike for a perfect party in their garden; Mita Vail and the Norfolk Book Ladies, who are always available to toss a champagne-driven literary fête; my next-door neighbor Judith; Susan and Doug; my architect cousin, Bridget; the ladies of the Denver Debutante Ball, and the awesome cowgirls of the National Western.

I am grateful for all the Connecticut Kelloggs and the Colorado Davises; for my darling mother's grace, courage, and sense of adventure; for Major Hunter R. Kellogg, USMC, his elegant, remarkable wife Courtney, and their Duncan and Delaney; Peter and his fiancée, Bede; our wire fox terrier, Kick, who makes me laugh all the time, and, of course, for my beloved Peter, who never stops taking my breath away. Finally, I thank God, because the fact is, I just get up in the morning and say, "Okay, Lord, what's up for today?" And these stories come out, it's as simple as that.

Marne Davis Kellogg
Denver, Colorado

PERFECT

PROLOGUE

"When did you last wear these?" Bradford picked up the long diamond-and-emerald earrings and held them close to his ears.

"I'm not sure," Elizabeth—Lilibet to her friends and family—answered. "Montreal perhaps? You're the one with the list. What does it say?"

Bradford put down the earrings and picked up his clipboard. "You're right. Montreal."

"May I tell you something, Bradford? Strictly entre nous?"

"Of course, ma'am."

She looked into his gray-blue eyes. "I don't want to go on this trip. I'm actually quite dreading it. If you would change your mind and come along, it would make all the difference."

His eyes filled with tears. "Oh, ma'am. What can I say? If you order me to go, I will. But my back is in such terrible condition. . . ." He patted his midriff where a heavy back brace made an uncomfortable outline through his jacket. "I would be more of a burden than a help."

"I know." It appeared for a moment that she might put her hand on his to comfort him, but then she remembered herself and withdrew the nascent gesture. "Of course I won't make you go, but I'm going to miss you so."

A blast of icy wind threw sheets of cold London rain against the windows, making them rattle.

"On the other hand," he said, looking outside, "when I think of the stop in the Seychelles, that warm air on my aching back—perhaps I'll resume my duties there."

"That could be arranged."

Although her formality—even with close friends and family—was legendary, she gazed at him with real tenderness, affection, and heartfelt gratitude for his decades of service. He'd been her most-trusted servant and confidant. He'd never let her down, had never been indiscreet, was always there, right at her elbow, ready to do whatever she required or requested without complaint or question—all that in spite of his increasingly frail health, that in her heart of hearts, she attributed mostly to his hypochondria. He was her Rock of Gibraltar. She stepped to the next ensemble. "Let's finish," she said.

"Evening clothes are last." He picked up his clipboard and turned to the beaded gowns and silk evening suits that hung around the perimeter of her enormous dressing room like costumes from an extravagant opera. Each had a folding wooden camp table in front of it, arranged with the handbag, shoes, gloves, jewelry, and medals to be worn with the ensemble. All the elements of each outfit had been tagged and numbered and were accompanied with written instructions as to where and when they were to be worn. There was no possibility for mistake or confusion.

Across the room, six black metal trunks the size of regular suitcases—they were, in reality, heavily armored transport safes—stood open on heavy-duty luggage racks beneath the windows, ready to receive the jewels as soon as each outfit was completed. At that point, Bradford would close the jewelry boxes—many of the pieces were still in the cases in which they'd been received, the leather and velvet linings worn with age and use, their original gift cards tucked inside—and place them in one of the trunks.

"What are your plans?" she asked as he double-checked his list.

"I'll be at my cottage in Sussex. You know how I love to garden, and I have an excellent man helping me until my back gets stronger."

She smiled. "I'll miss your roses."

"I'll send them up regularly."

"Good. I'll like that."

They had stopped in front of a plain white satin ball gown with a pleated décolletage and elbow-length sleeves. Wide bands of seed pearls and brilliants circled the cuffs and hem. The gown's attendant regalia was so complicated, it required two tables to hold it all.

"So beautiful in Sussex," she said, and picked up a five-inch-tall diamond tiara, each of its five points punctuated with a large emerald. The scrolls and festoons of its design were so intricate it almost looked like a crown of starched lace. " 'May's best tiara,' " she said. "That's what Grandfather called it."

"Yes, madam."

"This is for Delhi."

"Yes, madam."

"I haven't seen the whole parure assembled for over forty years. It's quite breathtaking, isn't it?"

"Indeed. There is nothing else like it."

Lilibet picked up the emerald-and-diamond necklace with its negligée of diamond-and-emerald pendants of unequal lengths.

"Granny quite moved heaven and earth to get these pieces assembled, didn't she?"

"And"—Bradford's eyes sparkled—"it's said she cracked a few skulls in the process, as well."

They shared a little laugh.

She studied the necklace. "I'm not sure I want to take it with me— not sure it should leave the country." She turned to him. "Perhaps I should take the copies."

Bradford shook his head. "Don't worry, ma'am. They will be well looked after. You haven't made a tour like this for many years. It requires such a show."

"I know you're right. As usual." She replaced the piece lovingly in its velvet case. "I wonder if it will really be my last, my farewell tour."

"I rather doubt it, but it will be stupendous, a royal tour of all the Empire's former colonies. It will be a grand time—practically all of Africa. When was the last time you were in Kenya? Or South Africa and Mozambique?" As he spoke, he stacked up the individual cases that held the parure—except for the tiara, which had its own traveling box—and carried them to their designated transport safe. He kept his back to her as he set the jewel cases in the trunk and swiftly replaced their contents with strings of marbles he'd stashed in the trunk earlier. The original pieces slipped into his pocket more smoothly and quickly than the eye could see—at least an old, trusting eye, like Elizabeth's— tumbling silently into a nest of shredded cotton. "I understand the people in the Seychelles have planned a parade around all the islands! India, Australia, Hong Kong, Canada, a state dinner at the White House. Oh, my. It will be positively majestic. A true 'Progress,' ma'am."

"More majestic if you were along to make sure everything goes just so." She was starting to sound a little peevish.

"Now, ma'am, we've been over this before. All will be meticulously looked after by Michael. I've seen to that."

Bradford and Elizabeth were well trained—possibly the best trained people in the world—in the art of keeping their emotions under complete control at all times. And he gave no indication that not only was he impatient with her growing petulance, but he was also concerned that she would change her mind and insist he come along. She certainly had the power to do so and he'd seen her impose her will more than once. This was no time to slip up, no matter how difficult the good-bye. They moved to the next table.

He picked up a sapphire blue evening suit and held it up in front of her. "This is the most perfect color. It is exactly the color of madam's eyes. Just beautiful."

She smiled.

"It's to be worn at the state dinner in Cape Town." A black leather jewel case with a faded blue velvet custom-molded lining sat open on the table. "I thought the Lesser Stars would be the right touch."

"Brilliant. You always think of the right thing. Michael won't be able to think of this sort of refinement." There was the tone again, getting close to a whine.

"Oh, ma'am, that's not true," Bradford reassured her, hiding his irritation at the bead of sweat that rolled down the back of his neck from beneath his toupee. "He's much more of a history buff and protocol expert than I."

"Hmmm," she said skeptically. "We shall see. I don't believe they've been back to South Africa since they left." She picked up the simple unadorned brooch, one diamond above the other. With their combined carat-weight of 158, the Lesser Stars of Africa—the *Cullinans III and IV*—were so enormous they didn't require any dressing up. "I never wear them and they're so magnificent." She gently placed the diamonds back in their case where they smoldered from the velvet like briquette-sized coals.

"Yes, madam." Bradford checked his watch. Her musing was beginning to put them behind schedule.

They continued their circuit, with Bradford naming each outfit and pointing out each suite of accessories and accompanying jewelry, and then, in a ceremony as old as time, she watched as he latched and locked each jewel case and melted a large disk of wax across the rim, sealing the safe shut. Together they pressed their signet rings into the soft red seal. Once the wax had cooled and hardened, Bradford zipped the cases into anonymous, tightly-fitted khaki canvas covers, turning them into ordinary-looking luggage.

It was time to say good-bye. Lilibet faced him from a proper distance. She kept her hands folded in front of her.

"How long have you been with me?"

"Over thirty years, madam. I was only twenty-three when I joined your household staff."

She shook her head. "It seems like yesterday." Her eyes took him in—his frail countenance, the wonderful bright eyes behind his tortoiseshell bifocals, eyes that never missed a thing. The expensive dark brown toupee.

"I shall miss you, my Bradford Quittle."

He bowed deeply. "It has been my honor and privilege to serve Your Majesty."

She turned and left the room.

Shortly, Bradford rang for the guards to take the boxes to Norfolk Airport, where they would travel in their own unmarked business jet to Cape Town, the first stop on the queen's farewell tour of the Commonwealth.

ONE

"Kick?" Thomas's back was to me as he stooped to toss another log and a bouquet of dried lavender onto the fire.

"Yes?"

"We need your help on something." He put his hand on the small of his back and straightened himself with a slight wince before turning to look at me, his bright blue eyes serious above his black-rimmed reading glasses.

It was wintertime in Provence and we were sitting in our living room, sipping hot cider laced with rum, and enjoying a rare snowstorm that hid the valley and Les Alpilles, the Little Alps, behind a wall of whirling white. Lamps on the side tables and my long book table beneath the picture window cast a warm glow, silhouetting the drinks tray and stacks of books against the starkness outside. The bookcases on the far wall were in shadows, but above the mantel a small light illuminated my most treasured painting, *La Polonaise Blanche* by Renoir— skaters whirling on a pond in an almost pink snowstorm. Our Westie, Bijou, was curled up on the cut-stone hearth, sound asleep, a fluffy little indoor snowball unconcerned by the change in weather and uninterested in anything not directly related to her stomach or her comfort.

" 'We'?" I said, feeling a little like the dog, fully enjoying the snugness of my champagne-and-salmon paisley armchair and ottoman, and the cozy softness of my cashmere warm-up suit and the persimmon cashmere throw over my legs. It was absolutely heavenly, and I was unreceptive to anything that might mar this perfect day. "That sounds rather regal, Thomas. Are the snow and cold making you homesick for England? Missing the royal 'we'?"

"Well, in fact it is the royal 'we'." He swept fallen bits of bark and spattered coals back into the fire before replacing the iron screen. He rubbed his hands together.

"Of course it is, darling." I returned to my needlepoint, a pale yellow canvas covered in bright red cherries with their stems and a few leaves attached here and there. I thought it would make an apt addition to the chaise in our bedroom. Some people have pillows scattered around their houses that say things like "Chocolate is Life." Or "If You're Going to Run Away from Home, Please Take Me with You." Or "Give Me the Luxuries of Life—It's the Necessities I Can Do Without." A statement I can relate to fully. But the fact is, I'm not a talking-pillow kind of woman. I'm more interested in subtleties and refinements, in living the message, not talking about it. Living a life, not intending to. I loved the cherries because, in fact, our life was a bowl of them. What a thing to be able to say after decades of running and hiding and lying. I've finally arrived at the safe harbor I pictured all those dozens of years ago. But interestingly, I'd never imagined a lover, a husband, a partner, a friend as a part of that vision, but here he was. My Thomas.

If people knew what a completely unlikely couple we are, they would never believe it.

"I'm not joking, Kick." There was an attention-getting sharpness to his voice.

"Excuse me?"

"We need your help. It's serious and highly confidential."

"All right, Thomas." I put down my sewing and sat up a little straighter. I was an expert at confidentiality. I have more secrets than the Sphinx. You don't get to be the greatest jewel thief in history by blabbing what you know. Correction: the greatest *retired* jewel thief in history. "Tell me what it is."

Thomas, one of Scotland Yard's most distinguished, highly decorated, and revered inspectors, also claims to be retired, but things keep cropping up here and there, assignments, secret calls. All very hush-hush. I don't care for it.

"The queen has a problem."

It was my turn to look at him over my reading glasses. "The queen? And she needs *my* help?"

Thomas nodded. "She does," he paused. "I do."

I studied his face. "I think you've had too much rum, my darling sweetheart, or else we need to go to the sun for a rest."

Being married, which I was very new to, is an extremely complicated affair. You make a number of serious promises, and if you want to keep a rich and honest relationship—honesty being something I was new to as well—you can't just say and do whatever you want, whenever you want. So I bit the inside of my lip to keep from saying no. Absolutely not. Whatever it is, I'm not interested. Find someone else.

"I know what you're thinking." Thomas retrieved my mug and took it to the cocktail tray, which he'd set on top of stacks of art and antiquities auction catalogues. "Just let me tell you about it."

He measured double tots of rum and poured them into our mugs and then dropped a spoonful of clove-scented butter into each. Then he added a small splash of steaming cider from a stainless steel electric pot that simmered away atop a massive volume of Impressionists that no one had looked inside of for years. He replaced the used cinnamon sticks with fresh ones and stirred absent-mindedly. The silence was deafening.

There was a small—I might even say smug—smile on his lips when he brought me my drink. "Careful, it's hot," he warned, and then circled the coffee table and sat down opposite me on the matching ot-toman. He took a slow sip of the steaming rum, placed his mug delib-erately on the table, and then examined his hands as though he were considering whether or not to have a manicure.

"Thomas, if all of this pedantic pondering is some sort of police tac-tic designed to make suspects crack and spill the beans, as I believe you all call it, it's extremely impressive, and I thank you for sharing it with me. Now, kindly say whatever it is you have on your mind or pick up your book and read, because you're coming very close to ruining my perfect day."

"Sorry." He grinned and put his elbows on his knees, clasped his hands together, and stared deeply into my eyes as though he were searching for something. I suspected, deep down, he was wondering if he could trust me.

"Thomas, I'm going to count to ten."

"There's been a robbery," he finally said. "Some of the queen's jewels are missing."

TWO

I'd be lying if I said that my skin and scalp didn't buzz up a bit at the mention of the word "robbery" in conjunction with the words "the queen's jewels." My heart skipped a beat or two. Like any addict, I had to remind myself almost on a daily basis that I was no longer a thief. I was rehabilitated. I was out of the business.

"Oh?" I said with as much disinterest as I could muster.

"The items vanished on the first leg of her world tour."

I squeezed my lips shut to keep from asking what was missing.

"A number of significant pieces are gone." Thomas pulled a piece of paper from the inside pocket of his jacket and scrutinized it. "Let me see. I'm not sure exactly what these pieces are—you might have heard of them. The Cambridge and Delhi Durbar parure . . ."

"Par-rheur," I corrected him. I worked to keep my voice steady. The emerald-and-diamond parure was one of the rarest and most beautiful ensembles in the queen's collection.

"Excuse me?"

"It's pronounced par-rheur. A parure is a set of five pieces: tiara, necklace, earrings, bracelet and brooch, or in the case of the Cambridge and Delhi Durbar parure, a stomacher." I touched my head, neck, ears, wrist, and bosom as I said each item. "And I seriously doubt the queen would take the entire set out of the country at the same time—they're far too valuable, and no one's seen that fantastically tall gingerbread tiara in almost a hundred years."

"I see. Thank you." He ignored my patronization and returned to the list. "And something called the Lesser Stars of Africa."

My mouth fell open. "You're not serious."

"Completely."

"Granny's Chips?"

"Pardon?"

"That's what King George called them because they're chips off the Cullinan."

Thomas was expressionless.

"The largest diamond ever discovered," I said. "Over three thousand carats. Ringing any bells?"

"Your point being?"

"My point, Thomas," I said indignantly, "is that it's the single most valuable piece the queen owns. It's made of the Cullinans Three and Four. I mean, good heavens. This is outrageous. How on earth did such a thing happen? It must have been a family member or one of her servants."

"Quite."

"Who discovered they were missing?"

"If I may proceed." Thomas was so dogmatic—heaven forbid one should veer off the course of process, but naturally that was what had made him such a gifted detective—I could tell he was becoming irritated with all my questions. "When the queen got to Cape Town on the first stop of her tour, a number of the jewel boxes were stuffed with marbles packed in cotton."

"And she's asked you to help?"

"Well . . ." Thomas couldn't help but preen. He had an ego the size of the Taj Mahal, which, of course, was one of the reasons I loved him so. His self-confidence was absolutely impenetrable. "There *is* precedent. I've worked covertly in the queen's service from time to time and I have pulled off some fairly major coups in my career. Besides, she'd rather not have this made public. If she were to call in Scotland Yard, word would inevitably get out."

"I'm beginning to understand. By major coups, I assume you're referring to our 'Millennium Star Affair.'" I held up my fingers to emphasize the quotation marks. "For which you received all the credit while I did all the leg work."

Thomas opened his mouth to speak, but I didn't give him a chance.

"Please don't get me wrong, darling. I'm delighted you received the accolades. You know how crucial anonymity is to me, but I've got the picture: she thinks you're the one who recovered the Millennium Star, and if you could do it once, you could do it again."

Thomas colored. "She's based her judgment on that as well as other services I've performed exclusively for her in the past. But all that's beside the point in this particular instance. The point is, I'm now far too visible a personality to take on any sort of clandestine work—everyone knows who I am. . . ."

"Really, Thomas. That's one of the things I love about you—you're so humble and self-effacing."

He gave me an almost impish smile of acknowledgment and appreciation. ". . . so I thought perhaps we could work together—something inside the law for a change of pace."

I caught the twinkle in his eye. "Where do you think they are?"

"I'm not one hundred percent certain *where* they are but we are fairly confident about who has them. The queen's personal footman, Bradford Quittle, retired, in good standing I must add, when she left on the tour, and vanished. He has recently been spotted in the company of Constantin."

"You mean King Constantin?"

"No. I mean the opera singer."

"Oh. How disappointing. It would be so much more interesting if it were the king of Greece." There was always such backstabbing and skullduggery going on amongst the royal families over their possessions, most especially their jewels, it had practically taken on the characteristics of a sport. And in spite of the fact that I'd retired, I would have loved to get in the middle of one of those notorious royal squabbles.

For instance, much of the queen's current collection is due to her grandmother, Queen Mary, who could spot an opportunity when she saw it and drive as hard a bargain as the most skillful rug trader. When her cousins, the desperate and beleaguered remainder of the Romanoff family, escaped the revolution and staggered into Sweden without tuppence to their name (but with much of the royal jewelry sewn into their hems and hats) and asked Queen Mary to care for them, give them sanctuary—naturally she agreed. They were, after all, family. But there were conditions, of course, though reasonable ones: they'd have to pay for their room and board with whatever they could muster, which of course turned out to be their best jewelry, which they grudgingly handed over because they had no choice. Today, many of those old Russian jewels comprise some of the most fabulous pieces in the current queen's collection, a fact that still rankles what's left of the disenfranchised, disinherited, disenchanted, and discombobulated Romanoffs to this day.

"The two men have been traveling together," Thomas continued. "My associate, David Perkins—he used to be my top aide at the Yard, retired the same time I did, wonderful, talented man—reports that the footman, who has changed his name to Sebastian Tremaine, has a large briefcase that he keeps with him all the time."

"And you think the jewels are in the briefcase?"

Thomas nodded with assurance. "Quite certain. What else could it be?"

"Constantin's music?"

"Kick."

"I'm sorry, Thomas. This just all seems so far-fetched to me."

"I know, it sounds crazy, but it's not. Here's what I'd like you to consider—you don't have to say yes or no right this minute. I'd simply like you to give it some thought. Constantin is giving a private charity concert in St. Moritz in a week, and I thought that would be a good place for you to start."

"St. Moritz, Switzerland? In February? You know I never even go outside when it's cold."

"I need you to."

"Why doesn't your associate, what's his name—David—just steal the case?"

"Nobody can get near these men. Constantin has so many body-guards, it's like a small army."

"What makes you think I could get through?"

"If anybody can, Kick, it's you."

Well, he was right, of course.

"You're our only hope."

"But . . . Switzerland?" I cringed.

He nodded. "It's all taken care of."

"What does that mean, 'taken care of'? How?"

Thomas had cast his line and now he sank the hook. "There's a large suite reserved in your name at Badrutt's Palace Hotel. We've also made train reservations for you to St. Moritz via Zurich, very comfortable, a private compartment—I know how much you love the train. As far as expenses go, the sky's the limit. Spend whatever it takes." He looked at me. "Will you think about it, Kick?"

"I'll think about it."

"Good." He sat down and picked up his book. He was completely re-laxed. His message delivered.

I, on the other hand, who had been so relaxed and happy, watching the snow from my cozy little living room, sipping my hot toddy, was now all a-spin.

How could he just sit there and read when the queen's jewels were missing? I wish I understood more about men.

I put down my sewing, picked up my mug, and headed for the kitchen. "Pick out a wine, will you?"

"I'll be right there."

THREE'

My kitchen in Provence has been the center of my universe since I bought La Petite Pomme twenty-five years ago. I am rooted to the earth in this wonderfully sunny room—as though an invisible magnet holds me in place. It has since the first moment I stepped through the door. Even for all the years I lived in London and could only visit the farm for an occasional week or two throughout the year, just transporting myself mentally to my kitchen brought me serenity and focus.

The walls are yellow, the cabinets white, and the counters are blue-and-white tile. My stainless-steel refrigerator door and the quilted stainless panel behind my six-burner range gleam—thanks to the elbow grease my houseman, Pierre, puts into them—as do the copper pots and pans stacked conveniently on open shelves beneath the counter. We are old friends. Beautiful food and cooking bring me almost as much pleasure as precious gems, which, until I met Thomas, provided the only long-term relationship I'd ever fully committed to in my life.

I have so many things to say about food and its place in our lives, I could probably write a book. Let me simply say, there's more to life than watching one's weight. I'm not saying we should all just eat whatever we want whenever we want, that would be dangerous and foolhardy, but I was born with an extra twenty-five pounds. Now, I could lose the weight and spend the rest of my life watching everything I eat, denying myself the pleasure of things I love for the sake of . . . what? Wearing a bathing suit? And where on earth would I do that? I've never been in the sun for more than a few minutes at a time, and even then I'm completely covered. No. I choose to accept that I am beautiful enough as I am. I have plenty of beauty to go around. I'm more interested in taking full advantage of all the richness life has to offer because you never know. You might be the next in line to leave the planet— wouldn't you hate to do that having had just celery, carrot sticks, and a yogurt for lunch?

Much better to have just had a steaming bowl of thick vegetable soup, a crusty baguette with butter to sop it up, and a glass of clear, ruby red burgundy.

Anyhow, many of the most pleasurable things we remember through our lives have happened around the table. You might not remember the rainstorm that drenched you on the way to meet your lover for lunch, but you will remember sitting and staring at him across the table, the tall windows fogged and streaked from the weather. The laughter and the wine and the pleasure of the meal. The excitement of the conversation and the stolen touch of your knees beneath the table and the entwining of your fingers across the top. You might not remember specifically the dense flavor of the herbed butter on the grilled steak, the salty crunch of the pommes frites, the tartness of the braised leeks, and the wonderful dense fruit of the Bordeaux, but you will never forget the mounting anticipation of dessert or the chocolates and Champagne as you loll under the covers in the room upstairs afterward. You will always remember that the entire occasion was centered around the sheer sensuousness and intimacy of that wonderful, unforgettable meal, whatever it was.

A pot of lamb-and-olive ragout simmered on the stove, filling the kitchen with the aromas of fresh rosemary and garlic. I put on a clean white chef's jacket and checked my lipstick before going to work. I always have to be completely squared away before I can do anything, including cook. My kitchen and my makeup must be in perfect order. I looked wonderful—healthy, calm, relaxed. Except, unfortunately, I saw just the slightest dart about my expression. I didn't want to look myself in the eye too closely. I was afraid of what I would see. A little too much sparkle, possibly. That little fizz of excitement brought on by the queen's misfortune? The possibility that I might have the opportunity to touch the Cambridge and Delhi Durbar parure and the Lesser Stars of Africa with my own two hands, see them face-to-face? Hide them in my pockets?

No!

I separated three cloves of garlic and crushed them with the side of a knife, separating them from their skins. I dropped the cloves into the mortar and sprinkled them with salt and mushed them around a bit before adding olive oil and pulverizing them completely. I set them aside and then began to assemble the ingredients for a chocolate soufflé.

Soufflés are a staple of my repertoire. When in doubt, or a small hurry, a cheese soufflé, a fresh green salad, and a bottle of burgundy are always the right solution. And when it's cold and storming outside, there couldn't be a finer combination than rich lamb stew, an arugula salad, crispy garlic crostini, a big bottle of Syrah, and a mouth-watering chocolate soufflé with Grand Marnier cream.

The Lesser Stars of Africa.

How on earth did he get away with such a robbery? Even if he was her closest aide, the security around the queen and her jewelry is among the tightest on earth.

The queen's collection was the finest in the world—dozens of magnificent, irreplaceable pieces that I knew by heart. I could name and describe practically every single one of them in intricate detail, as well as the permutations of each: which brooch came apart and became ear clips or the twinkling centerpiece in a tiara. Which ones hooked together to make a stomacher—a grand, complicated cascade of jewels falling from the center of a monarch's bust to her waist, a creation seldom seen today at public affairs—as opposed to a corsage, an elaborate piece draped from side to side across the corsage of a low-cut or strapless gown. Often, a jeweled corsage could also double as a necklace.

For centuries, the royal family has had a staggering stockpile of jewels, but Queen Mary raised the bar when it came to assembling a massive and breathtaking collection of large, and often priceless, stones. The majority of her efforts—in addition to the Romanoff pieces—comprise the current queen's favorite jewels.

What a wonderful coincidence that many of the largest diamonds in the world, including the largest diamond ever discovered, the whopping 3,106-carat Cullinan—uncut, it was the size of a large brick—were discovered in English colonies during her husband, King Edward's, reign. What a terrible waste it would have been if the reigning queen hadn't cared about the unprecedented, blinding haul that poured through her door, as though Ali Baba's cave were being delivered to her palace every day. I like to think that the fact that she personally received all 102 cleavings of the Cullinan as a gift from the South African government made her as giddy as she could get. I'm quite sure she dreamed about them and fondled them and loved them more than she loved her children, even more than she loved her dogs.

The Cullinan cleavings—in the gemstone business, *cleaving* or *cleavage* is the term used for rough diamonds that have at some time in their history been cleaved from a larger stone—are all numbered: The 530-carat Cullinan I, the Greater Star of Africa, sits atop the royal scepter like a transparent, slightly blue, baseball-sized pear. The Second Star of Africa, the 317.4-carat Cullinan II, is in the imperial state crown, placed there in 1911 by George V for his coronation. And so on and so forth down through the Cullinan number 102, which I must admit I have no idea where it can be found today. Some lesser royal's lesser brooch, no doubt.

Queen Mary had power, vision, and a will of iron. In her official

Durbar portrait—where she wears the now-missing Cambridge and Delhi Durbar parure—there is no question that she is empress. Although she was petite, she had the attitude of a giant.

I love to study portraits and photographs of her—I have never seen such a stern, inflexible countenance. And, in the few images where she appears to be trying to smile, it's clearly such a distasteful, unnecessary, *unfamiliar* exercise that it's agonizing to look at—she always looks as though she's just taken a bite of a pickle. She was aloof and unreadable. Did a real woman's tender heart beat behind that battleship of a bosom or had the circumstances of her position, duty, and life force it to become as impenetrable as lead at an early age?

Her family had been publicly humiliated when she was a young woman, just sixteen. Her father, Francis, duke of Teck, and her mother, Princess Mary Adelaide, had lived way beyond their means and were financially supported primarily by Mary Adelaide's brother, the wealthy duke of Cambridge. At some point, brought on by I don't know what monetary crisis, the duke of Cambridge had had enough. With Queen Victoria's full knowledge and support, he demanded that the Tecks give up their "grace and favor" residence at Kensington Palace, publicly auction their furniture, and move to Florence, which they did, and where they managed to survive for a while on a very tight budget.

I suspect after that, Queen Mary's only real pleasure came from her jewels; they were her lovers and comforters. They kept her warm on cold nights and secure from revisiting the mortifying, impoverished circumstances she suffered as an impressionable and possibly sensitive young woman. Her jewels gave her power and independence. They would never let her down.

Queen Mary and I have a lot in common.

FOUR

I removed the lid from the stew pot and let a billow of fragrant steam envelop me. I stirred and then tested a piece of lamb, cutting it with the edge of my spoon. It was as soft as butter. I put the lid back on and lowered the heat. I turned the oven to 375 degrees and double-checked that every soufflé ingredient was laid out in proper order.

There are a number of things you need to know about making a chocolate soufflé. Unless you're a very gifted cook, you can't just assume it's like anything else and jump in and get it together. After years and years of experimenting, and experiencing one version of a flop after another, I now follow exclusively Julia Child's chocolate soufflé recipe. For me it is foolproof. This is a very different creation from other dessert soufflés because chocolate is heavy—you use potato starch instead of flour to make the roux, three rather than four egg yolks; it will need ten to fifteen minutes longer to bake (up to forty-five minutes); and the temperature of each element must be just right. One more thing: no matter how many times you've made a soufflé of any kind, do not talk to anyone while you are preparing it. The steps are easy to do and easy to follow, but they are precise and cannot be short-cut, tinkered with, or relaxed about. Just keep your eye on the target, there will be plenty of time to talk later when you're all sitting around admiring the airy extravaganza and praising what a genius of a cook you are. I've always forced myself to adhere to this rule of total concentration, but today it was a struggle to keep my mind on the subject at hand and from sailing off into one scenario after another of how this person, this footman, could have absconded with such a huge haul from his queen. It was unbelievable.

I buttered a six-cup soufflé mold and, in another allowance for the properties of chocolate, sprinkled it with flour, not sugar.

I took a large, sharp knife, slivered three and half ounces of semi-sweet chocolate off a one-pound block, scraped it into the top of a double boiler over scarcely simmering water, and added a little espresso.

St. Moritz. One of the most exclusive, expensive resorts in the world. Thomas obviously didn't have a clue what he was saying when he said "St. Moritz" and "unlimited budget" in the same sentence. But, then again, if the queen were paying . . . was there something else to this? Something Thomas hasn't told me? What did he mean when he said he'd performed a number of covert services for the queen over the years?

I stirred the starch and milk together in a saucepan, added a little sugar, and let them come quickly to the boil. Within seconds it was a thick, gluey mess. I immediately pulled the pan off the heat and beat in the hot, melted chocolate, laid a few pats of butter over the top, and set it aside to cool. Letting this mixture reach close to room temperature is one of the key steps to a successful chocolate soufflé.

Now for the eggs. Five whites into a large bowl and three yolks into a small one. I threw away the other two yolks. Some cooks keep extra whites and yolks in the freezer for future use, but when I need them, I need them and I can't use them if they're frozen, and that's assuming I even remember they're in the freezer in the first place.

A large suite at the Palace Hotel. I have a policy about traveling: I'm not interested in staying anywhere that isn't nicer than my own home. But from what I'd heard over the years, I was quite sure Badrutt's Palace would come close.

The egg whites quickly came together into stiff peaks before I added a little sugar and by then the chocolate batter was cool enough to receive the yolks without cooking them. In they went, whisked until well blended. Then the egg whites folded in delicately. Then the whole affair went into the baker and into the oven.

I sliced a loaf of bread for the crostini, laid the slices on the grill, and kept a close eye on them while they browned.

"I thought a nice fat Syrah would be perfect with the ragout," Thomas interrupted my reverie. He set a bottle of 1999 Chapelle Jaboulet Hermitage on the counter and began to remove the capsule.

"Absolutely." I brushed the toasts with olive oil, scrubbed them vigorously with sliced garlic, and sprinkled them with crunchy crystals of Fleur de Sel and ground pepper.

Well, it can't hurt to ask a few more questions, can it?

By the end of lunch, he'd sunk the hook in fast and reeled me in. Thomas can be very persuasive. I agreed to take on the assignment.

The soufflé was perfect. We ate it in bed with a bottle of Champagne.

I slept little that night. I focused instead on creating a feasible strategy and scenario, and each time I created a plan, I ran through it from beginning to end, testing every possible angle and pitfall. Many ideas were discarded, but finally, about two-thirty in the morning, all the pieces fell into place and after another couple of hours of testing its merits, I felt confident I had a bulletproof strategy. It would be complicated and possibly even dangerous, but it would work. I got up and made a pot of coffee and sat quietly in the living room, just staring across the now moonlit valley, testing and testing, examining every contingency.

Pierre, my houseman, arrived at seven to drop off the newspapers, croissant, and baguette. I was already dressed in my favorite pink warm-up suit and soft leather ballet slippers.

"Pierre," I said. "I think Monsieur has time to look at the new tractor-mower this morning. Does that suit you?"

He nodded.

"Good. I'll let him know."

After breakfast, Thomas and Bijou left for town to pick up the mail and to meet Pierre at the tractor dealer in Salon. They would be gone for at least two hours.

As soon as his Porsche disappeared down the drive, I went into my bathroom and locked the door. I pushed the rug aside and pressed a tiny, invisible button that is flush with the bottom of the window sill. With a scarcely distinguishable click, a panel of floor tiles was released. Beneath it lay a large safe containing my emergency stash—millions of dollars in diamonds and cash, both U.S. dollars and Euros, dozens of identities, passports, driver's licenses, license plates, as well as other critical tools of my trade: my highly prized jeweler's tools that fit so familiarly and comfortably into my hands, it's as though they're physical extensions of myself, night-vision goggles, digital scanners, and indestructible, undetectable space-age-plastic lock-picking sticks, to name a few. I'm slightly ashamed to say I haven't yet had an opportunity to tell Thomas about this safe or, actually, about any of the secret vaults I'd had built into the structure of the house when I bought it. One day I must. Possibly.

The section of tile swung aside smoothly and I knelt down on the floor, leaned over, and entered the electronic code. Seconds later, the seal released and the vault opened with a satisfying hiss—the most beautiful sound a jewel thief can hear. A breath of cold, sterile air blew over my face as I hefted up the heavy door and locked it into place, much the way one opens up and secures the bonnet of a car to check the engine. Then I sat back on my heels and ran my eyes across the twelve large safety-deposit-type boxes that were lined up vertically. I removed the boxes one at a time and withdrew what I needed to complete my mission.

Next, a thick shawl draped around my shoulders, I tiptoed through the melting slush across the gravel stable yard to the garage. I backed my British racing green Jaguar XJ-8 convertible out of its space and then pushed a small button concealed behind the track for the automatic garage door. A large section of floor opened hydraulically, revealing a secret stair that leads to my archives—arguably the most complete library in the world on the subject of jewels, gems, and the people who own them. I quickly located and copied every image and description I had of the missing loot.

Finally, I went to my main jewelry safe, which is hidden behind the kitchen pantry, and pulled out a few especially impressive wintertime pieces.

By the time Thomas got home, lunch was on the stove and everything was secure in the false bottoms of my Hermès canvas-and-leather overnight cases.

FIVE

"Here's David's phone number." We faced each other in the private compartment of the train. Thomas handed me a slip of paper and an envelope. "I know you haven't met him, but after twenty years of working together hand in glove, I would—and have—trusted him with my life. If you need anything, anything at all, David will be right there. Please don't hesitate to call him. He'll meet you in Zurich—he's a tall, thin fellow, sandy hair and blue eyes—and will help you make the connection to St. Moritz. He'll be on your train to St. Moritz, as well. Different compartment, of course."

"Thank you, Thomas. That's very reassuring. It sounds as though you've thought of everything."

"And this is five thousand pounds' worth of Swiss francs for you to travel with. You do have the bank card and cell phone I gave you?"

I nodded and raised a sleeping pill to my lips and swallowed a glass of water. I caught a glimpse of myself in the mirror on the back of the door. I was as pale as a ghost.

"I'm so sorry you don't feel well, Kick. Please call me as soon as you get to Zurich. I'll be there tomorrow—I think my flight lands about two—so I'll be within a stone's throw of St. Moritz. Now, here's the phone number of the Baur au Lac in Zurich where I'll be staying, but you know you can call my cell phone anytime."

I tucked the paper into my pocket.

"I can't tell you how much I appreciate your doing this—if there were any other way to make it work, I would have done it. But you're the only one who even has a chance of pulling this off." He checked the tiny bathroom in my train compartment, a stainless-steel work of art when it came to making maximum use of minimal space—there was even a small portholelike window in the shower. "Very nice. I wish I were coming with you."

"So do I."

The porter had secured my two large Louis Vuitton suitcases in a storage closet. My overnight cases were stacked on one of two over-stuffed armchairs that could swivel. The compartment, like the train, was sleek and high-tech. It was paneled in burled walnut and uphol-stered in brown-and-gold industrial fabric in a flame-stitch pattern. There was a banquette that converted to a bed opposite the armchairs. A shiny chrome vase of yellow rosebuds sat on a table beneath the large window. Outside, the platform bustled with departure preparations.

"How's your headache?"

"Excruciating."

"Maybe this will help." Thomas pulled the semitransparent privacy shades, putting the cabin in pleasurable twilight and blocking prying eyes from outside. "See if you can get some sleep—you've got almost seven hours."

"I will—I'll probably be dead to the world before we even leave the station." I put my hands on his cheeks and looked into his eyes. "I love you, Thomas."

"I love you, too, Kick. Thank you again for taking this on."

We kissed good-bye.

"Remember," he said, standing at the door, "call me anytime you want. Have a safe journey and lock this behind me."

He disembarked and stood outside my cabin. I raised the shade enough to wave and blow him a kiss before pulling it back down. I checked my watch. The train didn't leave for five minutes.

I dropped the sleeping pill that had been tucked under my pinkie finger back into my pillbox, and while I didn't think Thomas would come back in, I switched on the radio in the bathroom full blast and closed the bathroom door, just in case. I also laid the cell phone he'd given me on the side of the sink. It was a British government-issued phone and I was quite certain it had a GPS beacon attached to it so he could keep an eye on me and my whereabouts. Then, I turned my black mink coat inside out, converting it to a tan raincoat, tied an uninteresting brown scarf over my hair, grabbed my canvas travel cases, and moved as fast as I could down four cars before sticking my head out the door. Thomas was still there, his back to me, talking on his phone. I put on my dark glasses, stepped off the train, and dashed through the station to the taxi stand.

"Airport, *s'il vous plait. Vîte.*"

The secret of my success is that I have never had a partner, and from the moment I began to contemplate taking on this rescue project, I knew I would do it on my terms and without assistance. I appreciated all the trouble Thomas had gone to, the hotel, the train, the phone, cash and credit card, and even though I loved him more than I'd ever loved anyone and trusted him as much as I could—he was still a policeman. If I were going to commit to using my highly developed skills and signature techniques, I wouldn't dream of putting myself in jeopardy or making myself vulnerable to capture by letting him, or anyone, see into my secret world. My secret world of Swiss bank vaults packed with stones and currency and identities. I could vanish in seconds.

In fact, I just had.

SIX

Thomas and I are grown, well into the second halves of our lives. Neither one of us had been married until a year ago. We were willingly, happily single—both of us spoiled by our independence and richly fulfilled by our careers, not looking to muddle them up with love, especially a love where any sort of compromise or making allowances would be required. I think to both of us, "love" and "entanglement" were synonymous. Don't get me wrong. I'm not a man hater. I just never had very good luck in the romance department. Actually, I gave up on love when I was fifteen.

Actually, I gave up on my life as it was when I was fifteen. It was so different from my life today, and I was so different from who I am today. Sometimes when I look back on it, which I seldom do, it all seems like a highly improbable, practically impossible transition.

My mother, little more than a girl herself, dragged her trailer, with me inside it, around the Oklahoma oil fields and made her living entertaining the roustabouts in the only way she could. I knew that wasn't the direction I wanted to go—I would never let myself live her life. When I looked at myself in the mirror, I saw someone special looking back at me. I was going to be somebody. Unfortunately, I got off on the wrong foot, and accidentally ended up pregnant when I was fifteen. So, I did what girls in trouble did in those days, I went off to the Florence Crittenden Home for Girls in Omaha to have the baby.

I'll never forget lying there in that clean, crisp, all-white room—having signed the papers to give away my baby, whose face I never even looked at, never even inquired if it was a boy or a girl—that I somehow had the grace to realize and accept that no matter what it took, I had to change. And I was the only one who could make that happen. I realized I couldn't go much further down, all I could do was go up. I was also aware that no one knew who I was or where I was. I could be anything or anybody I wanted to be. I'd been offered a second chance. I got to start over. I never saw my mother again.

The Florence Crittenden people—the kindest people I'd ever met in my life—found a room for me in a safe, clean boardinghouse and a job in a department store in Tulsa. The salary was an appropriate wage for a junior clerk, but I was in a hurry. I wasn't going to get anywhere on $1.65 an hour, minimum wage at that time. So that's when I started stealing, and before long, I realized I really had a knack for it. I was gifted! I was onto something—not only was I good at it, but the tiny jeweled pieces gave me a wonderful, confident power and an almost erotic pleasure. They provided me with independence and more than doubled my income. Some people search their whole lives for their calling—I'd found mine with little or no effort just by being willing to take a risk, by making the best of a bad situation, by being willing to try to make lemonade from the lemons of my life.

I took just small items at first, little pins and lavalieres, but soon I had my eyes on bigger targets. I honed my skills by constantly manipulating marbles and stones in my hands, sensitizing them, making them flexible and quick. Hot goods could vanish into my pockets and bodice in the twinkling of an eye and I could sell or pawn them quickly, leaving no trace.

I got up my nerve to apply for a job at one of Mr. Homer Mallory's Fine Jewelry stores. "I'll get back to you soon," he'd said. I was still within earshot of his office when I heard him and his secretary share a mean-spirited laugh. "Can you imagine hiring a fat girl like that in our business? She's got no class." This coming from Mr. Mallory himself, who was hairy and dirty and had boils on his face and bad teeth. Evidently they thought fat girls couldn't hear.

Well, Mr. Mallory and his secretary receive the dubious credit for bringing clarity and righteous justification to my criminal activities, and launching my brilliant unbelievable career. Their unkind remark and arrogant white-trash attitude crystallized my vision and gave rationale to my crusade to steal things from people who were cruel to those who were less fortunate, or more corpulent. I slipped so many goods from Mallory's Fine Jewelry stores into my overdeveloped bosom, I was able to buy myself a little yellow Corvair convertible for my sixteenth birthday. I was a one-girl crime wave. Of course, even though I thought I knew everything, I didn't. One day I walked into his newest shop and was no more than two feet inside when they nabbed me. I was sentenced to a year in the Oklahoma State Home for Girls— a nice way of saying reform school.

I'd stay awake many nights just thinking and thinking, because I had all these big plans, but they weren't working out. I didn't understand. And I didn't have anyone to ask. Certainly not the other girls in my "class." They were all doing time for stealing hubcaps and hairspray. I intended to be someone, the best jewel thief in the world. And in order to do that, I needed the one thing Mr. Mallory—quite rightly—said I didn't have: class. But who would show me the way?

One Saturday night—which was movie night when they would shoo us all into the auditorium where we would smoke and talk while they'd put silly movies up on the screen—it happened. The movie was *Pillow Talk* with Doris Day and Rock Hudson. I saw what I could become. She was beautiful, successful. She had her own apartment and a beautiful wardrobe. She had elegance, independence. She was her own woman, her own boss. I would be Doris Day. I even took her name as my middle name: Kathleen Day Keswick. Kick, for short. I began to work on my posture, took a jewelry-making class, put my makeup on every morning and kept my nails polished.

By the time my time was up, I'd chipped off a few of the rough edges and was awarded a full scholarship to Oklahoma State University, where I studied geology and made up an entire family history for myself, claiming I'd been orphaned when my parents burned to death trying to save their dairy herd from perishing in a barn fire. It was such a ghastly and gruesome demise, no one ever asked for further details. I pledged Kappa Kappa Gamma, and spent my spare time figuring out how I could rob my sorority sisters and their rich parents, although I never did. While it was very instructive to study their homes and habits, and the casual way they took their valuables for granted, they were wonderful, gracious girls—not a single one of them came anywhere close to meeting my criteria for being one of my victims. But, in spite of the warm welcome into their circle, and fixing me up with their brothers and cousins, deep inside, I knew I wasn't cut out for any regular sort of country club Junior League life.

It was the late '60s and the college put on a thirty-day, twenty-city, summer tour to Europe, which I took because I had nothing else to do and nowhere else to go. I was bored out of my mind on that god-awful, stupid, sophomoric tour, standing in endless lines of unwashed, strong-smelling foreigners, waiting to see famous paintings that were no larger than postage stamps and, in any event, were behind sheets of bullet-proof glass so thick and scratched you couldn't see through it in the first place. I couldn't take it anymore. I had to get onto a different track. I was too busy to waste my time sitting on a hot bus in a foreign country watching people actually living.

When we got to London—it was all happening in London in the '60s, the Beatles and the Rolling Stones, Carnaby Street and "mod" everything, Twiggy and Verushka, Petula Clark and *Blow-Up*—I ditched the group and took off, leaving all my worldly possessions in the luggage compartment of the bus except for my purse, which contained my makeup, money, jeweler's needle-nosed pliers, jeweler's loupe and lock-picking sticks. I happily traded all my money for a psychedelic minidress, pink vinyl go-go boots, and a professional Mary Quant makeover that included bright blue eye shadow, platinum lipstick, and false eyelashes even bigger than Twiggy's. By the time I left the shop, I was quite certain I was pretty much the sharpest "bird" on the face of the earth. Then it started to rain. And every drop of rain seemed to drill into me the complete pathetic futility of my actions. There I was, my pink-and-purple mini glued to my voluptuous body like a bathing suit, leaving nothing to the imagination, blubbering my eyes out—no money left, nowhere to go. Oh, what a mess I was. What a mistake I'd made. I wasn't Twiggy. I was Kick Keswick from Oklahoma City and I'd really screwed up.

That was when the Rolls Royce Silver Cloud pulled to the curb. The rear door opened and a man's voice said, "Get in, miss. Get in out of the rain." It was Sir Cramner Ballantine. But to my eyes and ears, he looked and sounded just like Cary Grant in *That Touch of Mink*.

The car took us to Claridge's where we spent two days in a suite, at the end of which time he offered me a position in the executive suite at Ballantine & Company Auctioneers, one of England's oldest and most esteemed auction houses, founded in 1740 by Sir Cramner's ancestors. Sir Cramner saved my life, made my life. He bought me a spacious flat on leafy Eaton Terrace, home to tycoons and diplomats, and placed the Pasha of St. Petersburg around my neck: a thirty-five-carat brilliant-cut perfect diamond suspended from a gossamer-fine platinum chain. I have worn the Pasha every day of my life since then—it is always there, nestled in my bosom, keeping me grounded.

He educated me about the finest the world had to offer—furniture, paintings, wine, food, jewelry, clothes. He taught me refinement, poise, discretion, and discernment. He turned me into the lady I am today. I loved him until the day he died at age ninety-two, seven years ago.

SEVEN

Thomas and I met when he was chief inspector on a bombing case that involved Ballantine & Company. Sir Cramner was gone by then, but I'd been with the company for thirty years, and it was hard to leave. I'd also promised Sir Cramner I'd continue as executive assistant to his ineffectual son and heir, who was doing his best to run 250 years of family history into the ground.

During the course of the investigation, Thomas invited me out, twice. Wonderful, sophisticated invitations such as a Schumann concert and an afternoon at the Victoria and Albert looking at the Raphael cartoons, the sorts of invitations I'd waited all my life to receive from a sophisticated, witty, urbane fellow, but never had. I demurred, turned down his offers because by then, due to a number of circumstances, it was too late.

As London's notorious, elusive Shamrock Burglar—Scotland Yard never had a clue who I was (and they still don't)—it didn't seem very intelligent to strike up a friendship with the city's superstar inspector. And I was seeing someone else (a misguided affair if there ever was one, which only served to confirm my belief about men and trouble) and, finally, and most importantly, I was getting ready to take my stash and move permanently to my beautiful little farm in Eygalières outside of St. Rémy. La Petite Pomme, with its quiet view, lavender beds, and hyacinth blue shutters.

Actually, Thomas did invite me out a third time, just for a quick hot-curry dinner at the Indian spot in Cadogan Square around the corner from my flat in Eaton Terrace. I had accepted and he stood me up! Not without a call or anything—a homicide had gotten in the way, as I recall—but I'd simmered alone for about twenty minutes before hearing from him, sipping single malt scotch and excoriating myself. Reconfirming, yet again . . . Men. Romance and I seemed fated never to end up in the same place at the same time.

Two days after the nonexistent dinner date, I padded my body with several million in diamonds and cash from my safe, boarded an Air France nonstop to Marseilles, and decamped to Provence, where I was finally able to stop looking over my shoulder and breathe.

After I'd settled in, I thought about Thomas from time to time—he would drift into my consciousness every now and then, especially when my old friend, Flaminia Balfour—she and her husband, Bill, live on a beautiful hilltop farm down the road in Les Baux—would trot out some relic who was ancient enough to think that I was *"une tomate."* And I still was (and am) a *"tomate"* in many ways—beautiful, full-figured, luscious, rich, and extremely well maintained—but I had virtually zero interest in spending my time taking care of a groping nonagenarian.

One evening at Flaminia and Bill's, my dinner partner died, not from any sort of strenuous or amorous activity beyond the effort required to sip soup or white burgundy but simply from being old. Right in the middle of the soup course. He gave a startled little peep, fell face first into my lap—bringing his bowl of cream of asparagus with him—and died. From old age. He was simply too old to be alive anymore.

"Oh, for heaven's sake." I held my hands in the air and stared at the bottom of the yellow-and-blue Limoges bowl that covered his wizened old bean like Don Quixote's helmet. My favorite pink-and-gold bouclé Chanel dinner suit soaked up the thick pale green liquid like a big expensive sponge.

I'm embarrassed to say the three of us got completely hysterical.

"What on earth are you thinking, Flaminia? Do I really seem that desperate to you?"

"I'm so sorry, Kick," she said, helping Bill curl the old gentleman onto the floor, where he lay comfortably until the authorities arrived. "I just want so much for you to be happy. To meet a man."

"Why? It doesn't make any difference, Flaminia. I couldn't possibly be happier."

"He was very, very well fixed."

"So what? So am I. Please, please, give it a rest."

She nodded as the ambulance drivers wheeled away the shrouded remains. "I suppose you're right. I did push this one a little too far—I should have let him bring his nurse."

"He had a *nurse?* Oh, my God. This is getting worse by the second."

Half-Persian, half-French Flaminia had the grace to blush, probably for the first time in her life.

It was at times such as that—thankfully there weren't too many of them—that I'd recall Thomas. He'd seemed such a completely decent man, but timing is everything and the timing hadn't been there.

One afternoon my phone rang. "Kick," Flaminia said, "can you come to dinner tonight?"

"Don't tell me," I said. "You've met a man."

"*Toujours.*" She laughed. "There's always that chance. But truly, come just because it's a wonderful group and will be a beautiful October evening. Get dressed up. Seven o'clock."

The evening was chilly, so I draped a black pashmina over my black silk evening pajamas and secured it with a large art deco diamond brooch, put on three graduated strings of sixteen-millimeter pearls and diamond-and-pearl earrings, all of which I feel obliged to point out I'd bought legitimately at auction at Christie's in Geneva. On my wrist I clasped the one piece I'd stolen and kept because it was too magnificent to break down and I couldn't bear to sell it: the Queen's Pet, a cuff of five rows of 5-carat diamonds with an egg-sized clasp encrusted with a diamond melee. The clasp concealed a locket with a miniature of Prince Albert painted by Winterhalter for Queen Victoria. The bracelet was unfenceable and no one with a brain in his head would break down such an exquisite creation, reduce it to its basic elements of gemstones and precious metal and sell it for scrap. On this particular evening, it seemed like the perfect thing to complete my ensemble.

And there, at Flaminia and Bill's cocktail party, was Thomas Curtis.

My heart stopped, and not from any romantic notion or pleasure at seeing him again. I was filled instead with the deep-down sorrow and grim realization that he was there to arrest me. That my beautiful life was finished. That all my years of meticulous planning and disguise and secrecy had evaporated like fog. That he had tracked me down and would now unceremoniously haul me off to the hoosegow like a common criminal.

I glanced up, and far off in the distance I thought I could almost make out the lights at La Petite Pomme where my little Bijou was curled up asleep in her basket waiting for me. My head ached as though in a vise and my eyes filled with tears.

EIGHT

I stared at his hand. It was strong and square and had a firm hold on a tumbler of scotch, not a badge or a pair of handcuffs. His other hand was casually in the pocket of his tweed sports coat and he smelled vaguely of Trumper's Lime cologne.

"I didn't like the way it ended between us," Thomas said. "With me standing you up."

"Really?" I said casually. "How did you find me?" My voice sounded completely normal even though my mouth felt filled with cotton and I was quite sure I would need to be defibrillated to get my heart and breathing to resume. The headache arced through the center of my head like lightning bolts and would have buckled a weaker person's knees.

He didn't answer. He studied me up and down, not in a lecherous or leering way but with appreciation. "I'm so glad to see you, Kick. You look sensational. You're even more beautiful than I remember." He admired my bracelet. "That's an impressive piece."

You know, it is true that criminals are compelled to reveal themselves one way or the other. They—we—cannot stay away from their works because their works eat them alive. At some point they have to say the truth about themselves if they're going to have any sort of real life at all. It becomes an unstoppable mandate, almost a crusade to tell someone. To confess. You cannot restrain yourself from freeing the swarm of bees that lives in your mouth. This was that moment for me.

This would be when the truth flew out of my mouth like a beautiful flock of liberated bluebirds—I would not live the lie any longer, no matter the consequences.

"I stole it," I answered evenly, now fully prepared to present my wrists for the obligatory handcuffing. "I'm the Shamrock Burglar."

"Of course you are." He raised his glass to me in a mock toast. "And I'm the Samaritan Burglar." He was alluding to another of London's "celebrity" burglars, but one that was a do-gooder. The Samaritan stole priceless works of art from peoples' homes and left the paintings at police stations with notes warning the owners to take better care of their valuable property or some real thief might get his hands on their goods and actually steal them for good.

We both laughed and laughed—the Shamrock and the Samaritan. What a ridiculous idea. I felt wonderful, lighter than air. Because no matter the outcome, the fact remained, I'd told the truth. For the first time in my life! I was liberated. It wasn't my fault he didn't believe me.

Later that evening, when we returned to my house and I was whipping up a little midnight snack—a tarte Tatin, one of my specialties—he brought a painting in from the car and hung it over the fireplace in my living room.

"Come here a minute, Kick," he said from the living room door. "There's something I want to show you."

I recognized the painting immediately, *La Polonaise Blanche,* by Renoir. I'd last seen it in Sheilagh Winthrop's bedroom when I was in her pitch-black closet cleaning out her safe while she was at her father's ninetieth birthday party. I'd watched, horrified, through my night-vision goggles, as a masked burglar entered the room, replaced the painting with a note card, and then for some reason unknown to me, came into the closet. I had no choice. I whacked him with my little hard rubber ball peen hammer and he'd fallen like a ton of bricks. I got out of there as fast as I could. In the newspapers, the theft of the painting was attributed to me, the Shamrock Burglar, a bit of notoriety I never cared for. Any hack could break and enter and swipe a painting off a wall, it took virtually no skill or finesse. Clearly, it had been the work of the Samaritan Burglar, except the painting was never recovered.

To discover that night, in my living room, that Chief Inspector Thomas Curtis actually was London's Samaritan Burglar absolutely stunned me. That he had conducted these robberies while the people who owned the works were out to dinner or out of town and had asked the police to keep an eye on their homes left me with my mouth hanging open. It was as egotistical as it was disgraceful.

We sipped Champagne and made love all night long.

Beyond acknowledging the reality of our former lives, Thomas and I had never gone on to discuss the subject in any significant detail—we didn't talk about methods or favorite heists. He'd never asked me about my techniques, my various identities, or my stash, which, depending on the market price of precious gems—mostly diamonds—and metals, could maintain my lifestyle at the height of ultimate luxury for two or three hundred years at a minimum.

And I'd never asked him.

Our pasts weren't hidden from each other, but we'd both come to Provence to become new people, learn new things, to look to the future, not spend a lot of time reflecting on the past. Our histories sat like expensive books on a coffee table that you walk by and see every day and maybe even pick up occasionally but never really delve into. Like the giant volume of Impressionists in my living room that serves as the stand for the drinks tray, they finally became fixtures in our existence, window dressing or decorations. They were just there.

One thing I do know, though, is that Thomas had been a do-gooder, a helpful thief, a scolder and a disciplinarian.

I, on the other hand, had no altruistic or philanthropic motives at all. Not only was I an unparalleled burglar, I was also a master jeweler and made perfect copies of pieces I stole from the auction house where I worked. So while many of the thefts from residences—where I knew the owners were out of town or out for the evening, and where I left my lovely, famous bouquet of fresh shamrocks, tied with an ivory satin ribbon in place of their precious gems and jewels—were made public, the majority of my robberies had gone undetected. As a matter of fact, even Thomas didn't know of my jewelry-making skills or the auction-house switches. It was actually from those thefts that I'd realized my greatest gains.

There were many, many other things Thomas didn't know about me and, I'm sorry to say, it seemed as though that was how it would stay. Throughout my life, "truth" has always been a relative thing. Nothing about me has ever been as it seems. And while I've revealed many truths about myself to him, the body of my life remains out of sight, like the proverbial iceberg under the water, or actually, like my body itself. I don't think anyone should be forced to look at anybody's middle-aged skin from the neck down. Unless they want to, of course, and the bedroom door's closed and the lightbulbs are pink.

We fell in love, got married at the little Anglican church in St. Rémy, and settled into a wonderfully comfortable life filled with beautiful food, lovely wine, long walks, books, art, and love in the afternoon.

Our lives of crime were over, behind us, part of our history. And that's where they would stay—in the past. Everything at La Petite Pomme was on the up-and-up.

NINE

Five minutes after walking into the ladies' room at the Avignon airport, I walked out as somebody's grandmother in flat shoes, a gray wig, beige-rimmed glasses, and an unbecoming maroon wool coat that was slightly snug. Before leaving the restroom, I took my personal cell phone out of my pocket, snapped the front off it, removed the battery, and dropped the pieces in separate trash bins, rendering it fundamentally unreconstructable. I proceeded to the ticket counter.

"Any baggage to check, Mme. Garnier?" the Air France agent asked without giving me a glance.

"*Non, merci.*"

"Your flight to Paris departs in fifty minutes. Gate three. You can enter security just there." She pointed to her right and slid my driver's license and boarding pass across the ticket counter. "Have a nice flight."

"*Merci.*"

There are certain rules to major-league theft, to planning a big heist—not a standard hotel or residential robbery. You need to do it on your terms, control the circumstances as much as possible. Study your prey and create the scenario. I knew nothing about Bradford Quittle—now known as Sebastian Tremaine—the queen's retired footman. But I knew that if he had stolen the jewels and was hanging around with Robert Constantin, the world's leading concert tenor, he'd been stealing for a long time. And he'd amassed a pile of cash that had let him become something he wasn't. Sebastian Tremaine had been living a secret double life that had gained him access to Constantin's constellation. As Thomas pointed out, the superstar had an army of bodyguards to protect him from the millions of fans constantly trying to break through the visible and invisible cordons that surrounded him and get his attention. So Sebastian had done what I was preparing to do—created a setup that put him in that world in a way that attracted Constantin to him, rather than the other way around.

I knew little about Constantin's private life because like many classical superstars who live in the stratosphere, he was the darling of the superpowers, the highly wealthy, highly cultured elite who live behind the scenes in the anonymity of private enclaves and clubs. Constantin's privacy was protected not only by his own security team but also by the powerful security blanket of that exclusive world. He had more than succeeded in keeping his private life private.

I did, however, know two important things: showing up at a charity benefit concert in St. Moritz might get my picture in the paper—something I had no interest in seeing occur—but it certainly wouldn't get me into his inner circle. And number two: I knew where he lived.

Constantin lived in Mont-St.-Anges, quite possibly the most exclusive, most secret private club in the world. Located somewhere in the Swiss Alps, Mont-St.-Anges was owned lock, stock, and barrel by the richest man in the world, megabillionaire George Naxos. Nicknamed by the media as simply The Greek, Mr. Naxos stayed well hidden from the public eye. His reach and power were so great, the actual location of the club and its membership were known, as far as I could tell, only to the members and their closest friends and associates who could keep their mouths shut. Banishment was the punishment for indiscretion, and for the insiders in this world, the term *banishment* meant more than simple exclusion, it meant financial and social ruin. So far, no one had been willing to risk it and write an exposé of the whereabouts or goings-on at Mont-St.-Anges.

For me, breaking in to Mr. Naxos's world would be, without question, a far greater challenge than actually stealing the jewelry. But he was the critical, oblique doorway to Constantin—only Naxos could provide me with the entrée and credibility necessary to legitimize my plan.

Because he was such a powerful man, I'd had Mr. Naxos on my radar screen for a long, long time, just as I did many wealthy individuals who had the capacity for and interest in acquiring magnificent jewelry. I suppose you could say I was a little like an obituary writer at a newspaper who passes slow times writing the obituaries of famous or influential people just to be ready for when they die. I'd been planning and preparing for how to meet George Naxos for decades.

He and the Royal Ballet's former prima ballerina, Alma de la Vargas, had been married for over thirty years. She vanished from the stage a long time ago, maybe fifteen years, after suffering a torn ligament in a production of *Swan Lake* at Covent Garden. A short time later, the Royal Ballet announced her retirement. After that, she disappeared, simply evaporated into their hidden world. And she hadn't been seen since, which was unfortunate because as I remembered her—I'd seen her at a number of our auctions in London—she was one of the most beautiful women I'd ever seen in my life. We were exactly the same age, and I was curious to see how she'd handled it. She'd been black haired, blue eyed, and had that otherworld quality that prima ballerinas have that makes them seem as though they're floating above the ground. That every step they take is one of those suspended leaps when their partners carry them through the air one giant flying step at a time.

No one was too certain exactly where the Naxoses called home—their yacht, their island, their London flat, their New York apartment, their Swiss chalet, their plantation home in the West Indies, or any number of other spots no one knew about. Their residences were guarded like military installations. They didn't eat in public restaurants or attend public functions, and they moved among their properties privately so there was never any opportunity for their pictures to be taken.

Paparazzi wouldn't even begin to consider haunting them.

I had one shot at getting myself in his orbit, and I was now putting my long-dormant, carefully researched and planned strategy into play.

The flight to Paris-Orly was uneventful. I exited through security in the heart of the crowd, following a couple of women into the ladies' room in the main terminal. After a few contorted minutes in a cramped stall, I transformed myself back to somewhat more familiar territory. I pulled my mink coat from my overnight bag and shook it out, putting the maroon coat in its place, and tucked my blond hair under a glamorous black turban. I broke the beige glasses in two, stuffed the wig into a plastic bag, and tossed it and the broken glasses in the trash, fixed my lipstick, and put on my dark glasses. I could easily have been mistaken for Catherine Deneuve or Princess Grace back from the dead.

I checked my watch. Thomas wouldn't know I'd gone missing for another four and a half hours.

TEN

"Bienvenu, Princesse. We were pleased to receive your call." The gentleman smiled courteously at me when I emerged from the elevator.

Other than the doorman, who'd greeted me at the discreet street entrance three floors below—he was flanked by two dark-suited security
guards with clear plastic earpieces and the outline of guns visible beneath their jackets—it seemed we were the only people around.

Located in the upper stories of an office building owned by Naxos
on the Champs Elysées at l'Etoile, the boutique-style hotel—known
only as III, or Trois—had been created for the safety and convenience
of his friends and colleagues. It was also selectively available to those
who knew about it and who could pass the hotel's background check.
Trois was so exclusive its phone number was unlisted.

I knew about it the same way I knew about Mont-St.-Anges—it used
to be my business to know who and where the wealthiest were, their
hiding places and haunts. And I must admit, I've continued to keep my
antennae tuned to a certain degree. It's part of me. Like breathing. I still
keep my hand in. I stay up to date. I listen at cocktail and dinner parties more than I talk.

"Please." He indicated a straight-backed armchair in front of a large
Boule desk behind a screen of potted palms in an alcove off the empty
lobby. The only things on the desk were an enormous vase of white
roses, a telephone, and a sheet of paper. It looked like a still life. "Be
seated."

"I'm pleased you have room for me at the last minute."

"We are at your service." He slid the paper across, laid a black pen on top. "Your signature, please."

I signed. "Margaret Romaniei." And slid it back.

"Do you have baggage?"

"*Non.*"

In the sedan on the way into the city from the airport, I'd considered a number of answers to this inevitable and reasonable question about my nonexistent baggage, and decided no answer at all was the best. He could draw his own conclusions.

Over the years, I've worked hard to develop a number of identities. Some are very disposable—such as Mme. Garnier, who flew today from Marseilles to Paris—requiring only a driver's license and a working credit card or two. Others, such as Margaret Romaniei, Princess Margaret of Romania, I'd worked on for a long time.

Her history was detailed, complicated, and private. In fact, she had never existed, but her late husband, Prince Frederick Romaniei, had.

Frederick Romaniei had been an oddball, a drunk and a café darling, a heavy marijuana smoker and LSD user. A devotee of the hedonistic hell of the '60s, Prince Frederick would fall into the category of what's known today as a combination of unredeemable loser and Eurotrash—a poorly raised young aristocrat with a fool's arrogant, unfounded aura of entitlement. The possibility of his assuming the nonexistent responsibility for which he'd been birthed—the throne of the kingdom of Romania—was virtually zero. In fact, at that time, Romania was very much behind the Iron Curtain and under the rule of a totalitarian despot, and even if it hadn't been, Frederick was way down the line in the order of succession. He'd never been to Romania and probably wouldn't have recognized the language if he'd heard it. Freddy, as he was called, was killed in an avalanche in Switzerland in 1967 when he was twenty-three, skiing where he shouldn't have been. He'd never been married, that anyone knew of, but he'd lived such a reckless, useless life and was forgotten so quickly, no one knew or cared about him anymore—not that they ever had in the first place. His parents, from whom he was famously estranged, were now both dead and there were no siblings.

His widow, me, "Princess Margaret," was from an aristocratic Norwegian family, the daughter of a diplomat, brought up and educated in England. Appearance-wise, I could easily pass for a Norwegian, and as far as being married to Prince Freddy . . . well, the antics of any number of today's solid citizens, centers of influence and decision makers, captains of industry and elected politicians who did things in the '60s and '70s under the influence of mind-bending drugs, would leave most people with their mouths hanging open.

There were many, many long-ago marriages to someone met on a beach in Majorca or Ceylon or Hawaii, the wedding ceremony attended by stringy-haired, guitar-playing, barefooted, unwashed, like-minded strangers in tie-dyed T-shirts and sarongs, conducted by a self-proclaimed, flower-draped, stoned swami or guru of the Temple of Eternal Bliss, or some such similar phony-baloney sect dreamed up while on a "trip." Everybody singing and full of love. The bride or groom's horrified parents—when they were finally informed of the union, generally in a spaced-out phone call from the newlyweds asking for money—put hysterical calls in to their lawyers, paying dearly, whatever it took, for annulments. It was a very strange time with many unwise actions lost in the fog of hallucinogens.

It was entirely possible, even likely, that Freddy had been married. Maybe even more than once.

Freddy and George Naxos had been roommates at Le Rosey, the exclusive all-boys boarding school on the shores of Lake Geneva.

———

"May I offer you a little lunch or a snack?" the fellow at the check-in desk asked.

"A bowl of tomato soup and a pot of coffee would be wonderful."

"Let me take care of that immediately." He picked up the phone and spoke quietly, authoritatively. "The princesse would like hot tomato soup." He glanced over at me. "A little cheese sandwich?"

"*Oui, merci.*"

"*Un croque-monsieur et café. Merci.*" He replaced the receiver. "Do you know how long you'll be with us?"

"*Non.*"

"Please stay as long as you wish. We are at your service." He raised his hand and another man, dressed similarly in a well-cut business suit, materialized. "The princesse is in the Blue Suite."

The porter picked up my case and I followed him down a short corridor to the elevator.

E L E V E N

The Blue Suite opened onto the Etoile where gray clouds had descended and begun to spit out a steady gray February drizzle. The normally busy traffic that circled the Arc de Triomphe had, for the most part, disappeared, leaving me with an extraordinary bird's-eye view of what the Etoile and the Champs Elysées must have looked like in the middle of the last century when there were about one-tenth as many cars.

In spite of the gray day, my rooms were large and bright, extremely cozy and feminine with pale blue and white toile everywhere—on the furniture, the walls, the bed. Comfortable downy cushions filled the chairs and sofas. A gold-rimmed plate with the Roman numeral III sat on the coffee table with five neatly arranged petit fours. I picked one up, a little mocha confection iced in coffee fondant, and went into the bedroom, which was done up in the same fabric. It was just beautiful. The bathroom was as large as the bedroom, with two windows and what looked to be a dozen thick towels stacked on heated racks. A hint of carnation scented the air.

In the distance, I heard the doorbell chime and by the time I got back to the living room, my lunch was waiting on the desk—small silver domes covered the soup and sandwich—and the waiter had vanished.

A number of foods revitalize me. Cream of tomato soup with a dollop of sherry, grilled cheese sandwiches, chocolate and Champagne are close to the top of the list, right after my complete favorites: nut bread sandwiches with cream cheese, apples, raisins, and chutney. Of course, the petit fours didn't hurt. I am well aware that experts claim that the high that comes from sugar has an immediate and opposite effect—a deep, depressing down. I have not experienced that phenomenon and can only surmise that the experts aren't getting enough sugar in their diets.

I'd just swallowed the last bite of sandwich when the phone rang. It was the man at the front desk.

"Mr. Naxos wishes to know if you will join him and his wife for cocktails."

"Well, yes," I answered, surprised. "Of course. I'd like that very much. Thank you."

"Someone will call for you at eight o'clock."

"*Merci.*"

Of course, I wasn't really surprised. Step one complete.

An hour and a half had passed since I landed, and I needed to accomplish a great deal by eight o'clock and . . . I needed for all of it to be in white. That's what I'd decided years ago when I created the persona of Princess Margaret of Romania: she would wear only white. It would be her signature, add to her mystery and cool demeanor. The rightness of the concept was confirmed when I met Odessa Niandros in London, the smoky, sultry, latte-skinned sister of the late Princess Arianna. Odessa had come to Ballantine & Company to have her sister's jewelry auctioned and she wore only white and always looked like an unapproachable ice goddess. I thought that would be a good look for enigmatic Margaret. Everything white. I would be as cool and mysterious as Bianca Jagger.

Back downstairs, the doorman helped me into the hotel car, a custom-made black Mercedes 500S with an extended wheel base, dark-tinted windows, and nicely worn black leather seats. It was not as big as a proper limousine but had significantly more leg room than a regular sedan and smelled of leather and citrus, which unfortunately gave me a quick, rueful twinge of Thomas and his brisk lime cologne. I wondered if he was in his study, or walking the dog, or packing his bags to go to Zurich tomorrow.

"Where may I take you, Princesse?" the driver asked when the door was closed.

"Carita, please."

Carita, one of Paris's leading *maisons de beauté* for more than fifty years, has grown from a small salon frequented only by those in the know to an international presence in the world of beauty products. Its modern salon and spa now fill three stories on the Faubourg St. Honoré, three stories dedicated to nothing but beauty and well-being. It is a delicious eucalyptus-scented sanctuary.

"This way, please, madame," a sylph in a tight black dress said. She escorted me to the second floor, showed me into an all-pink powder room and handed me a smock. "Francois will meet you at the desk."

"Thank you," I said. I locked the door. It was a huge relief to take off the glamorous dark glasses and tight black turban, pull the pins out of my French twist and shake out my shoulder-length blond hair that I spend a fortune on to keep just the right shade. I hated to see it go. I put in contact lenses that tinted my blue-green eyes to enough of a deeper hue that they were completely different.

By the time I left Carita, no blond remained. My coiffeur was now much darker. Francoise had dyed all my hair a sort of medium brown and then streaked it with three different shades of light brown, tan and gold. He cut it to chin length, parted it in the middle and pulled each side back with tortoise shell combs. It was a sophisticated, elegant style that suited my face and coloring and, besides, I'd always wanted to be able to use matching combs—some of the jeweled ones from the '30s and '40s are stunning. The makeup artist had created a whole new palette for my face.

I was unrecognizable.

My next stop was Galleries Lafayette, Paris's landmark department store. Entering its multistory atrium is to be transported to a vast wonderland filled with the best the world has to offer. Thank goodness, they've moved all the domestic goods, such as gourmet delicacies, kitchenware, linens, and garden tools to their new Maison store across the street. It used to be agony for me to go through the gourmet department where you could find a canned, jellied canard next to a basket of rare black truffles, or a jar of tapenade and ten different brands of marrons glacée, or the latest in cookware. But now all those traps are gone, replaced by chapeaux and cosmetics, somewhat slightly easier for me to move past the escalator, and get to the business at hand.

I went to the second floor and began assembling the proper wardrobe for a wealthy Romanian princess, widow of a long-forgotten Romanian prince, to take to the Alps.

Here's what I learned: buying an entire all-white wardrobe isn't as easy, or as interesting, as you may think. First of all, it's not particularly flattering unless you're terribly petite and have, like Bianca or Odessa, a little tone to your skin, which I don't. Secondly, it doesn't bring out the roses in your cheeks—just the opposite, actually. And finally, white doesn't show diamonds off to their best. Unless you're wearing quite dramatic colored stones or displaying a décolletage full of healthy, taut, tanned skin, white pulls the fire out of diamonds and the luster out of pearls. Why on earth I ever thought Princess Margaret should wear only white, I have no idea. I think I'd gotten carried away envisioning myself ice-skating on a frozen alpine pond in a hooded, full-length white mink cape and a white velvet dress. I don't know. But the fact was, this entire alpine caper was about jewelry, about showing it, and me, off to our absolute best, and a major expanse of white on my body was just not going to do it. I made a number of strategic adjustments and ended up with a collection that included some white, but also lots of black, taupe, and coffee bean, and trimmed with wonderful passementerie stitching and mink, fox, and leopardskin collars and cuffs.

All right, I'll admit it. I did buy that full-length mink cape with a hood, a hat, and muff to match. But I got it in black. And it looked sensational. Who knew, I might get an invitation to go ice-skating, and black would look much more dramatic twirling on the ice than white.

On I marched, up to Lingerie—a wonderland of frills and femininity. Choosing was so hard, it almost made me cry—I was afraid the time pressure I was under was going to make me sick. It did give me a headache. A fairyland of silk and satin and lace, ruffles and bows in every color of the rainbow, the negligees and peignoirs, cotton nighties, robes and pajamas, bras, panties, bed jackets, bustiers and teddies poofed out of the racks like the corps de ballet's wardrobe room at an especially lavish production of *Sleeping Beauty*. I wanted all of them. It made me lightheaded.

I couldn't help it—lingerie has been one of my passions since Sir Cramner rescued me on Carnaby Street. I'm an addict. He taught me to appreciate myself—all of me.

"You are absolutely delicious," he said one day when I was apologizing about my extra pounds. "Don't lose an ounce."

I'd realized by then there was no possibility that I was going to lose that twenty-five pounds. And Sir Cramner helped me see I didn't need to penalize myself for that my whole life, and feel obliged to wear Carter's cotton shorts and bras that covered my bosom like catcher's mitts. I made the decision then that I would wear only beautiful underthings that would show me off to my best advantage.

So now, today, you can imagine how the selection that lay before me in the lingerie department at Galleries Lafayette was a terrible, heart-tearing wrench because I had so little time. Darling Cramner would have loved it.

After much back and forth, I settled on sixteen or seventeen silk, satin, and lace peignoirs ranging from champagne to silver pink to black, and three quilted pale pink silk robes (I have a number of these robes at home. They're like security blankets to me.). Two cashmere robes with leopardskin trim, because I was going to Switzerland where it was freezing, several sets of lacy bras and panties, camisoles and slips, and stacks of lightweight cashmere socks and stockings.

Finally, I was almost totally set. I had evening gowns, cocktail clothes, a dozen pairs of lightweight wool slacks and cashmere sweater sets, an entire wardrobe of ski clothes(!), slippers and shoes, several colors of kid gloves, scarves, shawls, fur mufflers with matching hats and muffs, a number of handbags and a set of large Vuitton suitcases.

"*Et en suite, Princesse?*" my driver asked. "Back to the hotel?"

"No. Please take me to Chanel on Avenue Montaigne."

"*Bien.*"

I've never considered myself a power shopper, but after a total of three very fast hours, I got back to the hotel fully equipped for any contingency—you name it, I could dress for it. I was completely exhausted. My Galleries Lafayette purchases had already been delivered—shopping bags and boxes filled the living room. It was an extraordinary array and while I was searching through them for one of my new pink robes, the doorbell rang and in came the porter with my packages from Chanel. (I'd already stowed my purchases from Cartier and Van Cleef in the bottoms of my Hermès travel bags along with the rest of my jewelry.) As I've said before, I wasn't sure exactly what budget Thomas and the queen had had in mind for this adventure when he'd said "St. Moritz" and "unlimited," but it was very dear of him to think he could imagine it, and in fact, no matter what it was, I'd exceeded it in the first six hours. And I wasn't any closer to Switzerland than I'd been when I got up this morning.

I gave the porter twenty euros, double locked the door behind him, and turned on a Rachmaninoff concerto. A bottle of Dom Perignon sat chilling on the sideboard in the living room so I poured myself a glass, and then slowly pulled off all my clothes and tossed them on the bed and dragged my robe behind me into the bath, and turned on the tap. While I waited for the tub to fill, I studied myself in the mirror. Age has wonderful compensations. Not a single one of them, however, is physique related. My body was my body, what can I say? Nothing is where it used to be, except the Pasha of St. Petersburg that Sir Cramner had hung around my neck on a terrace at the Hôtel du Cap in Cap d'Antibes, all those years ago. Now almost a part of me, it lies there—a reminder, a comforter, a constant companion. I held the diamond between my fingertips and twisted it so it caught the light and sent a shimmering kaleidoscope of color across my body. I loved my body. We'd been together a long time. I patted myself on my heart and climbed into the steaming tub and stretched out luxuriously under the bubbles.

Any minute now, Thomas would hear from his associate, David Perkins. "She wasn't on the train," he would say. And Thomas would know exactly what had happened, that I'd disappeared and he'd never be able to find me until I let him. He'd lost control of the situation.

"Dammit to hell," he would say, and slam his tumbler of scotch down on the kitchen counter, scaring the dog. "She's done it to me again."

Hundreds of miles away, from my bubble bath on the Place de l'Etoile, I raised my glass.

"Trust me," I said.

TWELVE

I dressed with intentional understatement, new black Chanel jacket with black and navy blue fringe, straight-legged trousers, a simple black T-shirt, sling-back pumps, several strings of pearls and plain pearl earrings. No diamonds, no sparkles at all. My entire operation to recover the queen's stolen jewels depended on my success this evening. It was important for me to be relaxed, elegant, and low-key.

At precisely eight o'clock, there was a sharp rap on my door. A man with a serious expression, an earpiece, and an expensive suit waited. It didn't look like he had a gun, but I imagined he did.

"Princesse," he said. "If you're ready, I'll escort you to Mr. and Mrs. Naxos's residence."

"Thank you." I gathered up my pashmina and short black kid gloves, tucked my handbag under my arm, and followed him to the waiting elevator. I was prepared for whatever happened. I wondered where they lived—in a grand *hôtel particulier* in the eighth or a villa on the grounds of the Bois or in a restored multistory seventeenth-century town house in Place Dauphine on the Ile St. Louis with an upriver view of the entire city. Wherever it was, I knew it would be extraordinary. I wondered if there would be other guests.

He slid a plastic card into a slot, placed a key into a lock and up we went. It hadn't occurred to me that they would live in this building. But why not? It was a lovely location—not the best, but after all, Naxos did own it. I was a little disappointed.

The elevator door opened into a small, bare, pure white chamber—almost like an air lock except there was no sealed door at the end. There was, however, an unattended airport-style security setup. It was bizarre and creepy and it did cross my mind that maybe I'd gone a little too far in my pursuit of George Naxos. Maybe he was a crazy recluse, like Howard Hughes or John Paul Getty, Sr.

I turned around and the man was gone, the elevator doors were closed, and there was no visible call button to summon it back.

One thing was certain: the only way out of here was forward.

A little shiver of excitement sped up my spine as I laid my purse and shawl on the conveyor, which started up immediately and silently, controlled by some invisible being. It was like being in a James Bond movie. I crossed through the gateway and found myself before two white front doors, one of which clicked open automatically. I retrieved my belongings and stepped into an entry hall that was unadorned with the exception of an astonishing composition of branches laden with orange blossoms in a large square vase on a glass table. The arrangement was so massive, it was as though someone had cut off the entire top of the tree and brought it inside. Behind their fresh fragrance, I discerned an almost undetectable back note of chlorine, as though there were a swimming pool nearby.

A butler greeted me, a tidy little man with lively eyes and a friendly smile.

"Welcome, Your Highness. I am Cookson. Mr. Naxos asked if I would escort you to the sitting room." He indicated the direction down the hallway. "Please."

"Thank you, Cookson."

He made no allusion to the high-security welcome process, but then, what could he say? It was what it was.

The look of the place surprised me completely. For Paris, which so often basks in the opulence of its Bourbon and Napoleonic excesses, it was contemporary and uncluttered. The floors were pale, almost caramel-colored wood and the fabric-covered walls were white, with the smallest tint of sage or eucalyptus. A handrail ran along the wall beneath lighted paintings by contemporary artists. At the end of the gallery, we entered the living room, which was surrounded on three sides by floor-to-ceiling glass walls and ran the entire width of the building. Outside was a wraparound terrace with now leafless trees in gigantic pots spaced every eight or nine feet apart. The trees were dimly lit. The view of Paris was beyond spectacular. Dame Joan Sutherland and Robert Constantin were singing *"Un dì felice,"* from *La Traviata.*

Did I wish my Thomas were there to share this amazingly romantic, once-in-a-lifetime moment with a view of the most beautiful city in the world—the trees, landmarks, and boulevards ablaze with lights— accompanied by one of the most romantic duets ever written? Well, I'd be lying if I said I didn't feel a small twinge. Did I let it get in my way? Heavens, no.

"Mr. Naxos will be here shortly. What may I bring you to drink?"

"Scotch, please. On the rocks."

"Twist?"

"Please."

He went to a mirrored bar set into the wall. And while he fixed my cocktail I scanned the room's reflection in the windows with my thief's eye, as I always did, looking for ways in and ways out, hiding places, secret doors, and invisible panels—although I had virtually no intention of robbing the Naxoses. This part of the apartment was ideally protected in terms of access from outdoors. In front of each set of doors was an imperceptible pressure panel built into the floor. Tiny camera holes were positioned in each corner of the room. The huge sheets of glass were bulletproof. The terrace was three-foot squares of white marble and I assumed a number of them were pressure sensitive, as well. I was terribly impressed. Unless the system were completely disabled, there was no way for a burglar to sneak in from the outside.

And inside, any of the fabric-covered wall panels easily could have opened into another world, and probably did. The ceiling was high, maybe eighteen feet, and the furniture modern, chrome and glass, upholstered in tan leather, almost the same color as the floor. There were a few white area rugs under the seating arrangements, but the general feeling was one of sparseness. I was surprised to see a dining table at the far end of the room. The table was set for two. It seemed they weren't expecting me to stay to dinner. Well, I would do what I could to change that.

Although I was posing as the widow of Mr. Naxos's prep-school roommate, poor, long-dead Prince Freddy of Romania, there was no way George and Alma Naxos were going to invite me to dinner sight unseen. I needed to be vetted. Seriously vetted.

I heard sharp footsteps coming down the hall and turned to see George Naxos striding toward me. What a wonderful-looking man. Not handsome in any traditional sense, but so confident, it made no difference. Of average-to-short height, short waisted and quite, quite round, his face glowed with good health and his light brown eyes sparkled with vitality behind rimless glasses. He was impeccably dressed in a dark gray suit, white shirt, green-and-blue silk tie and glossy black banker's shoes—everything clearly made to order. It was like watching a king arrive at a press conference. He had a warm smile on his face and extended his hand as he approached.

"Princesse," he said. "George Naxos. What a wonderful treat that you're able to join us tonight on such short notice."

"Please, call me Margaret, Mr. Naxos—I'm a princess only by a long-ago marriage. And the treat is all mine. I'm delighted, and I must say a little surprised to meet you."

His smile was warm. "Please call me George. The front desk keeps me informed of all our guests and since my wife doesn't go out in public, I try to bring the world to her, on a very limited basis, of course. I'm glad you were available for a drink—I imagine you have a busy schedule. Everyone does in Paris."

Cookson, the butler, handed me a crystal tumbler of scotch and handed Mr. Naxos the same, and then disappeared behind one of the padded panels.

"Alma will be here shortly. Would you like a tour of our paintings while we wait?"

"Between the view and the paintings, I'm not sure which to look at first."

He smiled. "It is beautiful. We are extremely blessed."

Blessed? Did he say "blessed"? Because of my long career at the auction house, and my brushing up against Flaminia and Bill Balfour's powerful friends occasionally in Les Baux, I have been in close contact with any number of movie stars, industrialists, royals, dictators, and wealthy individuals. This was the first time in my life I'd ever heard a single one of them say that he was blessed, or give credit to anyone but himself for his success. I imagine I've become jaded, but I have little respect for people of influence or privilege who are simply spoiled and feel they not only deserve what they have but need and deserve more. These were people with the power to damage and crush with a single instruction, and many didn't hesitate to exercise it if they didn't get their way. To hear the richest man in the world say he was blessed amazed me.

"Oh," he turned to the hallway. "Here she is."

I hadn't heard her coming but turned with him and saw Alma. She was as beautiful as I remembered. And she was in a wheelchair.

THIRTEEN

I knew my expression didn't betray any of the bewilderment I felt, but was this something everyone on the planet knew but me? That Alma de la Vargas was in a wheelchair? No. This was tangible evidence of the far-reaching power of Naxos—if you were fortunate enough to see into his world, you knew enough to keep your mouth shut. I was sure that although various media outlets were aware of Mrs. Naxos's condition, none would dare publicize it—they counted on his favor too much for hard news items and advertising revenue.

I stepped toward her and offered my hand. "Mrs. Naxos, what a pleasure to meet you in person. I've always been such an admirer."

Her nails were dark red and her hand was snow white. As delicate and fine boned as one would expect a prima ballerina's hand would be. Except it was tight with arthritis and fragile and soft as a bird. I took it very gently and looked into her eyes. Large, dark blue eyes that had flashed from the greatest stages in the world, electrifying sold-out audiences with the pathos of Juliet, the innocence of Aurora, and the terrifying anger of a wronged, brokenhearted swan. They were clear, unforthcoming, and assessing. Even from her physically vulnerable position, she was still Alma de la Vargas, the epitome of grace and elegance, commander of center stage. She was magnificent.

"Thank you. I'm glad you could join us on such short notice." Her voice was deep and modulated. Her accent British.

The butler handed her a flute of Champagne and then took up his place behind her chair, ready to follow directions.

"Just at the sofas, please, Cookson." She had on a fitted navy taffeta jacket with a portrait collar and a single string of perfect, very rare, slate gray eighteen-millimeter pearls. They gleamed like blue steel. Her earrings were matching pearls encircled by diamonds that sparkled with the fire-like energy that comes only from perfect stones. Her black hair was pulled straight back into a chignon topped by a flat velvet bow and her strong-boned face was nicely toned up for a woman her age, firm but not tightly pulled. When she turned her head to talk to the butler I saw the iconic profile that had made her one of the ballet world's most powerful, recognizable images. It was undiminished by time or illness. She had the profile of Queen Nefertiti.

A smooth navy cotton blanket covered her legs and feet.

The room's sparseness now made sense. Whereever there was a seating arrangement, there was room for a wheelchair to become a natural part of the setting without any fussing or rearranging. Cookson placed her at the end of a coffee table, where a normal chair would normally be. She put down her Champagne and opened a silver cigarette box. Cookson held the lighter.

George sat to her left in a low-backed armchair and I sat to her right on the sofa.

"Are you in Paris for long?" Alma asked. She had a way of speaking and a demeanor that wasn't rude or cold or unfriendly, but distant, wary and weighing, possibly even sedated. I had the feeling that those eyes were looking right into the innermost part of my soul, but I couldn't tell if they liked what they saw.

"I'm not sure." I took a salmon canapé from a white-uniformed maid who had materialized from behind another of the panels with a tray of hors d'oeuvre. "I'm . . . between things at the moment."

She raised her eyebrows slightly. "Ah." She nodded and waved off the toast points and took a puff of her cigarette. "Between what sorts of things?"

I was gauging Alma as closely as she was me. Her husband had done everything in his power, short of ceasing all communication with the outside world, to protect them from schemers and users, kidnappers and extortionists. They were large targets, and she wasn't going to let an unknown princess, a minor royal, even if there was a long-ago, completely uncultivated—and as yet unacknowledged—connection of our husbands, breeze through their door and rip them off. She intended to put me through my paces and I had to deliver. I required acceptance by both Mr. and Mrs. Naxos, not just one or the other.

There would be no funny business with Alma de la Vargas, no inane social chatter. No name dropping.

I returned her look and smiled. "Now, Alma. Don't you think we should at least hold hands and kiss before we tell each other all our secrets?"

She laughed, caught off guard by my candor. "You're right. Forgive me." She ground out her cigarette and removed another from the silver box. "I find other people's problems so much more interesting than my own."

"Don't we all? Actually, I'm on my way to a spa in Switzerland, but need to be in Paris for a few days. I've heard so many wonderful things about your hotel, and I was delighted when there was room."

"This is your first visit to Trois?"

I nodded. "I usually stay with friends but they're out of town and redecorating, so I decided this was the perfect opportunity to see what everyone's been talking about."

Alma's laugh was breathy and smooth and, unfortunately, followed by a painful bout of coughing. "I hope you enjoy your stay."

"Are you ready, madam?" The butler asked.

"Not quite, Cookson. Margaret, are you by any chance free for dinner? We'd love to have you join us."

I'd passed the first test—I didn't have two heads.

"That would be splendid."

"Cookson, I think we'll have another drink." She turned to me. "My mother used to call the cocktail hour 'the hour of charm.'"

"How delightful," I said. Charm might as well be my middle name.

FOURTEEN

The three of us had a wonderful time getting to know each other, although the maid with the salmon canapés never reappeared and there was not a nut or an olive in sight. I was starving to death. Finally, after an hour and ten minutes and another cocktail, we proceeded to the dinner table, where the candles reflected from the windows and softened our faces. Cookson pushed Alma to her spot and once she was in her place, George held my chair for me. Alma spread her snow white Madeira linen napkin in her lap, and George and I followed suit. It was very formal, ritualistic, proper. Cookson filled our water glasses, and Alma asked me if I'd grown up in Romania, which made me laugh.

"No. You know, I'd never even visited there until four years ago. I grew up in London and outside of Oslo. My father was a diplomat."

"Lovely cool climates. Pale-skinned climates."

"Yes. They suit me. I love cool weather."

"I love London. We haven't been there for years."

Cookson placed plates of thinly sliced duck pâté sprinkled with chopped cornichons and capers in front of each of us, and then filled George's wineglass with the unmistakable fresh ruby glow of fine burgundy.

George held out his hands to Alma and me. "Shall we have a grace?"

His blessing was brief and to the point, and he crossed himself when he was done.

"George always insists on saying grace at every meal," Alma explained, as though she found the blessing tedious and it needed explanation or apology.

"I think that's nice," I answered. "I need all the help I can get."

Alma just stared at me, expressionless. She was very, very tough.

"You know," George said, after he'd tasted the wine and nodded to Cookson to fill our glasses, "your husband and I were roommates in school."

I frowned. "Which school?"

"Le Rosey."

"Are you certain?"

"Quite. Your husband was Frederick Romaniei, correct?"

I felt Alma's eyes on me. Taking it all in.

"Yes. I'm sorry, I'm surprised. I know he went to Rosey, but I don't remember his ever mentioning you being a roommate. Although he might have." I gave a small shrug. "It was a long time ago and we were under the influence much of the time. He's been dead for almost thirty-five years."

"I'm embarrassed to say I never knew he had gotten married."

"Well, we weren't married for very long. Only three years when he was killed."

"What an unnecessary accident," George said. "He knew better than to ski there at that time of the year. He was the most beautiful skier I've ever seen. I've never been able to figure out why he did it."

"Surely you remember what Freddy was like. He lived for adventure and attention. And vodka. And pot. And any number of other recreational drugs. In fact, if he had lived, I'm quite sure we would not have been married for very much longer. At some point one of us—and I can guarantee you it would have been me—was bound to sober up and seen how unsuited we were and how totally inane our life was. Did you ever meet him?" I asked Alma.

She shook her head.

"I'm making him sound terrible. In fact, he was one of the most delightful, gentle people I've ever known. But he was a Lotus Eater and I'm a Scandinavian. We Norwegians can flit around for a little while but then we must get to work. We take our 'duty' very seriously." I put a small amount of butter on a crust of bread and added a slice of pâté. It was tangy and delicious. The burgundy was ambrosia.

"A Lotus Eater." George grinned. He picked up his bread but at a cruel look from Alma, put it down again. "A perfect description of the Freddy I remember. I think that's what I liked about him so much—he had an irreverence, a devil-may-care attitude about everything, which I envied. I was very serious in my studies and he just skimmed through—of course he failed most of the subjects—but he enjoyed everything completely."

I looked at George over my glasses. "And? What? He's dead and you're the richest man in the world."

Alma cried out a laugh. "You have the most wonderful, direct way of putting things. Where did you and Frederick meet?"

"At the Sorbonne."

Alma rolled her eyes. "The Sorbonne in the '60s. Those were forgettable days."

"Certainly not anyone's finest hour."

Cookson reappeared and while he cleared our plates, Alma had a cigarette. The next course was grilled sea bass on a bed of steamed julienne vegetables flavored with soy sauce. The plates were plain white china.

"And you've never remarried?" Alma said it more as a statement than a question. She carved off a small bite of the fish, but didn't put it in her mouth. George and I both watched and waited for her to take the bite. I got the impression he was as hungry as I was. Cookson had not replenished the bread. My stomach growled. It was torture.

"No," I said. "I'm far too set in my ways. And, may I add, too happy in my ways. You know better than anyone that when you have resources, you're vulnerable, and I've been around that mountain enough times to spot a phony from a hundred miles off."

"One can't be too cautious." Finally, she nibbled.

George breathed a sigh of relief and put his fork in his mouth quickly, as though he were afraid she might change her mind and make him put it back.

"It's true," I agreed. "So I own a small place in Barbados and a flat in London, and like you, have a small circle of close friends whom I trust. I live very quietly."

The sea bass was followed with a salad of fresh greens lightly dressed with oil and vinegar and a dessert of tart pomegranate soufflé. Alma ate very little and smoked between each course.

"Which spa are you going to?" George asked.

"Clinique La Prairie."

"Wonderful," Alma said. "It's the best. Have you been there before?" I noticed a quick glance pass between her and George.

"Yes. I'm looking forward to getting back. I'm a spa devotee—every now and then I feel the need for a major overhaul."

"Are you going for beauty or revitalization?" She stifled a yawn.

"Both." I looked at my watch. "Oh, heavens. I can't believe it's after ten-thirty," I said. "I'm sorry to stay so late. Thank you for inviting me."

"It was our pleasure." Alma said. "Please forgive me if I don't accompany you to the door."

Cookson pulled her chair from the table. I took her offered hand and kissed her on each cheek. She looked exhausted.

"Call me in the morning and let me know your plans. Do you by any chance play gin rummy?"

"Yes. I do. Quite brilliantly, in fact."

"If you're free in the afternoon, say about three, please come for tea and we'll have a game. Good night, Margaret."

"Good night, Alma."

FIFTEEN

When I got back to my room, I was practically weak with hunger. No wonder she was so thin—she didn't eat anything and obviously had put George on a strict diet as well. Poor George. What good did it do to be the richest man in the world and not be able to eat whatever you wanted? Thank goodness, a new plate of petit fours waited for me, along with a beautiful platter of sliced baguettes, apples and four kinds of especially pungent, runny cheeses. A feast. I could save the world given nothing but apples and cheese. And a little wine.

The rain had stopped and stars were visible through patches of dark gray-blue clouds. Traffic on the Champs Elysées and around l'Etoile had resumed its regular frantic late night pace.

I slipped into my bathrobe and snuggled into a downy bergère chair, poured myself a healthy glass of port, and reviewed the evening as I spread thin slices of baguette with thick slices of Brie de Meaux.

The brief look that passed between George and Alma when we were talking about the spa, Clinique La Prairie, was a critical step in the right direction. Among other amenities, Mont-St.-Anges was rumored to have the most complete, most luxurious spa in Europe. And, after a lot of weighing of the options, I'd realized I didn't have many strategic or tactical alternatives for getting myself onto the property. So I deduced that if I said I was interested in going to a spa, that would at least open the subject and hopefully provide the entrée I sought—it was certainly a benign approach. At any rate, this was an all-or-nothing deal. If it worked, it worked. If it didn't, I'd return most of the clothes, none of the jewelry (I'd picked up some truly amazing pieces this afternoon) and go home and Thomas and David could move on to plan B.

Regardless of that downside view, I had a strong hunch my tactic would work and I was excited about the possibility of going to Mont-St.-Anges. To me, it had taken on the aura of a fantasy almost like Shangri-La or Brigadoon, as though a magic window would open in the scenery and let you step through.

According to various ladies I'd eavesdropped upon in various powder rooms in various exclusive establishments who thought they were in there alone, (and actually why wouldn't they, when I was hiding in a locked stall with an out-of-order sign on the door? I know it's shameful, but I picked up most of the information I needed about who was going where and whose house would be empty and thus available to rob. It's how thieves make their living. What can I say?) Mont-St.-Anges is a fairyland, a perfect little village. No cars or motorbikes, just horse-drawn sleds and sleighs in the winter, and wagons and carts in the summer. The only way in or out is by helicopter or train from Geneva or Zurich.

It's also not really a club in the traditional sense of the word—there's no board of directors or nominating committee. Naxos alone controls the membership.

It is a grace-and-favor reward, where handpicked hardworking rich people can go and just be rich without putting up with a lot of judgmental, jealous nonsense from those less fortunate.

Also, according to my "sources," spectacular chalets dot the hillsides while the magnificent Hôtel Grand Anges anchors the "town" center. There are all sorts of rules: members and their guests must dress appropriately at all times when they're out in public, no wild parties in the hotel, no public drunkenness, no profanity, no noise of any sort coming from the hotel rooms after nine o'clock at night. Any infraction results in immediate expulsion. There is a strong incentive to follow the rules because there is no court of higher appeal. Naxos is judge and jury.

There's also a private hospital where some of the finest doctors in the world are given the green light and financial wherewithal to practice leading-edge medicine, from heart surgery to cancer treatments to reju-venation injections to face-lifts.

I've also heard that the health spa takes its health and fitness seri-ously, operates hand in glove with the hospital, and offers services not found in the menu of most beauty regimens in luxury spas. Unfortu-nately, I didn't have any clue what those services were because the ladies who mentioned them only would smile knowingly and roll their eyes, but my imagination roamed from brain-boosting vitamin shots to all sorts of transplants and lifts. I was ready to find out for myself.

If all went according to plan, by tomorrow, or the day after at the lat-est, I would be on my way.

SIXTEEN

Alma was too sick to play gin rummy the next day, and the day after that, and I was starting to run out of time.

Of course, no one should ever complain about being in Paris. After all, I'd spent two full days in the Louvre and had dinner one night at Alain Dutournier's Carré des Feuillants, where I treated myself to Gillardeau green-tinged Marennes oysters with bite-sized foie gras sandwiches, pheasant-and-chestnut soup that was more like a light chowder, Pyrenees noisettes of lamb with a crispy little potato galette, a half bottle of 1995 Madeleine-Collignon Mazis-Chambertin, and finally, a gingerbread crumble that made me homesick for London.

The next evening, I went to Chez George and after a martini, I ordered celery rémoulade, a steak, and pomme frites. But I didn't give my dinner the attention it deserved, I was too distracted. At the far end of the long, narrow bistro a man was having dinner with his two snow white Westies. They were perfectly groomed and sat with their paws on the table and evaluated everyone with their beady little black eyes. They made me want to go home and snuggle up with Bijou in front of the fire and forget the whole deal. I was getting anxious. I should have been well on my way to Switzerland by now. But I'd concocted my plan without the knowledge that Alma de la Vargas was an invalid, giving me even less control over what was already a mostly uncontrollable situation. I ordered another glass of wine and forced myself to remain calm and optimistic.

Finally, on the third day, her secretary called and asked if I'd come to tea at three.

The day was brisk and clear, the sky pale blue, and I walked over to Hédiard on the Place de la Madeleine and bought her a package of their famous fruit jellies. I knew she wouldn't eat them—Alma was clearly as uninterested in food as I was passionate about it—but it would be rude to show up empty-handed and I loved their fruit jellies, so maybe I'd eat them.

As a precautionary measure, I stopped at a café for lunch and ate a baguette with country ham, butter, and hot mustard, a glass of chardonnay, and a cup of espresso and a small raspberry tart.

Cookson, their butler, called for me at three o'clock and once upstairs and through the security system, he showed me into the library, a much smaller aerie than the living room, but light filled and with a view down the Champs Elysées to the Place de la Concorde. Alma was waiting for me, sitting at a card table in front of the windows. She had a stunning large spray of diamonds pinned on the left shoulder of her black cashmere turtleneck, and matching earrings. Two decks of cards and a score pad were in the center of the table. A silver cigarette box and ashtray sat on the edge. A stark white Rosenthal china tea set—two cups and a pot—and a decanter of sherry were on a sideboard. A fire burned in the fireplace, making the room uncomfortably warm.

"Are you feeling better?" I asked.

"I am. These diseases are very complicated. But today I've been able to spend the morning in the pool and now have things back in as good a working order as possible." She smiled. "Do you have any arthritis?"

I shook my head. "No. Thank God. I know how agonizing it can be."

Alma smiled into my eyes. "No, you probably don't."

I smiled back. "You're right. I haven't a clue."

"The sort I have, rheumatoid, is a constant challenge. But now that the sky has cleared and there's no rain in the immediate forecast, it's

abated for the moment. So, onward." She opened the silver box, removed a cigarette and held it to her mouth, her fingers almost quiver-
ing, until Cookson lit it. She inhaled with relief. "Tell me, would you
like a cup of green tea or a glass of sherry?"

"Tea sounds perfect, thank you."

Cookson poured a cup and placed it before me. Thank God I'd eaten
something—there was neither milk nor sugar, cookie nor cake in sight.

"The same for me, please, Cookson," Alma said.

"Anything else, Mrs. Naxos?" He asked.

She shook her head. "No, thank you."

"Do you have your bell?"

"I do." She held up a small silver bell that had been lying in her lap
and rang it.

"Please ring if you need me." He stoked the fire and left, taking the
fruit jellies with him. It sounded as though the door had locked behind
him. The little bell was a curious prop, a ruse. There was a panic button
on the bottom of the table.

Alma cradled her cup in both hands, blew on her tea, and then took
a small sip. She placed the cup carefully back on the table and then
raised those enormous dark blue eyes. They were as flat as slate.

"Now," she said, sitting back in her wheelchair. "Let's get down to
business. Precisely who are you?"

SEVENTEEN

I am very seldom caught off guard. But Alma had succeeded. It took a second for me to gather myself.

"What do you mean?" I said. "I'm Margaret Romaniei."

She shook her head and stared straight into my eyes. "No, you're not."

"Excuse me?"

"You are not Princess Margaret of Romania. There is no such animal."

"I beg your pardon."

"Frederick Romaniei may or may not have been married but he was most definitely not killed in a skiing accident. So now tell me what you want."

"I don't know what you're talking about." My heart pounded and I was having trouble getting my breath—I couldn't believe that all the years of research I'd put into creating Margaret Romaniei had gone out the window like a puff of Alma's smoke. It didn't make sense.

"You're here for a reason and I want to know what it is."

"I'm here because you invited me." I was mad and I could feel the color rising in my face. I hadn't failed at anything since I'd gotten caught in Homer Mallory's jewelry store almost forty years ago. I stood up. All I wanted to do was get out of there. Make a graceful exit.

"Please sit down," Alma said. Her face had turned very pale.

I remained standing.

"How did you find out?"

"Find out?"

"Please stop playing games," she insisted. "How much do you want?"

"Excuse me?"

"How much do you want? Let's be done with it."

I stared at her. I'm old enough to know that when you don't know what to say, don't say anything.

"All these years have gone by." She shook her head sadly and turned to look out the window. "I thought it was dead and buried. This is my worst nightmare to be caught in a blackmail scheme at this point in my life. Nothing can ever be hidden, can it?" She gazed up at me and her face was filled with anguish. "Poor George. He hates scandal and this is such a small, dirty, meaningless one."

She and I stared at each other. "Mrs. Naxos," I finally said. "I have absolutely no idea what you're talking about."

"I was with Frederick when he died. And it wasn't in an avalanche."

Hell. The overly warm room suddenly grew hot. I'm not sure whether or not my mouth actually fell open, but it felt as though it had, and I didn't know what to say but I knew I'd better come up with something pretty quick. "Oh, dear," I said. "It seems I've overplayed my hand."

It wasn't much but it was the best I could do at the moment.

" 'Oh, dear,' indeed. Do you want to tell me who you are and what you want—you've obviously gone to a great deal of trouble to get inside our house—or should I ring my bell and summon help?"

From the tone of her voice, she may as well have said, Shall I summon the firing squad.

I felt as if I were having an out-of-body experience. My mind churned, flashing between retreat and truth like a ball on a roulette wheel. "I don't know what to say."

"You're saying you aren't here to blackmail me?" She looked as confused as I was.

"Truthfully? The thought never even entered my mind."

Alma and I studied each other. It was a standoff.

"Well, this is very strange position to be in."

"An understatement, to say the least. May I?" I opened her cigarette box.

"Please."

I lit the cigarette and inhaled. "Would you like a sherry?" I asked.

"I believe I would."

I fussed about the cigarette and pouring the sherry for a minute or two, long enough to gather myself. "Alma," I said. "The fact that you, Frederick Romaniei, and I are joined in this conversation is pure chance, coincidence."

"And? Surely you're something more than a simple con artist or thief. You know there's virtually no chance you can get out of here with anything of value. As a matter of fact, you can't get out of here at all unless I let you. And even if you're a member of the media, you're wasting your time. If your lipstick is a camera, our security machines have killed your film and your story will never see the light of day. At least not on planet Earth. My husband will see to that."

I hadn't had a cigarette in ages. It tasted wonderful and seemed to quiet my brain, which continued to flail. There was no choice. I had to tell her the truth and take her into my confidence.

"You are still a British subject," I said.

Alma nodded. "I am."

"I need your help. The queen needs your help."

"The queen?" She didn't look in the least surprised. Actually, her expression almost said, *What does she want now?* For all I knew the queen called her on the phone and asked her for help all the time. Oh, well. So Alma calls her up to check me out. How much worse could it get? I was beyond having anything to lose at this point.

I nodded. "Alma, I am an undercover British agent and I, we, need your help to get into Mont-St.-Anges. We picked the Frederick Romaniei connection to try to attract Mr. Naxos's attention, not yours." I laughed. "This is unreal."

"Why do you need to go to Mont-St.-Anges?"

"One of the club members, Robert Constantin, has a constant companion who goes by the name of Sebastian Tremaine."

"Yes." Her face was expressionless. I couldn't tell if that meant she knew Mr. Tremaine or if she was just encouraging me.

"His real name is Bradford Quittle and he is the queen's former head footman. Her most trusted valet. Mr. Quittle-Tremaine is in fact a highly skilled jewel thief."

Alma's eyebrows arched a millimeter.

"He has stolen many of the queen's most famous and valuable jewels, including the Cambridge and Delhi Durbar parure."

"You're not serious."

"I'm very serious. Furthermore, he's probably planning to rob a number of ladies in Mont-St.-Anges. We intend to get him, and the queen's jewelry, back to England as quickly and quietly as possible."

"A jewel thief in Mont-St.-Anges? Never."

If she only knew, I thought.

"Yes," I answered.

"That is simply not acceptable. Naturally, we have a huge security department there, but we've never even had a call for a lost dog," she told me.

"Will you help?"

"Of course. But let me be clear, I'm very pleased if this helps the queen, but I'm doing it more for myself. Mont-St.-Anges is the only place when I am able to go out in public. If word got out there was a thief on the grounds—it would be a disaster."

Grounds here being a relative term since we were talking about more than five thousand hectares of private property, an entire alpine valley.

"I understand," I said.

She and I agreed that although I was British Secret Service agent, Margaret Kistler, I would keep my alias as Princess Margaret of Romania.

"What if there's someone else out there who knows how Frederick died?" I asked.

Alma shook her head. "No. His parents are gone and I had the death certificate fixed by a Swiss doctor for an absurd amount of money. It was a bad day in a cheap hotel and I was the only one there. No one knew I was with him and I was on a plane back to London hours before his body was even officially 'found.'"

My imagination spun with the possibilities of what on earth could have brought the Royal Ballet's prima ballerina into a cheap Zurich hotel room with a no-good, alcoholic, aristocratic deadbeat like Freddy. I couldn't ask what she'd been doing there but it wouldn't hurt to inquire as to how he'd died.

"None of your business," was all she said. The subject was closed. "I'm going to have my friend, Lucy Richardson, contact you. Do you know who Lucy and Al Richardson are?"

I shook my head no. But of course, I knew who Al Richardson was—he was up there near the top of the annual list of international billionaires. I'd seen his and his wife's pictures in a number of publications, but I thought her name was Monica.

"He's chairman of Globe Exploration and one of George's best friends. Lucy will be a nice contact for you to have. She's one of my closest friends. She and Al just got married a few months ago. I'll call her this afternoon and ask her to introduce you to a few of the members."

"That's very kind, thank you so much."

"Are you ready to leave tomorrow?"

I nodded. "I'm ready to leave today."

"Tomorrow will be plenty of time. I have to make some arrangements for you."

I didn't try to change her mind. One thing I'd learned about Alma—it was her way or the highway.

EIGHTEEN

Early the next morning, the hotel car with the blacked-out windows sped through light morning traffic to the green expanse of Paris's Le Bourget Airfield. On the opposite side of the A-1, traffic inbound to the city was already heavy, at a standstill in some places except for the ever-present motorcycles and motor bikes that raced like mosquitoes at sixty and seventy miles an hour between the lines of stalled cars.

I couldn't help being a little excited. I'd never flown on a private jet before. Many of our clients at Ballantine & Company arrived on their own planes and occasionally I'd gone to the airport in the company sedan to greet them. But they'd never invited me onboard for a look-see or a little tour and I'd rather have slashed my wrists than been so gauche as to ask if I could come inside. I knew enough to have a conversation about the different models and so forth, but actually to be entering this exclusive realm as a passenger was thrilling to me.

So far, almost everything about this situation was turning out to be a first. I was operating on the inside of the law—stealing jewels for the government. Flying on a private jet. Going to a private club. And . . . I had an accomplice.

The driver turned into the airfield and continued down the long service road to an enormous, unmarked hangar where five-story-high front doors were rolled open enough to let a big car in and a small jet out. The hangar was filled with the most beautiful fleet of private aircraft I'd ever seen, or even imagined. There were two Grumman G-5s, the ultimate in corporate jets, large enough to cross oceans and continents without refueling; four big Learjets, the most elegant of corporate craft with their sleek trim lines and wraparound windscreens; and a helicopter. I don't know much about helicopters but this looked like a good-sized one to me. They were all pure white, clean and polished and shining like stars. Other than their tail numbers, their only markings were a small Greek flag and George Naxos's Napoleonic corporate logo, a gold N inside a gold laurel wreath.

One of the Learjets was sitting in the center of the hangar, jet steps down and its nose pointed out the door, ready to go.

The sedan stopped at the foot of the steps, where two sharp-looking young men in black uniforms with gold trim waited. For me. They were very good-looking.

"Your Highness," said the man who was slightly older, maybe in his early forties and who had a great deal of gold braid on his shoulders and hat. "My name is Alan and I'm the captain of your flight today. This is Mark, my copilot." Mark gave a quick little halfbow. "Are you ready to board?"

Alan sounded American.

"I am," I answered. "Thank you."

I followed him up into the narrow cabin while two maintenance men in blue coveralls began the Herculean task of loading all my suitcases into the cargo bin. It was a good thing I was the only one on the plane because after my shopping spree in Paris, there wouldn't have been room for anyone else's gear.

The cabin, which in a business configuration could carry fourteen passengers, was arranged for six. Four chairs, two on either side of the aisle, facing each other across long, rectangular tables, with a sofa and two more seats behind. It was done in the same colors as the Naxos's apartment: creamy caramel-colored leather seats and carpeting. The tables and fittings were blond wood. There was nothing to jar the eye—it was soothing and comfortable.

"Please sit wherever you like except for that seat," he indicated the well-used, forward-facing armchair on the right side of the cabin. "That is reserved for Mr. Naxos."

"I didn't realize he was coming with us."

"He's not. It's reserved for him at all times."

"I understand." I smiled.

"Yes, ma'am." Alan returned my smile. "He's the boss."

I chose the seat opposite that which I assumed would be Alma's if she were along. Morning papers in three languages were arranged on the table. Outside the window I saw the copilot conducting his pre-flight check. He stooped and shone his flashlight under the belly of the plane and then stood at the end of the wing and tried to wiggle it around. The car was already gone.

"Allow me to show you some of the amenities of our aircraft. As I'm sure you know"—Alan indicated toward the back of the cabin—"the restroom is aft. Each seat is equipped with full communications capability." He flipped open a panel to reveal a telephone, an Internet hookup, headset jacks, and a pair of high-tech earmuffs with a little boom microphone. "Your CD/ DVD player is here." He flipped open another panel. "And the video library is in that cabinet if you want to watch a movie." He pointed to closed cabinet doors near the small forward galley. "There are fresh juice, coffee, and croissants in the galley in case you didn't have time to have breakfast. Or if you'd like a glass of Champagne, a Bloody Mary, or a chicken sandwich and potato chips, we also have that." He grinned. He had calm, intelligent eyes and a slightly crooked smile. He sounded like a Texan. "May I offer you something before we take off? Once we're in the air I'm afraid you'll have to fend for yourself."

"Café au lait would be wonderful, thank you. I'll get myself something to eat after we take off." I wanted a glass of Champagne to celebrate this momentous occasion—momentous to me at any rate, a career benchmark of some sort—but I had a long day ahead and needed to keep my wits about me. Starting with a Champagne breakfast would not be productive. Unfortunately.

"With pleasure, Your Highness. Sugar?" He had a wonderful way about him, so American. He was polite and deferential but with a sense of ease and camaraderie.

"Please. Two."

I watched him measure two teaspoons of sugar into a butter-colored mug with a white inside and then pour the hot coffee and steaming milk together expertly. He placed the mug in a recess in the table and laid a white linen napkin and spoon beside it. "Just to reconfirm our itinerary, because I'd hate to take you to the wrong town. Our first stop is in Zurich and then we'll fly on to Sion where the helicopter will take you into Mont-St.-Anges."

"That's right."

"Okay. Enjoy your flight—let us know if you need anything. We'll be right up here. Would you like the cockpit door open or closed?"

"Closed, please."

And then he left me and took off his hat and jacket and hung them somewhere inside the cockpit, climbed over the edge of his captain's seat, and that was that. The cargo door locked with a thump behind me and then the copilot boarded, pulling the air stairs and door closed behind him. I watched him and the captain fiddle with switches and talk on the radio as a tug pulled the plane from the hangar. Once we were well outside, the copilot reached around his seat and shut the cockpit door, then the engines started up and off we went. As we turned for the runway, I saw that the hangar doors were already closed. Mr. Naxos ran a very efficient operation.

I fastened my seat belt as the little craft taxied into position at the end of the runway. We paused there for a moment while the pilots turned the engines up to high and then they took their feet off the brakes and we shot forward as though we'd been launched from a catapult and were hurled into the sky like a javelin. And we just kept climbing. Higher and higher. Minutes later they slowed down the engines—actually, for a heart-stopping moment or two, I thought they'd turned them off altogether, it got so quiet—and we leveled off at our cruising altitude. Forty-four thousand feet it said on the altimeter gauge in the wall.

The sheer exclusivity and luxury of it all were really unparalleled. I wished Thomas were there. He would have loved this. I wanted to call him up and tell him everything, tell him about the last twenty-four hours and Alma Naxos's offer to do whatever she could to help. But that was missing the point, wasn't it? I was trying to stay out of Thomas's sights, not share my adventures with him.

As it was, I was running a risk by going into the heart of Zurich. Zurich was where Thomas was by now, unless he'd gone to St. Moritz after all in the hopes of spotting me there. But I'd assessed the downside and decided there was little chance of our running into each other. First of all, he wasn't looking for me in Zurich or expecting to see me, so I held the element of surprise in my hand. Plus, I'd changed my appearance completely. And finally, I didn't have any choice—that was where my connections were.

I got up and helped myself to more coffee, a brioche, butter and orange marmalade, and then I just looked out the windows and enjoyed the incredible spectacle of the snow-covered Alps passing below.

NINETEEN

The driver's eyes looked at mine in the rearview mirror. "Where may I take you, madam?"

The car was identical to the Naxos Mercedes sedan in Paris.

"The Baur au Lac, please. I'm meeting friends for brunch."

"Very well." He pulled out of the unmarked hangar at Zurich International Airport and drove swiftly into the center of the city. I got out at the front door of the hotel, passed quickly through the main lobby—my eyes were constantly on the lookout for Thomas, but thankfully, I didn't see him—and out the side door into the frigid morning wind that came off the frozen lake.

I'd spent a great deal of time in Zurich and knew exactly where I was going. I crossed the bridge and stayed along the bank of the canal until I reached the nondescript antiquarian bookstore marked by a chipped black sign with gold letters. A bell tinkled when I opened the door and an old man looked up from a desk heaped with books and papers in a dark corner.

"Madame?" He squinted over the tops of his smudged glasses. Between him and the piles of ancient manuscripts, the smell of unwashed body, mold and mildew was staggering.

I reluctantly closed the door behind me. "I collect letters of Madame de Pompadour and I understand you might have some new arrivals."

The old man studied me. "Oh?"

"I'm interested in one in particular—a note she sent to Choiseul."

"She sent numerous notes to Choiseul. Sometimes ten a day."

"You're right." I laughed. "This one calls for Voltaire's head."

"Ah. Good." He stood up from the desk and, after giving his creaky old bones a moment to accustom themselves to the shock of being erect, shuffled past me and locked the front door. It was painful to watch. "Follow me."

He creaked through brocade curtains that I wouldn't touch without rubber gloves, and down stone steps into a cellar that could only exist in an ancient city. It smelled disgusting. He cranked an ancient wall switch and a hanging bulb cast dim, watery light over old filing cabinets, more endless stacks of manuscripts and—half-concealed by a door hanging from broken hinges—a toilet I'd commit suicide before I'd use. He moved a stack of boxes aside with surprising strength and revealed a modern steel door. He placed his index fingers on an electronic scanner and the door rolled back automatically.

I stepped in and the door immediately sealed shut behind me with a hiss.

This was EKM Elektronika—the secret Mecca of the most advanced electronic espionage gadgets and gizmos on earth, most of them considered illegal in most civilized countries. Its existence was known only to select international government agencies who purchased and used the contraband gadgets in spite of the ban against them, and to certain individuals, such as I, who could afford them. It could be compared to a decorator's showroom, with its exclusive Open to the Trade sign on the door. But this was a much more expensive, selective, elusive consortium, hidden in the murky demimonde of acceptability, with price tags to match.

The halogen lights in the showroom were intense and focused. They blazed off long, gleaming stainless-steel counters and walls of glass-fronted displays. A man in a work apron approached. He had thick black hair and thick black-rimmed glasses. Although we'd done business with each other for years, I didn't know his name and he didn't know mine. We were both professionals and I trusted him implicitly.

"Yes, madam. How may I help you today?" His English had only the faintest accent.

Thirty minutes and many, many thousands of U.S. dollars later I had assembled items that provided for every contingency I could imagine. It was an enormous lode of goods but since I was going to a place with no easy access to the outside world, I needed to cover all the bases. Even for me, who always made sure to have the latest technology on hand, this was a significant purchase. He was happy to ship all my purchases but one, a huge handgun, able to stop an elephant, according to him. It made my purse heavy on my shoulder, and my whole right arm still tingled from the shooting lesson he'd given me in their soundproof target range.

Other than the shotgun I had for trap and skeet shooting, I'd never possessed a gun for my own protection, but again, there would be no second chance to provision this caper and I'd hate to end up in a situation where I needed to defend myself and not have the capability. My prey was successful and stealthy, and having the weapon made me feel more secure. It certainly packed a wallop.

My next stop was the shop that manufactured the most perfect synthetic stones in the world, undetectable from the real thing. I gave the owner the specifics of what I needed—dozens of diamonds and emeralds, along with a few other touches.

He nodded. "This is no problem, madam. When do you need them?"

"Forty-eight hours," I answered.

"Oh, ha-ha." He smiled.

"I'm serious."

"There will be a significant rush charge. We will have to stop all our current production just to accommodate this order. Our factory is swamped right now."

"I don't care how much it costs."

"That's a good thing. For you, we will do it."

I'd been a good customer over the years and I had sufficient cash on hand to pay not only for the stones but also for the rush charge, which precisely doubled the price.

I checked my watch—I'd been gone for almost two hours, not an unreasonable amount of time for a nice brunch with a good friend, but the fact was, I hadn't actually eaten and, even if it added half an hour or so, it was almost lunchtime and I couldn't be in Zurich, and within a block of Kronenhalle, and not run in for a quick bite. I sat at the long, busy bar, surrounded by their stunning collection of Picassos, Modiglianis, Klees, and Cassatts, and ordered my favorite Swiss lunch: rösti—perfectly sautéed, crispy, buttery grated potatoes—veal sausages, and a glass of pilsner, and prepared for a delicious experience. About halfway through my meal, I looked up and saw Thomas and another man, presumably David Perkins because he was, as Thomas had said, tall and thin with sandy hair and blue eyes. The bite of rösti and sausage turned into a lump of rock in my mouth. I turned quickly back to my book and swallowed and kept my eyes on them in the back mirror of the bar.

Thomas looked tense. David looked jumpy. He stood a step or two away, obviously familiar with and respectful of his boss's temperament. The hostess greeted them and after an abrupt word or two from Thomas, led them to a table near the front. He sat facing the door.

I paid my check and put on my dark glasses and looked at myself in the mirror. There was no way he would recognize me. I walked past their table. I even looked at him and he glanced briefly at me. Seconds later I was on the street, trying not to laugh. It was exhilarating. I had hit my stride and for the life of me couldn't remember why I gotten out of the business.

———

We took off from Zurich and flew to Sion—one of the few airports in the interior of Switzerland that has a runway long enough to accommodate small jet aircraft—and taxied into another private hangar where a Naxos helicopter waited to fly me to Mont-St.-Anges.

A light snow fell from broken clouds.

TWENTY

I am not a prideful person. I'm far too assiduous for pride. Pride leads people to believe their own publicity which perpetuates immaturity and leads to mistakes. However, I have always taken a certain amount of comfort in and reassurance from my sangfroid. I've always known I could rescue myself, no matter the circumstances.

One of the benefits of getting older is that you know what works for you and what doesn't, and as time passes you become less and less reluctant simply to stop doing things again, to scissor them out of your life permanently. For example, I've never liked sweetbreads of any sort and now I wouldn't even consider putting a bite of them in my mouth. No. Sweetbreads are over. Forever. Thank God. Same with bad wine, white panties, white bras, or diets. No. They're simply not worth it. I also know myself very, very well, particularly when it comes to plying my trade. There is no funny business about it, no seat-of-my-pants attitude. I know the ropes. I am the consummate professional.

I'm equally assiduous in regard to controlling my environment. What I mean by that is that I have never put myself in any sort of physical jeopardy, whether it's in terms of getting physically apprehended with hot goods in my possession, or in actual physical danger, as in falling off a window ledge, skydiving, going to Africa, ballooning, or shooting the rapids. I don't place myself in a situation from which I cannot extricate myself smoothly.

I am the queen of exit strategies. I've never moved forward with a plan or a heist if I haven't already provided myself with at least two or three reliable escape routes or backup identities. But, of course, that's one of the benefits of being a jewel thief, as opposed to an art thief or car thief or thief of stocks and bonds—I can dispose of my goods in the flash of an eye. They can drop down a sewer, hide beneath a cushion, or fly out a car window. In some instances, they can even be swallowed. They can be taken apart, the metals crushed or melted down and the stones smashed or recut in seconds, rendering them virtually unidentifiable and untraceable. Hot gems and stolen jewelry aren't cumbersome and there's no incriminating paper trail.

And while I'm on the subject of my personality traits, when it comes to physicality? Physical, athletic exertion has also never been a part of my life. I'm simply not interested. I've never been in what's considered "shape." I do have a number of cashmere warm-up suits—the pale, pale pink and the especially yummy taupe ones are my favorites—that I like to put on around the house or when I go for a walk, with matching anoraks in case it rains, but frankly, if the skies look the least bit threatening, I generally stay in. And, let me see, I did learn to play tennis in Portofino from that charming young pro, Guilberto. He really was absolutely precious. But that was the most exercise I've ever gotten.

I have virtually no interest in athletics, with the exception of sporting clays, which I do enjoy and which take a good eye, a steady hand, and a calm, sure finger on the trigger, or, in other words, sangfroid. Thomas and I constructed a trap and skeet range on the farm and spend hours shooting. I think we enjoy it the same way other people enjoy playing golf. I'm an excellent shot, if I do say so myself.

I've never skied, or played any kind of team sport such as volleyball or badminton, and so forth. In fact, the whole concept of a team is foreign to me and I cannot think of a single time in my life when it would have been in my best interest to depend on another person, much less a bevy of them. Like sweetbreads, exercise is simply not my field.

Occasionally I watch horse racing on television.

I treasure my marriage to Thomas as he treasures his relationship to me because we are like dessert to each other. We don't require each other's presence or expertise to survive, or even flourish. We require each other for fun and pleasure. My "partnership" with Alma is one I control completely. I can stop at any time because the fact is, I don't need to be doing this. Any of it.

I've made it a point to avoid extremes in all areas of my life.

In short, I am a woman who is in control, bolstered by skill, experience, prowess, and nerves of steel, even in situations of extreme duress.

All of this became mere braggadocio when the helicopter lifted off, hovered for a moment as though gathering its skirts together, and then charged, bolting forward—jet engines screaming like bats out of hell—dead center at a massive, craggy, snowy solid rock wall. I almost lost control of myself. I have never been so frightened in my life. I wanted to scream but my throat was paralyzed. I was sure I was going to die, from either the impact or the heart attack I would suffer just prior to the impact. Forcing myself to remain calm and even appear blasé as the ice-encrusted granite cliff approached at five thousand miles an hour, to act as though I were totally accustomed to crashing and dying, was one of the biggest challenges I've ever confronted. In fact, when we were only inches from slamming into it and I was just about to put my hands over my face and burst into tears, we suddenly went straight up, pivoted, and headed toward another one. I became completely disoriented and couldn't trust my eyes or my senses. It was terrifying—for the first time I began to question if I'd made a mistake all these years not having faith in anybody but myself. I looked at the rock wall and wondered what would become of me. Would Thomas have to trudge up these mountains in a blizzard and make a grisly identification? Oh,

Lord. What a mess. This speeding, stopping, rising, falling, turning, churning went on for only about half an hour, but it seemed like forever. I looked at the pilots—what a gruesome way to make a living. Poor things. It was absolutely horrible, and the unpredictability of our motion kept my stomach in my throat the whole time, right up there next to my heart and my rösti.

The landing was as hair-raising as the flight—a shuddering, rocking, noisy descent onto an elevated platform. But the issue was, I didn't know the platform was there. I could see terra firma way down below and when the pilot shut the engines off thirty feet above the ground, I assumed that was it. The end. We'd just drop like a rock and smash ourselves to smithereens onto the charming, snow-packed cobblestones. I closed my eyes. Seconds later when I opened them and saw people walking toward me, I admit, I did burst into tears. I wanted to tear off my seat belt, jump out the cabin door, and throw myself into their arms. No wonder Mr. Naxos said how blessed they were— anybody who did this on a regular basis and survived to tell the tale was leading a charmed life.

I'd go by train when I left.

"Welcome to Mont-St.-Anges, Princess Margaret," said a well-tanned fellow in a loden green ski parka with dark red piping. He had white teeth, an Austrian accent, and a jaunty loden hat with a deer-tail brush tucked in the braided hatband. His gold name badge said Jurgen. He took my hand and helped me down the steps to the ground, which I saw was a wide cement platform that banked into a hillside. A long hangar ran the length of it, and I could see a number of helicopters inside with a variety of markings.

I couldn't control the slight tremor in my hands and knew my face was as white as a sheet. I smiled at him as best I could. "Thank you. I'm so relieved to be here. I'm embarrassed to say I'm not a very comfortable flier."

The fact is, now that I was out in the air, if the terror hadn't already given me the shakes, the cold would. Even in my fur coat, it was absolutely freezing. This was without question the stupidest thing I'd ever done. I wanted to leave, to go home, or back to Paris or Portofino, back to some sort of civilization, but then I looked at the now-dormant helicopter, lurking there like a giant sneering torture chamber, and said to myself, *Never again in my life no matter how long I live, will I ever get back on one of those things.* I could feel my gall rise, prickling up my neck into my hair. I could feel myself growing angry and belligerent, which would accomplish nothing. I drew in a large breath and let it out slowly, a little at a time, in an attempt to get my heart rate to slow down.

"It is a bit of a hair-raiser, isn't it?" Jurgen smiled. "We'll take good care of you—get you a good hot mug of gluhwein to make you forget." He put a protective, sure hold on my elbow and guided me down a wide staircase to a gaily painted horse-drawn sleigh. A similarly dressed man sat in the driver's seat and he tipped his hat. Once Jurgen got me settled, he opened a wooden box the size of a large storage freezer at the foot of the stairs and pulled out three faux fur lap robes, which he tucked around me. They were heated!

"Better?" His eyes looked into mine with concern.

"Much." I could feel the color beginning to return to my face.

"Now, this will set you right." He handed me an earthenware mug with green trim, filled with hot, steaming, spiced wine. The scent of apples, cloves, and cinnamon curled up and filled my head with their warm, homey fragrance.

"Thank you," I said. But he had no idea of the extent of my gratitude. I'd been cold and frightened and way out of my element, and now this gracious young man was knocking himself out to make me feel warm and safe and welcome. Finally—I'm embarrassed to say even a little bit grudgingly—I raised my eyes and looked around at where I was and what I was doing, and saw the magnificent snowy valley and sharp classic peaks, the massive gray horse stamping its foot and shooting steam from its nostrils. I heard the sound of the sleigh bells and the hollow echo of the wind. I noticed the healthy, vigorous men and their obvious relish of what they did. It was surreal, as though I were in a movie, or a dream.

My life in England had been so closed. Filled with privilege to be sure, but save for that one weekend in Cap d'Antibes with Sir Cramner thirty-odd years ago, my domain had never extended beyond the borders of my own secure, totally controllable little world of London, Provence, Paris, and an occasional trip to visit my vaults in Zurich and Geneva. I marveled at the steps that had brought me to this place and time, and, now that I was on the ground, I could feel my legs coming back, my confidence restoring itself.

The driver turned and raised his eyebrows with a question that seemed to say, "Ready to go?"

I raised my finger. "One moment." I took a healthy sip of the hot wine. It felt warm and invigorating on the way down. I took another. I think there was a very strong dose of ginger schnapps in there as well. My head opened as though I'd been asleep. "Ready," I said, and actually felt as though I meant it.

He snapped the reins and off we went.

I was ready. Let the games begin.

TWENTY-ONE

On those quick trips to Zurich and Geneva, I hadn't ventured outside the cities into the Swiss Alps. In fact, I'd never been in the mountains. Any mountains. So my impression of Switzerland was that it would be like its photographs and postcards. Steep and snowy in the winter and bright green in the summer, with rosy-cheeked dirndl-dressed women and lederhosen-clad men who did a silly dance where they slapped their legs and boots, and they all ate cheese fondue and milk chocolate day in and day out, sitting just beneath their cuckoo clocks while their St. Bernards slept in the sun waiting for winter, and they watched their brown dairy cows out the windows of their charming little huts where they had everything they needed to live a happy life. And everything was just as cute as a button.

As a little girl I'd sneaked into the movie *Heidi* several times. Who could forget the little girl with braids and a checkered apron tending her goats, their little bells tinkling across the steep, grassy mountainsides? Her calling out, "Grandfather! Grandfather!" Who could forget Grandfather and his hunk of cheese (Swiss) that he carved with a big knife for lunch? Who could forget how much Heidi and Grandfather loved each other and how he was forced to send her away to Zurich or Berne or wherever to care for her sweet invalid cousin, Clara, who had that hateful mother. Oh, how I sobbed when she had to tell Grandfather good-bye. And then, Poor Clara, trapped in a wheelchair with those horrible steel braces on her legs, having tantrums and hating everyone and throwing her hairbrush at them. And lovely little Heidi befriending her, giving her courage and *getting her to walk!* And then, taking Clara to the hut in the mountains, but Grandfather was dead. Oh, God.

That, to me, was the real Switzerland.

Little wonder I came to Mont-St.-Anges with an expectation of what it would look like: a charming little town, every building and chalet made of either brown wood, its eaves and porches adorned with carved filigree, or else covered with white stucco, with colorfully painted murals and borders around the windows and doors, a red tile roof, wooden shutters with heart-shaped, peephole cutouts, and flower boxes filled with pine boughs in the winter and red geraniums in the summer.

I wasn't disappointed.

Our sleigh glided through a narrow, snow-packed street and into a small square—Place de Bonhomie—with storefronts of chic boutiques I'd never heard of, with window displays of irresistibly beautiful goods. Alma had told me the shopping was the best in the world but to protect the privacy of the place she hadn't let any of the luxury-goods shops that would typically be found in such an upscale environment come in. Instead, the shops were all owned by the club and operated by individuals who passed the Naxos acid tests for employment. We passed a few bundled-up people who were either walking or skiing, some apparently on their way to or from lunch, judging by the racks filled with skis outside the restaurant and café. It was busy and buzzing but not crowded. Most of the people waved as we passed and my driver tipped his hat to them all, greeting most of them by name.

On we sailed into the central plaza, Place de Bonne Santé. A large snow-filled fountain sat in the middle of what I assumed were spectacular gardens in the summer. An old-fashioned bandstand was off to one side, its floor and railings buried in snow. Directly across and dominating the plaza was the Hôtel des Anges, a wonderful, welcoming, classically Swiss sight with the mountains rising behind. Three stories tall, the building had a pitched red-tiled roof and was as white as the snow, except for wide borders of flowers painted around the windows, each of which had green wooden shutters with fancy peepholes and yellow window boxes. There was a main portico as well as a ski-in entrance. Three empty sleighs were lined up like taxis, their horses bundled in loden green blankets with red trim. Other than our sleigh bells, there was little sound.

Similarly styled but smaller buildings banked the hotel. Alma had told me that the larger was the hospital and the other the spa. Place de Bonne Santé indeed. I'm sure the hospital emergency room did a thriving business resuscitating people who'd just arrived by helicopter.

Evidently, my white-faced discomfort had been radioed ahead because when I walked through the front door, I was greeted immediately with another mug of hot wine, which I accepted gratefully. I think it was the high-octane schnapps that made it so bolstering—like dipping ginger snaps into red wine, or biscotti into Vin Santo and letting them soften and crumble in your mouth. Whatever it was, it had the calming, soothing effect I needed.

The spacious lobby was warm, high ceilinged and smelled of woodsmoke and spices. Stone fireplaces burned at either end and five or six dogs were stretched out comfortably on cushions near the hearths, sound asleep. Rustic, rough-hewn, peeled-pine furniture with red-and-white checked cushions was grouped in comfortable seating arrangements. Each chair had a good reading light and long, low wooden coffee tables that invited putting your feet on them. Neat stacks of books and magazines were everywhere and there were three tables with in-the-works jigsaw puzzles. Except for two people reading quietly, and a table of four playing bridge, the room was otherwise unoccupied.

On the opposite side of the lobby, floor-to-ceiling windows provided a spectacular view of the steep, snow-covered piste upon which were dots of human beings plunging down its face on skis. I saw one skier fall, skis and poles shot like missiles in all directions. The body tumbled and bounced down the hill for several feet and then disappeared behind a large pile of snow. Other skiers stopped and headed for the accident, gathering up the loose equipment along the way. I looked at the other people in the lobby. No one seemed alarmed or even to have noticed. A head appeared over the mound and then an entire body. The person brushed off the snow, accepted the return of his gear that had been littered along the hillside, put it all back on, and hurled himself down the slope as recklessly as before. He must have had bones made of rubber. Or a head full of sawdust.

There was no question about it: for me, skiing was out. Not that it had ever really been in, but I have to admit I'd toyed with the idea, a romantic notion that came into my head on the flight from Paris to Zurich on the private jet, when everything had been so comfortable and civilized with the fresh brioche, orange marmalade, and café au lait. The image had flown out the window on the helicopter ride when I saw how steep and jagged the Alps actually were face-to-face, but even then, I hadn't grasped that those were the mountains people actually skied on. Skiing had passed me by—at least in this lifetime.

The snow was falling hard now, a flurry of white—it made me cold just to look at it. One of the ski runs ended right at the edge of the terrace and a gondola terminal sat about thirty feet away. Two skiers swooshed gracefully into the boarding line, making a rooster tail of snow as they turned. At the edge of the terrace, a handful of diehards had gathered around a roaring outdoor fireplace to warm their hands, their breath coming out in puffs. A waiter emerged with a tray of steaming mugs, which the rosy-cheeked guests accepted with good-natured gusto.

I watched, enchanted and fascinated. I'd never seen a place like this—it had a warm, intimate feel—almost as though I'd stepped across a threshold into the heart and home of a large happy family.

TWENTY-TWO

My reverie was interrupted by the arrival of a tall woman of thirty-five or forty wearing a dark gray faille Armani pants suit. She had short streaked blond hair, smartly cut, and low-key makeup. "Your Highness," she said. "I am Lisle Franklin, the club manager. Welcome to Mont-St.-Anges. How did your helicopter ride go?"

I rolled my eyes. "Ooh la la. I think I'll take the train home."

"I know. It can be terrifying, even under the best of circumstances, but on a day like today when a storm's blowing in, it can frighten the wits out of you." Her accent was unidentifiable. "Would you like for me to show you around or do you prefer to go to your room directly?"

"I'd like to get settled first, if you don't mind."

"Wonderful. The elevators are right this way."

We rode to the third floor and I followed her down a short hallway to an old-fashioned wooden door with an old-fashioned drop latch. "We've put you in one of our 'for-ladies-only' suites. I think you'll be comfortable here, but if you're not, please let me know and we'll find something more to your liking."

Well, the suite was so welcoming, I could have been comfortable there for the rest of my life, if I didn't already have a life that I'd left back there somewhere in my beautiful Provence with my husband and my dog.

It's not that the living room was so large, it wasn't, but it was incredibly well appointed. The ceiling sloped slightly. A fire crackled in the hearth behind a small black wrought-iron screen with a decorative sil-houette of a skier. I'd been expecting classically Swiss furniture—child-sized, childlike, delicate and most decidedly not built for comfort. But, like the lobby, the chairs and sofa were large and comfortable, with deep, soft cushions covered in an almost calico-type orange-red fabric. A bookcase held an excellent selection of bestsellers and classics, along with a large flat-screen TV, a DVD and CD player, and an equally fine li-brary of films and music.

There was a small catering kitchen with a separate entrance, and a study with a complete office setup: laptop, printer, high-speed access, and four phone lines. Next to the phone was a red leather book. The words Membership Directory were embossed in small gold letters on its cover.

The bedroom was out of a Swiss fantasy. An old-fashioned wooden bedstead painted with rows of flowers and a featherbed that looked as though it had at least three feet of eiderdown as a mattress and another three feet of eider on top, and a ladder to climb into it. Yet another cheery fireplace—this one with painted tiles—a good-sized dressing room and a gleaming white tile bathroom. The cabinets were decorated with hand-painted ribboned bouquets and the towels were embroi-dered to match. There were walls of mirrors, a small color TV, and so many toiletries—beautiful products in frosted glass bottles labeled with the initials SA—that I could have spent hours smelling and testing each one. Loofahs, sea sponges, mitts, slippers, robes, soaps wrapped like presents. It was the most luxurious bathroom I'd ever been in.

While Lisle and I toured the apartment, bellmen began arriving with the luggage. They were under the no-nonsense supervision of a stern-looking, formally dressed gentleman.

"Allow me to introduce you to your butler, Klaus," Ms. Franklin said. Klaus did a quick bow.

"I'll leave you in his good hands. Please let me know if you need anything at all."

"Thank you."

"Your Highness," Klaus said. "Mrs. Naxos didn't say if you were bringing your maid or not."

I shook my head.

"Then may I arrange for your unpacking?"

"Yes, thank you."

Klaus snapped his fingers and a hefty blond in a red-and-green dirndl and lace-trimmed blue work apron appeared and instantly began opening my suitcases, putting some things away, laying others aside to be taken for pressing. Everything was done within ten minutes.

"Let me show you the vault," Klaus said when the staff had left.

In my closet sat an actual safe, not a typical small boxlike hotel-room safe but a good-sized fireproof vault, approximately two feet high by eighteen inches wide and deep. Its walls, bottom, and top were two-and-a-half-inch-thick armor. I supposed it weighed about six hundred pounds—too much for a cat burglar to cart off. The door sat open, revealing a forest green, velvet-lined interior with four velvet-covered shelves and a mesh of embedded locking bars that would slide into place once the door was closed and the electronic lock activated. This was a serious affair. The sophistication of the steel mesh and electronic lock indicated how seriously Mr. Naxos took security.

"Are you familiar with this sort of safe?" Klaus asked.

"Somewhat," I answered. The fact was, I could break into it in about three seconds, but only because I knew what I was doing and had purchased the newest iteration of electronic digital scanners in Zurich. Otherwise, it would be impossible.

Klaus instructed me on how to enter my own code.

"Thank you so much."

"What more can I do for you, Your Highness? May I send up a little strudel and a hot cocoa for your afternoon snack or will you be doing the après ski at the café with the others?"

I didn't know what the après ski was and the strudel sounded extremely tempting. I checked my watch—it was already three o'clock. I'd only gotten to eat half my lunch in Zurich before Thomas had arrived and given me the jitters. But on the other hand, I needed to do a little reconnoitering before it got dark. "I think I'll just grab something light at the café. Thank you."

Klaus did a sharp bow. "I am at your service." He stoked both fires and was gone.

TWENTY-THREE

I settled into one of the comfy armchairs and stared out the window. The crush of self-doubt brought on by my rocky arrival was long gone, replaced by a flood of well-being and confidence. I could tell I was going to be very happy here in Mont-St.-Anges for however long my assignment took—nothing but blue skies and smooth sailing. I had a feeling, if I really put my shoulder to the grindstone, I'd be in and out of town in a flash.

Robert Constantin's concert in St. Moritz was in a little more than twenty-four hours. I wondered if Thomas would go there and just as quickly discounted the idea. Whether I was there or not, he wouldn't blow the operation by showing up in public near his quarry. I assumed his aide-de-camp, David, was already well-embedded and had left town just long enough to meet Thomas in Zurich for lunch. Thomas hadn't described his plan B to me, but they wouldn't put all their eggs in one basket, even if it was mine, any more than I would leave myself with only one identity or escape route.

I poured a glass of sparkling water, added a wedge of lemon, and flipped quickly through the club activities guide. The number of ways to spend one's day were mind-boggling: alpine skiing, defined as all downhill skiing ("Alps," hence "alpine") including slalom, giant slalom, downhill racing, schussing, and freestyle; Nordic (from Norse and Norway) skiing, which according to the book meant either cross-country, snow-shoeing or jumping; lugeing, bobsledding, tobogganing, overnight ski camping, ski touring (which according to the photograph and description involved putting on your skis and holding on for dear life to the reins of a galloping horse), ice-skating, ice-dancing. It was endless.

I next opened the membership directory and a low whistle escaped my lips. It was a billion-dollar roster of Who's Who in the world of finance, industry, and the arts. Each listing had the member's address and phone in Mont-St.-Anges as well as all their other residences and offices, faxes, and e-mails. It was extraordinary, filled with information people would literally kill to get. But that's what private clubs are for—they're havens of safety, anonymity, trust, and secrecy, and if a member were to abuse the privilege of possessing such personal information about another member, everyone else in the club would ostracize him. His calls would go unanswered and unreturned, forever. The members of this club could put a person out in the cold, permanently, in a heartbeat. And they wouldn't hesitate for a heartbeat to do so, either.

On the other hand, there was so much confidential information included, I could understand how a person like Sebastian Tremaine, or any nefarious type for that matter, any fox in the henhouse, could do irreparable damage to the members' sense of coddled safety, not only while at the club proper, but also in any of their other residences or yachts. No wonder Alma Naxos had been so distressed and receptive to quick corrective action when I told her about it.

"It's all about privacy," she'd said. "Members come in and out of Mont-St.-Anges whenever they want and no one keeps track. As the owners, George and I could find out who's on the property and who isn't, but we wouldn't. It's too much of an invasion, an abuse of power that would make people uncomfortable, feel as though they're being watched by Big Brother."

The directory also had a walking map, showing paths that wound round the valley, and identified the chalets by name. For instance, Schloss Naxos and Schloss Constantin were conveniently across the road from each other in a hillside enclave of eight residences.

It was so comfortable in my chair, I longed to spend what was left of the day luxuriating, possibly go to the spa for a steam bath, a facial, and a massage—the description of services and treatments available was completely seductive. I kept having to remind myself why I was there. I could picture an invigorating Rosemary and Sage Salt Scrub, followed by a Body Moisture Drench, and then a comforting, detoxifying nap while I experienced a Fresh Powder Wrap. I snuggled deeper into the cushions. Just imagining the treatments relaxed me.

Kick! my conscience scolded: *Get up. Get dressed. Get to work. Now.* I did, but only after booking a cardio evaluation, a fitness physical, and a few spa appointments for the following day. I couldn't expect myself to work every second.

One of the many credos by which I've lived my life is: You never get a second chance to make a first impression. It was crucial that I hit the right note for my first venture outside. So after sorting through my new alpine wardrobe, which the maid had neatly arranged by color, I decided all black was safest: the black Bogner parka with the black fox trim, black slacks, black fox hat, Prada snow boots and good-sized—four-carat—diamond stud earrings, nothing fancy but large enough to draw attention without being showy. I tucked my book in my pocket—a biography of Winston Churchill, always a good choice if you're trying to strike up a conversation in a strange place with a proper kind of stranger—and set out, intending to have a coffee and possibly a little pastry at the café and find out what this après ski business was all about.

In direct contrast to the main plaza in front of the hotel, the little Place de Bonhomie bustled with people. Sleighs sailed around the perimeter—all kinds of sleighs, large enough for six, small enough for two. One of them was a jaunty one-person affair with its front, as well as the bridle, mane, and tail of its white horse, trimmed with bright blue-red-and-yellow ball fringe and little gold bells. I watched one man come in on skis behind his horse—ski touring—guide him to a gentle stop, step out of his skis and tie his horse at the hitching post.

"You really have to know what you're doing to do that," I said with admiration. "Wonderful."

He smiled. "Believe me, it's taken a lot of practice. For both of us."

He pulled a handful of sliced apples out of his pocket and fed them to the beast and then kissed him on his nose and patted him on his flank, talking to him the whole time.

"Kahlua café?" The waiter asked.

I'd settled at a small table on the terrace along the rail and fairly close to the outdoor fireplace. I wanted to sit inside where it was warm and where any sensible person would sit during a snowstorm, but inside was empty and outside the tables were filling up fast with people I felt as though I almost recognized, people whose pictures appeared only slightly occasionally in major newspapers or on CNN business news or in yachting magazines. They all seemed to be drinking the same thing out of a tall glass mug with layered contents: two inches of dark brown, half an inch of lighter brown and three inches of whipped cream.

"Please," I answered. It was cold and I was certain a cup of coffee with a little shot of liqueur would warm me up perfectly. Well, I had it backward. It was approximately six ounces of Kahlua with a two-ounce shot of espresso and a ton of sweetened thick cream—Viennese *Schlag*—and it was the most delicious thing I'd ever tasted. It occurred to me that everyone here looked happy because between the hot wine and the Kahlua cafés, they were all, to use the vernacular, half-bombed most of the time.

The activity and camaraderie picked up around the square as people went about what many consider humdrum, normal activities of everyday life, doing the marketing, shopping for wine, picking up prescriptions and drycleaning. This crowd, in the city or wherever they normally lived, had their maids or cooks or personal assistants run their errands. Here, they were doing it themselves with an ebullient aura of sheer enjoyment, as though it were real-life. It was charming and endearing.

By the time I finished my drink, I was inured to the cold. I signed the tab and went to join the crowd next door at Fannie's Delicacies.

I've been in dozens of specialty food shops in England, France, and Italy—Fannie's was the finest. It wasn't so big, it just had a little, just enough, of the best of everything. It was off the charts. And, I don't know if it was the gluhwein, the Kahlua or the overriding luxe of the place, but I felt as though I was at a cocktail party in the world's friendliest and best-stocked larder and pantry.

"How was the skiing today?" a man with a British accent asked me as I examined the marmalades.

"I'm embarrassed to say I didn't go," I answered.

"Neither did I. Too cold. It's supposed to be sunny tomorrow." He selected a jar of Marmite, the vile, vitamin-tasting, yeast-based toast spread that people either love or hate or love to hate.

I couldn't help but make a face.

"Don't look at me." He laughed and moved along. "It's for my wife. She's a health nut."

I put a jar of Fortnum and Mason lemon marmalade in my basket and stepped over to the caviar counter. I was trying to decide exactly how much beluga to buy for my dinner when I saw a shape out of the corner of my eye and then heard a voice.

"Oops!"

And then a slow-motion image of foamy latte flying through the air and hitting the front of my brand-new jacket, and then . . .

"Oh, my goodness. I'm so sorry." All said in a breathless lisp.

It was a very beautiful woman in a black mink jacket, thin as a rail and with perfectly coiffed dark hair. She had velvet brown eyes as big and lashy as Bambi's, which gaped with horror at my front—where the latte was rolling off my fancy new parka onto my fancy new boots— and a mouth that was a bright red perfect bee-sting. She pulled a lacy handkerchief from her pocket and her hand stopped midair, just inches from my chest, not sure exactly what the next step should be. Her eyes met mine. "Oh, my gracious," she said. "I don't know what to say."

I started to laugh—I couldn't help it. She looked like a child who was afraid she was going to get a paddling. I looked down at myself. "Not a problem at all," I said. "This is a parka—it's supposed to get wet. Now it's been christened."

By then Fannie herself had arrived on the scene with a damp cloth for me and a mop for the floor.

"Well," the woman said, repocketing her hankie. "This was a ridiculous way for me to introduce myself. Princess Margaret, I'm Lucy Richardson. Alma's friend." She offered her hand. "Welcome to Mont-St.-Anges."

I recognized her immediately. She'd been Lucy Sherman when I'd last seen her, and before that Lucy Von Buchner, and before that Lucy Wallace and who knows what before that. She was a regular at Ballantine's jewelry and arts and antiques auctions. One of our best customers. If she'd kept all the jewelry she and her husbands had bought from us, it would make her collection practically a rival for Queen Elizabeth's. She was as pretty as she could be and from what I'd heard, she wasn't particularly well liked by other women who said, among other things, she was not terribly bright, a little dingie, somewhat eccentric, a total narcissist, and completely nuts. In my opinion, judging by her parade of husbands and the stones she had on at the moment just to do her marketing, she was dumb and dingie like a fox.

"Thank you so much." We shook hands. She had on what looked like

a ten-to-twelve-carat, princess-cut diamond ring—possibly D flawless—
and shiny, bright red nail polish.

"Are you free for dinner this evening?"

"I am."

"I'm so glad. We're having a few friends, very casual. I'd love it if you
would join us. Eight o'clock."

"Thank you," I said. "I'd love to."

"It won't take you more than ten minutes to get to our chalet. Just
tell the driver Schloss Richardson." Those big brown eyes squinted a little and she cocked her head and frowned, pursing her lips into the
shape of a perfect little plum. Finally, I became uncomfortable.

"Yes?" I asked.

"I'm so sorry, you just look so familiar to me."

"I don't believe we've met before, but I could be wrong."

"I know I've got you confused with someone or maybe I've just seen
your picture in the papers. Oh, well. I'll figure it out. See you at eight."

Well, as they say in the best of circles, hell. A huge feeling of exhaus-
tion swept over me. This was just great. Just what I needed: to make my
way into the most secret place on the planet and have someone recognize me. But there was no way she could remember me—I'd only been
in the background at the auctions and I was now so disguised with my
dark hair and dark eyes, I scarcely recognized myself.

Back in my room, I checked the map. Schloss Richardson was up in
the same enclave with Schlosses Naxos and Constantin.

Thank you, Alma.

TWENTY-FOUR

Years ago, I learned that "casual" in a circle such as this means a low-key cocktail dress will do. So after a nap to recover my wits from the Kahlua café and Lucy Richardson's scrutiny, and a long delicious soak in the tub, I got put together in an silvery blue silk evening suit. I added a striking brooch of icy, light blue, thin-cut, square and emerald-cut diamonds piled on top of each other at angles to look like slabs of polar ice. A pavé diamond polar bear with onyx eyes and an emerald fish in his mouth stood atop the jumble. I put blue-and-white diamond-encrusted combs in my hair.

"Schloss Richardson," I told the doorman once he had settled me in the sleigh and covered me with heated robes. He relayed the destination to the driver who did an almost imperceptible flick of his hands and we slid away into the starry night. Within a minute or two we were out of the town center and in the open valley, sailing down the snow-packed road in the opposite direction from the heliport. Constellations galore packed the black sky and silvery moonlight gleamed on the pure white snow, making it look as though it were glazed. Shortly we slowed and turned right, and started up a hill. The Richardson residence was marked by a mass of white lights wrapped candy-cane style around an arched gateway—their chalet was an orgy of gingerbread and lit up like the Tour Eiffel.

A gigantic cowbell, at least two feet tall, with a leather strip attached to the dinger hung next to the front door. I pulled on the strip and the bonging was so loud, it made me jump.

Lucy Richardson opened the door. "Princess Margaret." She smiled and opened her arms. "We're so happy you could make it. Come in, let me introduce you around." She was wearing a dirndl. Well, not a full dirndl, if that's what one would call it. For instance, she didn't have on a peaked lace bonnet, but she did have on the long skirt with a blue apron covered with tiny yellow-and-white flowers, white lace-trimmed blouse tied at her neck, red hooked vest that was cut suggestively (and I felt a little inappropriately for a woman her age) around her bosom, white stockings with red hearts embroidered down the sides, and red shoes. She looked like a doll.

"You look wonderful," I lied. In my opinion, she looked like an idiot.

"Isn't it fun?" She twirled. "I like to go native wherever we are. Look at that pin, where on earth did you get it? Is that a Raymond Yard piece?"

I nodded. "It is—you have a good eye."

"That's an understatement." She grinned. "Jewelry is my greatest passion. Besides my husband, of course." Then she put her arm through mine and guided me down the entry hall toward the living room.

I felt a warning hidden in her benevolent marshaling of me. Her behavior was like that of a guard dog around his master that imposes himself physically on the guest, positions himself between the guest and the master. Not in a threatening way, in fact most often it's in an overly friendly way, but the point is to create a barrier.

"I'm so glad you could come tonight. This is the first time we've entertained since we finished redoing the house, top to bottom. I don't think Al's late wife, God rest her soul, had done a thing to the place since they built it twenty years ago. It was all in complete tatters. And cold as could be, just like a big old hotel. I told Al, this is Switzerland, honey. We need to look Swiss. I'm dying to hear what you think."

We'd reached the end of the hall which was hung with stuffed heads of deer, reindeer, moose, and elk—none of them indigenous to Switzerland as far as I knew—and entered what, in a word, could only be described as a cuckoo clock. It was the Swissest thing I'd ever seen in my life.

There were little red heart-shaped pine chairs with heart-shaped peekaboos cut in them, a collection of large and small cuckoo clocks on one pine paneled wall, and a collection of large and small cowbells on another. An ancient pair of very long skis crossed over each other in the shape of an X above the fireplace. The sofas and armchairs were all light pine and covered with forest green fabric bordered with red-and-white cookie-cutter stencils of men and women and cows. Every surface had throw pillows made in red-and-white and green-and-white pin-checked fabrics with ruffled edges. The lamps were made of antlers and milk cans, and rag rugs covered the plank floors. It was awful.

"Al, precious," Lucy called across to the fireplace where he was visiting with two other couples. "Look who's here. Princess Margaret of Romania."

"Margaret," I said to Lucy. "Please call me Margaret."

Al Richardson was older, but I'm not sure by how much. He was quite tall, trim, looked to be in tip-top condition, and had had some skillful work done on his face. He wasn't dressed in lederhosen, as I'd expected, but in soft cashmere slacks, a yellow turtleneck sweater, and a brown tweed cashmere sport coat. He was tanned and angular and came across as a man comfortable with his own power and influence.

"Very pleased to meet you," he said, and took my hand. "What may I offer you to drink? We have everything."

"Scotch on the rocks with a twist, please."

He relayed my drink order to a waiter who'd been standing by.

"Tell me," Al said, "what do you think of my precious's Swiss Miss hideaway?" He put his arm around Lucy's shoulder and kissed the top of her head. "Isn't she amazing?"

I nodded. "Truly amazing. I think you've out-Swissed the Swiss."

Lucy smiled. "I had so much fun doing it and my Al's such a good sport. He's just let me turn his world upside down and hasn't peeped."

I studied Lucy. She looked in her husband's eyes the whole time she spoke. She was completely focused on him—everyone else in the room could evaporate and she wouldn't mind. She was territorial and complicated. As the cocktail hour went along, I had the opportunity to watch her and she never took her eyes off him for more than a second or two. She was always watching to see if he needed anything or wanted anything, and not in a subservient way but with an awareness of wanting to make sure he had everything his heart desired, except for a conversation of more than two seconds with another woman. When that occurred, she would home in like an ICBM and break it up.

There are some women who are completely irresistible to men and Lucy was one of them. She needed them. She was helpless without them and she was so appreciative of any kindness, they would do virtually anything for her. She was the kind of woman who never raised her voice much above a whisper, and when Al looked at her, you could almost see him melt. He thought he was the luckiest man in the world.

I thought she was dangerous.

The dining room was as would be expected, with a collection of painted plates on one wall and a collection of copper pots on the other. A long pine refectory table with cute little Swiss chairs on one side and a long wooden bench on the other. Checked and ruffled seat cushions were tied on with ribbons and bows.

We'd just been seated when Lucy looked at me. "I know where I know you from," she blurted out. "It's been driving me crazy all afternoon."

My heart stopped. "Where?"

"Didn't we spend a couple of days together in Sardinia on the Batten's yacht?"

"I don't think so."

"Of course we did. Don't you remember when we all went skinny-dipping? It was a riot."

"Ignore her," Al said lightly. "She thinks she's met everyone at least once."

I laughed. "Well, I would definitely remember going skinny-dipping. You have me confused with someone else."

"Do you know Ann and Fred Batten?"

I shook my head. "Sorry."

"Hells bells," Lucy said. "I swear I'm going to figure it out."

"Lucy," Al said. "Let's move on."

I needed to get away from Lucy Richardson. Fast.

TWENTY-FIVE

The next morning, my day began with an authoritative knock at the door followed by the entrance of a Teutonic nurse who carried a stainless-steel tray covered with a white cloth. She was there to draw blood and so forth preparatory to my physical and visit to the spa in the afternoon. The Swiss take physicals very seriously.

"You have not had breakfast, have you?" she accused, as though she were going to hit me. She had a heavy German accent.

I shook my head.

"Three glasses of water only?"

I nodded.

"Good. Let me see."

I pushed up the sleeve of my robe and offered my arm.

"Excellent. Good strong veins. Well hydrated." She tied the tourniquet around my upper arm. "Make a fist."

I did.

"You will feel a little poke and then I will draw five vials. It will take only a second. Be still."

Only a masochist would refuse. I squeezed my eyes closed and heard the full vials clatter onto the steel tray one at a time. I also heard my butler, Klaus, arrive and begin to clatter about the kitchen.

Blood drawn, she handed me a small cup and gave more specific instructions than were required. Thankfully, less than five minutes after she arrived, she laid the white cloth back across her tray and left, stepping aside with haughty, tight-lipped impatience, and palpable contempt, to make way for Klaus, who was carrying a tray of his own. He swept past her as though she weren't there. Their mutual dislike of each other was so intense, it could only mean he had rejected her amorous advances sometime in the past. And knowing her as I did, which granted wasn't much, I further supposed Nurse Hell would pursue romance as aggressively and relentlessly as she pursued veins. She offered up a small, miffed snort before departing and closing the door behind her with a decisive and final click, off on her bitter rounds to torture and intimidate some other unsuspecting guest.

Klaus had set the breakfast table with wonderful china—white with silhouettes of primitive, forest green cows, birds (cuckoos no doubt), and hearts. He shook his head. "She is dreadful."

"Her bedside manner could use a little work."

"She didn't hurt you, did she?" He was immediately on the offensive and I got the impression he'd grab any opportunity to tattle and try to get her fired at best, or get a letter put in her file at the least.

"No. Actually, I have to admit she did an excellent job."

"Good," he said vehemently, although I could tell he was disappointed. "That's why she keeps her position. She's very good at what she does. Here, Your Highness." He pulled out a chair, "you sit down and look at the piste—what a beautiful sunny day it is—and let me pour you a cup of chocolate. It will calm you down."

I was already calm but loved Klaus's protective concern and attention. He filled the large breakfast cup with chocolate that was so thick it looked as though he were pouring cake batter, and then he added a heaping spoonful of sweetened whipped cream.

"I have brought you the Super Fitness breakfast as you requested and also two morning papers. I can offer others if you wish." He placed a folded copy of the *International Herald Tribune* in easy reach and on top

of it placed a stack of stapled photocopies with the headline Mont-St.-
Anges Report.

"This"—he tapped his finger on the report—"is what most members
prefer. Mr. Naxos says it's everything you need to know to figure out
what more you need to know!" Klaus rapped out a little laugh. "It's a
compilation of stories from the world's top newspapers. And finally, before I leave you to your peace, here is your schedule for the day." He
opened a leather folder and pulled out a typed sheet and laid it on top
of the report. "Now." He shook out my napkin and handed it to me.
"What more may I do, Your Highness?"

"I can't think of a thing, thank you."

"You're certain the nurse did not hurt you?" I caught the hopefulness
in his voice.

"Not even slightly."

He added a log to the fire and stoked it to a bright flame. "I am at
your service."

I sipped my chocolate and scanned the agenda for my day at the fitness center and spa. It was printed on bright white paper with green
trim that matched the china:

SPA DES ANGES

Margaret Romaniei

9:00 A.M.	Fitness Center
	Wake-up stretch—private session
10:00 A.M.	Cardio-fitness evaluation
11:00 A.M.	Cooldown
12:00 P.M.	Low-fat/high-protein energy lunch
1:00 P.M.	Spa St. Anges
	Dr. Schmidt, physical examination

and so forth with a myriad of rubs, soaks, and beauty treatments described in sumptuous detail.

I began my healthy Super Fitness breakfast with a glass of vegetable juice into which I squeezed and dropped a wedge of lemon. Next, a soupy bowl of muesli (this was Switzerland, after all) to which I added fresh blueberries, raspberries, a little dollop of cream, and honey. It was awful but I felt healthier already. I peeked under the linen that covered the pastry basket. It was full with slices of unbuttered multigrain toast and four small cinnamon rolls. I decided to start with a cinnamon roll. The top was sticky with praline and pecans and the thinly rolled dough had been spread with butter, cinnamon, brown sugar, and raisins prior to baking, which made the inside chewy and spicy. The praline stuck to my teeth before dissolving and coating the inside of my mouth with the sweet, buttery taste of caramel. I hadn't had a cinnamon roll in ages, and I had such a wonderful recipe for them. There was really nothing to them at all if you had the patience to let the dough rise. I'd make them for Thomas as soon as we got back home.

I ate another, starting at one end and unrolling it into my mouth like a paper birthday whistle.

I skipped the healthy toast.

The phone rang, startling me and interrupting my practically illicit affair with my breakfast.

"Hello?"

"Princesse," a woman said, "I'm sorry to disturb you but it is past nine o'clock. The instructor for your private stretch asked me to call. She is concerned that you won't have time to warm up properly for your cardio evaluation at ten. Shall I tell her you're on your way?"

Oh, God. I hadn't showered or put on my makeup yet. Too late. Besides, I didn't much care for the sound of that Low-fat/high-protein energy lunch. I have plenty of energy already.

"I'm so glad you called," I said. "I was just about to call you. Something's come up and I can't be there this morning."

"I understand. I'll let her know. Shall I hold your doctor's appointment and spa treatments for this afternoon?"

"Please."

"Thank you, Princesse. We will see you at one o'clock. Please let me know if you want to make any changes."

I'd go to the Fitness Center and exercise tomorrow.

Besides, I had some arrangements to attend to before I could really let myself relax and receive the full enjoyment of an afternoon in the spa. After breakfast, I showered and dressed in pink slacks and a pink cashmere turtleneck, pearl earrings, and a short white fur jacket, and walked over to the little square.

I looked like a princess on holiday.

TWENTY-SIX

"Good morning, how may I help you?" said the young woman in the real-estate office. Bright sunlight poured through the windows.

"At dinner last night, Mrs. Richardson told me one of her neighbor's chalets is available to rent."

"Yes. Schloss Alexander," she said. "If Mrs. Alexander hasn't had a change of plans. But you should know the lease is only for three months. If it's still available, would you like to see it?" Lots and lots of ifs in her voice. Lots of caveats and subtle screening.

I nodded. "Please. Three months is perfect."

She extended her hand. "I am Elsa Schick."

"Margaret Romaniei."

"Is this your first visit to Mont-St.-Anges, Mrs. Romaniei?"

"It is. And it's Princess Margaret, actually. Mrs. Naxos was kind enough to offer the invitation for me to stay at the hotel but I'm a painter and I'd like a quiet, private place where I can really set up and go to work."

"I understand."

"Here," I said. "Let me give you my card."

She accepted the heavy ecru card engraved with the Romanian royal crest and my name, Margaret of Romania. "Let me just telephone Mrs. Alexander—I'm sure there won't be a problem. Excuse me a moment."

Elsa stepped into a private office and picked up the phone. I could hear her talking and laughing. "All set," she said when she reemerged. "Let's go look."

She closed the office door behind us, hanging a sign with a movable clock indicating we'd be back in an hour. "This is Tati," she introduced me to her taffy-colored horse, which had bright ribbons braided into its mane and tail and was hooked up to a red sleigh. "Would you like to sit up with me or in back, which is much, much more comfortable?"

"No, I'd like to sit with you." I climbed up the step to the well-used, leather-covered bench. "Until yesterday, I hadn't ridden in a sleigh for years, almost since I was a child. I'd forgotten how much fun it can be."

"Where did you grow up?" She picked up the reins and gave Tati a little click.

"Norway."

"They have wonderful dray horses in Norway. What kind did you have?"

Oh, dear. When it comes to horses I can possibly tell the difference between a thoroughbred race horse and a Percheron, but that's the extent of my knowledge. I tried to recall what kind of horses pulled the queen's carriages in London. "I'm embarrassed to say I can't remember their name. But I do remember that they were sort of soft gray with darker spots."

"Ah," said Elsa. "Knabstruppers, no doubt. Quite rare."

"Exactly. Knabstruppers."

"Wonderful. Come, come Tati. You must wake up." We trotted along at a nice, reasonable pace. "Would you like to drive?"

"I'd love to try. But I've never done it before."

She handed me the reins. "It's easy, and Tati's just a big, fat baby."

Just my speed.

With Elsa's teaching and Tati's patient good humor, I drove the sleigh to the edge of town, turned uphill through a stand of snow-covered trees, and passed into the Naxos's little neighborhood.

Every now and then I saw a glint of light reflect off lenses of surveillance cameras in the trees.

While we drove, Elsa gave me a rundown of how many chalets and apartments were permitted by the covenants of the club. "This is the most there will ever be, unless Mr. Naxos changes his mind." She described what happened when owners died or left the club, how the residence reclamation was handled. "Members don't actually own their houses or apartments, they lease them from the club, and when a member dies or resigns, his estate is reimbursed the cost of construction or renovation and his, or her—we do have a number of women members—estate agents may come and reclaim furnishings and personal property. But the actual real estate and the membership themselves are not transferable to heirs."

We passed the entrance to the Richardson's Swissed-up chalet, where I'd had dinner last night, then Schloss Naxos, which was actually a huge Neuschwanstein-type white castle visible out on a point, looking as though it were out of a fairy tale. Robert Constantin's giant chalet was across the way. A tree-filled berm hid the ground floor. When we passed his drive, I looked back and saw that the berm concealed a good-sized parking area with a number of open horse stalls and six garage/stable doors. His road continued up the hill to what I assumed was a circular drive at the main entrance. A plain red mailbox sat at the foot of the driveway.

"Here it is to your right." Elsa pointed. Without any apparent direction from me, Tati turned down a snowy drive to Schloss Alexander. "It's quite small but I think that's what makes it so charming."

The gingerbread-trimmed, brightly painted chalet sat on a rise with a spectacular view of the entire valley. Woods circled it on three sides, giving the impression that it was a solitary house in the woods far, far from civilization. A bay leaf wreath hung on the front door and inside, after a few steps down a short entryway decorated with stylized, oversized classic ski posters of Garmisch and Gstaad, a generous living room opened to the right, treating you to a breathtaking view of the surrounding peaks. The room was decorated in what I would call Modified Yodel—much, much calmer than Lucy Richardson's house—with painted furniture, woven rugs on the plank floor, a white polar-bearskin rug in front of the stone fireplace, and the ubiquitous crossed antique skis above the mantel. To the left of the entry hall was the dining area, a long plank table and substantial cane-seated chairs with forest green cushions trimmed with red. Behind it was a counter fronting what appeared at a glance to be an extremely well-equipped kitchen. The master bedroom and sitting room were up a short flight of stairs beyond the living room. A private porch ran along the front of both of them. You had to go through the bedroom to get to the sitting room, making the suite a completely secluded little haven—ideal for my purposes. Staff quarters were in the walk-out basement with a seperate entrance. There were no guest rooms. The house was spacious and comfortably appointed, designed for relaxation.

Outside, in back, instead of a garage was a stable but no horses were in sight.

"What do you think?" Elsa asked.

"I love it. What's the staffing arrangement?"

"Mrs. Alexander brings her own household staff when she comes but we can provide whatever you need. A housekeeper three times a week is included in the rent."

"That will be more than sufficient."

"We'll make whatever arrangements suit you. Do you like to cook?"

"I do."

"So does Mrs. Alexander. Let me show you the kitchen."

It was sensational, really an exhibition kitchen. All-stainless-steel, eight-burner Miele cooktop, four Miele ovens, polished white marble countertops, sinks galore, and pinpoint work lights.

"She's a much more serious cook than I am," I said. "This is amazing."

"She's quite well known for her cooking, especially her desserts and pastries."

"Is this Tinka Alexander's house?" I said.

"Yes. Do you know her?"

I shook my head. "No, but I have all her books. She's one of my favorites. Tell me about the security arrangements and system. I've noticed the house alarm and the camera at the entrance." I'd noticed much more than that but didn't mention it.

"The house alarm rings at the police station down the hill and the cameras, actually there are four, go to these monitors." She slid open a panel under the lip of the kitchen service counter and flipped a switch. The screens came to life with views of the gate, the front door, the kitchen door, and the wooded area around the staff quarters downstairs.

"But these images don't go to the police station?"

Elsa shook her head. "We can arrange that, if you like. Most members prefer to protect their privacy."

I nodded. "I agree."

Did I believe her? I did. Club members wouldn't tolerate having their comings and goings observed twenty-four hours a day by anybody. It was an excellent system—I could spot only two blind spots: the side of the master bedroom porch and one section of the back of the house beneath the bathroom windows. The chalet was perfect for my purposes. Although I would have preferred to remain in the incredible luxe of the hotel, I needed to be able to set up a jewelry-manufacturing studio where I could work uninterrupted for long periods of time. I had a great deal to accomplish—perfect replication of the queen's stolen pieces—and little time to do it. Schloss Alexander would provide me with essential privacy.

"There's another set of monitors in the master sitting room, as well. The horse guard patrols every two hours, twenty-four hours a day. Although no one has ever needed them for any security breach or criminal activity. One of our members did get stuck in the bathtub once and the security patrol had to help her husband get her out."

"Oh, dear," I said. "How embarrassing."

Elsa nodded. "It was sad. Naturally, medical emergencies come up from time to time, and we have a fully equipped ambulance that responds. I don't want you to think you have to wait for a horse and carriage to get up here."

"That's good to know."

"I think you'll find Mr. Naxos has thought of everything. So. What do you think? We have two other properties that I'd be happy to show you if you'd like something larger."

"This is perfect."

"Wonderful. Let's go back to town and I'll get it all arranged. A horse and sleigh are included, along with Barnhardt, the groom/houseman, who can also drive you if you wish. He won't get in your way at all, he lives in the groom's quarters in the stable. Let me see, what else do you need to know? The hotel will bring your clothes up, there's no need for you to repack. I'll have the telephone, satellite dish, and DSL line activated in your name by the end of the day. I think that's it. When do you want to move in?"

"Tomorrow morning."

"Perfect. Schloss Alexander will be ready to receive you at ten o'clock."

When I got back to the hotel, I called the shops I'd visited yesterday in Zurich and gave my new address.

"Yes, overnight, please. Mark the packages as 'Art Supplies.'"

TWENTY-SEVEN

Luxury has so many definitions, and what's luxurious to one person may seem like nothing to another. I've found such fulfillment and pleasure in my métier during my life that I haven't taken the time to indulge in the myriad of creature comforts associated with great spas. I've read about them and thought they would be a good idea for me to check out more thoroughly but I've never taken the time to do it. So when I stepped outside the hotel for the dozen bracing steps leading to the Spa des Anges, I felt as though I'd entered a different world. It was transformational, like walking into a cloud or arriving in heaven.

The air was perfumed with verbena and aloe—it radiated good karma and good health. A man and a woman, both dressed in crisp white clinic smocks, sat behind a counter of illuminated glass blocks, topped by a thick piece of glass that was a mysterious, almost hypnotic mossy green. Behind them, a wall of backlit shelves held the different Spa des Anges products available for purchase as well as a display of robes and slippers.

"Good afternoon," I said. "I'm Margaret Romaniei."

The woman stood up. "Welcome, Princesse. I am Mirabelle. Follow me, please."

The front door opened with a gust of cold wind and in came Lucy Richardson wrapped head to toe in black mink with a red challis shawl tied around her shoulders. She opened her mouth to speak to me but I pretended I didn't see her and followed Mirabelle through a door into a long hallway of snow white, floating gauze panels that ruffled slightly as we passed. She held open the door to a small dressing room with a private bath and shower and a mirrored dressing table. The walls were covered with ecru flannel, which muffled all sound. She handed me a featherweight snow white terry-cloth robe and a pair of slippers. The tops were cotton flannel and the soles were inch-thick clear, springy cushions that looked as if they were made out of bubble wrap.

"When you're ready, Dr. Schmidt will take your history and perform your physical examination here in the spa clinic. I'll show you the way."

The spa clinic ran along the back of the building and was filled with bright light from Bauhaus-type ribbon windows that ran the length of the room in stacks of long narrow panes. The room was white and all the fittings were chrome or stainless steel. It was exactly how I expected a Swiss clinic to look. Clean and austere, cutting edge, completely professional.

A nurse led me into an examining room and immediately Dr. Schmidt arrived, a Swiss woman of indeterminate age but mature. A woman who understood women my age.

"Would you like to weigh?" she asked.

"I don't believe so."

"That's fine. Please be seated here." She indicated the edge of the examining table and for the next hour proceeded to question me about every aspect of my life—many of the answers I gave her were true—followed by the most thorough physical I'd ever had. She spent an inordinate amount of time on my hands, having me squeeze her fingers as hard as I could, which was hard enough to make her wince; flex my fingers and them spread them, then fold them in one at a time and then open them up one at a time.

"You have very interesting hands," she finally said. "They have the strength and flexibility of a much younger person. You're fortunate. By this time, most people's hands have begun to stiffen to some degree."

"Thank you," I said. "Must be my genes."

Genes, of course, had nothing to do with it. I exercise my hands constantly, manipulating various sizes and shapes of stones and marbles, hiding them under my fingers, letting them drop into my sleeve. The flexibility, sensitivity, and dexterity of my fingers have always been integral to my success. You don't become the world's greatest anything by wishing it so—it's just like getting to Carnegie Hall: it takes practice, practice, practice. I shared none of this wisdom with Dr. Schmidt.

She then reviewed and explained the results of the chemistry reports she'd gotten back so far and when she was finished, she pronounced me in very good health, for which I was grateful. "I don't see any restrictions to your fitness regime." She flipped through the chart. "I see you missed your cardio test this morning."

I looked at her over my glasses. I could lie, but why. "Cinnamon rolls."

She smiled and nodded. "Well, perhaps you'll be there tomorrow."

"Perhaps."

She extended her hand. "You can reach me twenty-four hours a day. Please let me know if you decide to undergo the cellular injection therapy and I will make the arrangements. It's an in-patient procedure and we need forty-eight hours' notice." She pushed a small bell and the door opened immediately. "Mirabelle will take you to your first appointment."

"Thank you, Doctor."

"Have a wonderful rest—I'm sure you've earned it."

The truth was, I hadn't earned my rest yet. I was still in the warm-up stage for what I expected would be the most serious test of my skills and endurance in my life. Did it make me feel better knowing that according to the doctor I was up to snuff physically? In excellent shape for a woman my age who had an undisciplined diet and did minimal exercise? Well, it didn't hurt.

"Follow me, please," said Mirabelle. "We will start with the steam."

I'd just drifted off on the hot tiled ledge when I heard the door open with a quiet whoosh. I quickly pulled my towels over myself and opened one eye just enough to see through the fog. Oh, God. It was Lucy. Didn't she have a steam bath at her own house? She was turning my afternoon off into a very stressful ordeal.

"Yoo-hoo," she whispered, and came and bent over me, trying to see if my eyes were open. "Yoo-hoo. Margaret. Are you asleep?"

"I was, but I'm awake now." I sat up and slid to the end of the bench, putting put my back against the wall.

"Oh, good. I'm glad I didn't wake you up." She stretched out flat on the ledge catty-corner from mine and casually threw off her towel. There was not one authentic thing about her breasts. They rose straight up like, well, the Alps. "I get so bored all by myself in these things. It's much more fun to have someone to talk to. Don't you think?"

"Much. But unfortunately, my time's up. If I stay another second I'll turn into a puddle." I reached out a leg for the floor, carefully holding my towel around me in a death grip. "Lucy, thank you so much for including me last night. It was very thoughtful of you. I'll see you again soon, I hope."

"Absolutely. Did Alma say if she and George were coming?"

I shook my head. "She didn't."

"I'll have to give her a call. It would be fun if they came for a few days and we could all just girlie it up together while the boys did their business thing. Do you play bridge?"

"I'm sorry to say I don't."

"Well," she said. "That's okay. We'll just find something else to do—shopping maybe."

"Unfortunately, I'm here to work. I'm a painter and I need to get some pieces ready for a show. But maybe we can have lunch in a few days."

"Oh, I love art. What kind of painting?"

"Mostly landscapes. I really have to go. This heat is starting to make me feel a little woozy." I pulled the door open and fled to my massage.

I wondered how long it would take for word to get out that I'd rented Tinka Alexander's chalet. I had visions of Lucy appearing on my doorstep wanting to have a slice of strudel and a chat.

Thankfully, our paths didn't cross the rest of the afternoon.

TWENTY-EIGHT

By the time I returned to the hotel from the spa, it was six-forty. In spite of the slight heartburn Lucy's presence had given me, I felt relaxed and happy, and very aware that the patron cocktail party before Constantin's charity concert in St. Moritz had begun ten minutes earlier. Had Sebastian Tremaine carried the briefcase with him or had he put it in the hotel safe? It didn't make any difference. He, and it, would be entering my lair soon enough—sometime within the next twenty-four to thirty-six hours, I imagined.

I turned on the TV while I bathed and dressed for the evening, and there she was, Giovanna MacDougal, my nemesis. The glamorous Sky-Word reporter who tried to steal my husband while I was in Portofino trying to salvage my reputation. Someone had been posing as the Shamrock Burglar and pulled off a number of fairly sloppy heists in Riviera resorts using my signature techniques. It became quite the story and Scotland Yard had asked Thomas to come out of retirement and apprehend the burglar. Every morning and every night on SkyWord news, I watched Giovanna interview my husband in one elegant, exclusive Riviera watering hole after another. They had obviously grown quite chummy. He, of course, claimed to have virtually no attraction to her, but still, I didn't trust her any further than I could throw her. I know this is extremely petty, but tonight I was glad to see she was on a different continent. She was traveling with the queen in Africa. She looked hot and uncomfortable and had to keep brushing a fly away from the corner of her mouth. I secretly hoped it would get stuck in her lip gloss, she had on so much of it.

"Today"—she squinted into the camera—"we are on the border of Kenya and Sudan in East Africa. As you can see it is a very different scene from last night's gala in Cape Town where Queen Elizabeth was feted in a celebration that was reminiscent of the days when South Africa was part of the British Empire."

Footage rolled of the queen and her consort proceeding into a dazzling banquet hall filled with lighted palm trees and colorfully dressed men and women of every color. Many of the black South Africans were in native dress, the men with leopardskin pillbox hats and capes, and the women with their heads wrapped in bright scarves, covered with jewelry.

The queen had on a very pretty pistachio green ball gown and the Girls of Great Britain and Ireland diamond tiara, a wedding gift from her grandmother, Queen Mary. The Lesser Stars of Africa brooch, the Cullinans III and IV, were suspended as pendants from her diamond necklace. They were fakes, of course. No one outside of her immediate circle knew the real stones were missing and I wondered how many standbys the royal household has for each major piece of jewelry. Three or four, I supposed. She also had a beautiful smile on her face.

As I watched, I put on a pearl gray light cashmere jacket and slacks, a large very attention-getting diamond bow brooch, a multistrand garnet necklace, and diamond-and-garnet cluster earrings. I was looking forward to a quiet, early evening alone with my book in the main dining room. The phone rang.

"Margaret? It's Lucy. We're meeting some friends—the Tripps, I'll bet you know them, Baxter and Barbara Tripp—at the hotel for dinner and thought you might be free to join us."

"I'm sorry, Lucy. I've got plans."

"Oh, well. Maybe tomorrow."

"Perhaps," I said noncommittally. What exactly was going on here? Had Alma assigned her to be my watchdog? Had she told her who I was? Was she reporting back to Alma on all my activities? Was she one of those types who go goo-goo around royalty and can't control themselves? Was she stalking me? Or was I just paranoid because she said she recognized me? I wanted to tell her to bug off but because she was such a close friend of Alma's, I didn't want to run the risk of offending her. However, I must say, envisioning her and Alma together was hard to do—they made a very unlikely pair.

I hung up the phone and called Klaus and ordered a double martini, ricotta agnolotti with sun-dried tomatoes and crunchy pancetta lardons, an apple-and-walnut salad, and a half bottle of Chianti riserva. Then I went into my dressing room and changed into a camel cashmere robe with soft curly Persian lamb trim. I could hear Klaus in the kitchen mixing my cocktail, and by the time I got back to the sitting room, he had placed a beautifully chilled crystal martini glass on the coffee table next to a little platter of dates stuffed with cheese.

"These magazines just arrived this afternoon," he said. "I thought you might enjoy them."

Paris Match, Paris Vogue, and the *Robb Report.* Required reading for billionaires.

It was a delicious, comfortable evening, and that night I had the best sleep I've ever had in my life. I needed and appreciated it—I might not get another for quite a while.

"We have the High-Performance breakfast for you this morning, Your Highness." Klaus lifted the dome from a plate arranged with a cheese omelet and grilled sausages. The basket with the cinnamon rolls was close at hand, as well. While I ate my breakfast and read the papers—I was pleased to see my name listed in the New Arrivals column of the Mont-St.-Anges Report—Klaus's battalion of maids and aides arrived to pack my goods. He shooed them into the bedroom like a mother hen and closed the door so they wouldn't disturb me. Fifteen minutes later, they departed practically without a sound, leaving my fur coat, hat, and gloves lying on the bed.

At ten, the phone rang.

"Your sleigh is here, ma'am."

"Thank you. I'll be right down."

"Take your time."

"My" sleigh turned out to be a grand antique affair. Not big but very bright and regal looking with a big curling swoop up the back. The entire thing was bright, shiny red with gold swirls painted all over it, a black leather driver's bench, and a tufted black leather passenger seat. My horse was black and shone from brushing and good care. She was a big, magnificent horse—her muscles rippled beneath a glossy coat and I could tell she wanted to go. Not that she was rearing or pawing or bucking. To the contrary. She stood quietly, but the energy was tangible. She had a white, diamond-shaped mark on her forehead. The rest of her body save one sock on her rear right foot was as black and shiny as coal. Long wavy curls fell from just below her knees and covered her shiny hooves. Her black mane was tied into little knots with red ribbons.

Atop the driver's box sat a rosy-cheeked, formally dressed gentleman in a loden suit and brimmed hat with a deertail brush. His jacket had buttons carved from reindeer antler. He had a beaklike nose, a crisp little gray mustache, and big blue eyes that were exaggerated by thick wire-rimmed glasses. He gave the impression of being wiry and agile, capable of anything physical or mechanical.

He turned as the doorman helped me up into the sleigh and tipped his hat. "Princesse," he said. "I am Barnhardt. And this is Black Diamond."

"I'm very pleased to meet you, Barnhardt. What kind of horse is that?" I asked.

"A black Clydesdale. Very, very rare. Excellent temperament."

Elsa's horse, Tati, had been a baby. Black Diamond was a babe. She got us up to Schloss Alexander in a flash—it felt as if we were speed skating.

TWENTY-NINE

"Do you need anything more, Your Highness?" Barnhardt stood in the kitchen door. He had lit the fire in the living room and made certain the hearth had an adequate supply of wood. "Would you like me to tend the fire?"

"I don't think so, thank you. I'm set until later this afternoon. I'd like to go to town for the après ski at four o'clock."

"Very well. If you do need me sooner, you can call my cell phone, the number is here"—he indicated a list next to the kitchen extension—"or use the intercom, which I think you'll find is most practical—or ring this bell." He pointed to a brass cowbell that hung to the right of the door with a little dinger attached by a thin leather thong. "Have a pleasant day, Your Highness. I am at your service."

"Thank you." I closed the door behind him and watched through the kitchen window. I was scarcely able to contain myself with excitement at finally putting my plan into motion. The complications and intricacies of planning the perfect heist were more energizing to me than chocolate, or wine or sex. It was in my blood. It had been my livelihood since I was a girl and seemed always to shimmer just below the surface of my skin like a fizz of temptation. As long as I was away from it, I was fine. As a matter of fact, at home, I didn't miss my former life at all. But now that I was back in the game, I was on fire. I watched Barnhardt on the monitor and as soon as he entered the stable, I locked the doors and went to work.

First on my list was to pull on a pair of tight latex gloves and conduct a thorough inspection of the premises looking for bugs, cameras, secret doors and cabinets. I always carry a small pocket flashlight with a powerful beam and I used it to look inside, under, above, below and around every square inch of the house. The only discoveries were a locked cabinet in the kitchen that I easily popped open—it contained Tinka's personal sets of chef's knives, cooking pans, rolling pins, baking tins, and secret recipes—and locked drawers and a locked closet in the master sitting room that I put off exploring until later.

All my packages had been delivered from Zurich and were stacked on and around the desk in the kitchen. I opened each box, laid out the contents on the counter and did a thorough inventory, confirming all was as ordered, which, with typical Swiss precision, it was. The array was quite impressive. I had purchased the latest, most expensive, most technologically advanced equipment available—everything was state of the art. Close to a million dollars' worth of electronic scanners that could do everything from find bugs and invisible beams, to mimic voice, digital and optical scans, to open the most sophisticated of safes. I had digital motion-sensitive cameras; cell-phone-looking gizmos that were actually complete audio/visual/communications centers; audio-sensitive microphones, and tape recorders, as well as a jeweler's bench, with all its contingent manufacturing necessities.

I'd done a good job provisioning myself for every possible contingency I could envision.

Now that I'd seen the exterior settings—Mont-St.-Anges, the chalets, and the terrain—I reviewed my preliminary plan. The final one wouldn't be developed until I'd had the opportunity to meet and watch the players—Sebastian Tremaine and Robert Constantin—and to surveil their style and daily schedule. Get my nose under their tent, so to speak. I wasn't taking anything lightly or for granted. Sebastian Tremaine had major talent and nerve—he'd made off with some of the

most highly protected jewels on earth and now it was up to me to figure out a way to rob him. I won't go so far to say that this was Holmes
versus Moriarty, but it takes a thief to catch a thief, and he was a good
one. Was he as good as I was? Very possibly. My plan was based on the
assumption that he was better.

The largest factor working in my favor was the element of surprise.
And actually, that's one of the most fun things about being a jewel thief
if you're good. You know what you're planning, but nobody else does
because you work alone. I imagined Tremaine had a few surprises of his
own up his sleeve, but until I got into his orbit, I couldn't begin to picture what they may be.

I wondered if they'd gotten home from St. Moritz.

I tied my new tool apron around my waist and slid two tubes of
paint and brushes into one of the pockets. Then I opened the tool kit
and laid it flat on the counter. It was a good-looking case packed with a
comprehensive assembly of stainless-steel implements with cushioned
red rubber handles. I selected three screwdrivers and a pair of pliers.
Finally, I clipped 10x magnification lenses (not the ultrastrong 55x ones
I needed for making jewelry) onto a headband and adjusted it around
my head, making sure it was snug and comfortable.

I changed the locks on all the doors. I installed specialized electronic
dead bolts on the master bedroom, sitting room, and master suite porch
doors. These locks were triple-controlled with voice recognition, eye
scan, and fingerprint readers, which I concealed in the bookshelves. I
programmed the devices and then painted the readers, locks, and locking bars brown to match the bookshelves or the wood of the door-
frames. Unless someone was extremely observant, they would never
even notice that new locks were there. I installed alarmed pressure pads
inside the front door, and outside the master bedroom and porch doors
and remoted them to one of my new cell phones. I found a step stool in
the utility closet and installed battery-operated pinhole audio and vi-

sual surveillance cameras in the upper corners of the living room, master suite, and above the porch doors. I hid another in the bay-leaf wreath on the front door. Their pictures broadcast to what looked like a cell phone but was actually a receiver with a remote that could also control each camera. The technology itself and the minuteness of these gizmos was amazing.

There was still much to do, but I felt better once these steps were accomplished. My personal perimeter was established, my drawbridge in place. I would add other cameras and motion-sensitive scanners outdoors when I went out for a walk later this afternoon.

I armed the exterior system, fixed a pot of coffee, put on a Mahler symphony full blast and hauled the rest of the boxes into the master sitting room, Tinka Alexander's private, personal hangout. Two walls had bookshelves with storage cabinets below. In addition to a wide selection of novels, the shelves had all of her cookbooks in every language and framed pictures of her from magazine covers and interviews with major journalists. The treadmill had a view of both the scenery and the television.

To me, however, the greatest attraction to this room was hanging over her desk—a four-by-six-foot horizontal color photograph of a shiny, moist chocolate cake—devil's food, judging by the rich, dark glow of the cake and icing. One glistening slice had been removed and was lying on its side on a plate with a fork. One bite had been taken from the slice, leaving moist crumbs. A glass of milk, a little froth circling the glass, sat to the side, slightly out of focus. It was a masterful photograph, the detail was so intense, it was as though this giant piece of cake was hanging on the wall waiting for me to take a bite. Every time I looked at it, my mouth watered and I felt a little weak in the knees. It was such a common, everyday cake, not the sort of thing you'd expect one of the world's most accomplished dessert chefs to focus on in her private study. No. You'd expect a spectacular creation. But this simple photograph told a much more powerful story than a soaring, floaty, filmy spun-sugar concoction could have. It evoked hunger, yearning, comfort, and happiness. It made you feel at home. I longed to have a piece.

I looked at my cold cup of coffee—it simply wouldn't do. I went to the kitchen and opened the refrigerator, which had been stocked with basic supplies until I could order my own. I selected a bottle of Veuve Clicquot, NV, poured a glass, and opened the old-fashioned tin bread box on the counter. Ahh. Just where I would keep them: dark chocolate truffles.

I placed half a dozen on a plate and headed back to the project, glancing at myself in the full-length mirror in the hallway. I almost screamed. With the headband around my forehead making a big dent in my hair and the magnifying lenses pushed up so they looked like little antlers, my reading glasses on my nose, my red tool apron bristling with implements and spread atop my hips in a most unflattering way, a stripe of brown paint swishing across my white cashmere bosom, a glass of Champagne in one hand and a plate of chocolate truffles in the other, I looked like something from outer space or an infomercial. The only things missing were flippers. Thank God the doors were locked.

I looked at the ceiling. "Please don't let me die now."

I always try to wear something I wouldn't mind being caught dead in, because, really, who knows? This was a horrible exception. If I were caught dead in this outfit, it would kill me.

I put my head down and hurried along to investigate the locked desk drawers and closet, reasonable expectations of privacy in a house you were amenable to letting a stranger use.

THIRTY

The locked drawers in Tinka's office were almost empty—just a few personal items such as check ledgers, a laptop computer, extra pairs of glasses. The only items in the closet were a full-length sable coat and a large bank safe with an old-fashioned spin combination lock, which I set about cracking the old-fashioned way.

I set a gauge wire above the lock and began, very slowly, to feel my way around the dial. After five minutes, I had all the numbers and began testing their combinations. On the fifth try, the dial began to tighten as the proper sequence fell into place, and seconds later, I heard the satisfying click of success. I took the worn brass handle and twisted it. The locking bars slid free, I tugged the heavy door open. Whoa. I leaned against the closet wall and bit into one of the truffles and just stared. The safe was jam-packed with cash. I counted it. Ten million brand-new U.S. dollars.

If Tinka's cakes began to fall, she'd made certain she'd have a soft place to land. My admiration for her grew. I replaced the cash, closed the safe and spun the dial. Most thieves would be tempted by the crisp new bills. Most would keep it. Not me. That's never been my style—I always have plenty of cash of my own.

I put a high-squeal, mega-decibel alarm on the closet door, so loud it would scramble the brain of anyone within a hundred feet with the sort of blanketing, staggering sound that you will do anything to get away from. I hate these alarms. Everyone does. But they absolutely serve a purpose.

It took an hour to assemble the portable jeweler's bench and manufacturing studio. It was quite ingenious—a collapsible rolling metal table, made like a sewing machine table with a lower adjustable work section in the front, and tool racks across the top. The racks were arranged in such a way that when the simple gray cotton cover was over it, it actually looked like a sewing machine. I clipped two high-powered lights onto the sides and clamped a flexible arm with a 55x Zeiss magnifying glass onto the top of the bench. I'd brought my own jeweler's tools from home. I'd had them made in Switzerland almost thirty years ago and they fit into the palm of my hand like old friends, my fingers clasped them effortlessly. I snapped them into the racks. It was just like old times.

Twelve-thirty. Almost done.

I heaved a heavy, briefcase-sized steel case up on top of Tinka's safe and undid the latches. The sides fell open and the setup became a small smelter with crucibles for gold, silver, and platinum fired by butane capsules. I arranged solid ingots and molds next to them and hid the cartons of butane refills behind the safe on the floor.

As a final touch to my studio's disguise, I set up a complete artist's studio: an easel, a box of oil paints with their assortment of necessary turpentines and linseed oils and so forth, a palette, a cup of brushes, and a medium-sized canvas over which I draped a white cloth. I leaned a stack of blank canvases against the bookshelves and draped a clean smock from one of the struts of the easel. The only things lacking were a beret and an overflowing ashtray. And a painting, of course. But I'd give that a go later.

I looked around. It was a very well-equipped manufacturing studio. I had everything I needed to duplicate the queen's missing jewelry. Except for one thing: the stones themselves.

I removed my headband and placed it on the jeweler's bench, which I rolled into the closet and covered with its sewing-machine-table cover; returned all my gear to its proper place then relocked the closet, restoring the room to normal. Confident that all was as it should be, I poured another glass of Champagne and took it into Tinka Alexander's perfect bathroom—solid white marble and mirrors—where Klaus's maids had reassembled my toiletries in just the right order. It was as though I'd been living there forever. The shower doubled as a steam-bath chamber and had a bench long enough to stretch out on. The tub, which had a Jacuzzi, ran horizontally to a wall of glass with a view of distant peaks. The sinks were white marble basins sitting at a comfort-able height on top of the counter. The commode and bidet were in a separate little compartment. The only color in the room was a mighty bouquet of dark purple hydrangeas in a cut crystal vase as big as a milk bucket.

I washed my hands—the soap was Alma Naxos's signature carnation scent—repaired my hair and makeup, changed out of my paint-stained clothes into a pink silk robe with white marabou trim, and returned to the study where I picked up the final unopened package.

It had been sitting on top of the desk waiting for me, like a patient lover. I sat down on the floor and sliced open the box. Inside, wrapped in tissue, were a number of black velvet bags tied tightly closed with black silk cords. A small tag was attached to each one with the descrip-tion of its contents. They were filled with stones of differing weights and cuts—diamonds and emeralds, dozens and dozens of them, made precisely to my specifications. Three bags held only one stone each: two had the Lesser Stars of Africa: the forty-five- and fifty-carat Cullinans III and IV that make up the queen's giant diamond brooch. And the third contained a very rare forty-carat pink diamond. Even larger than the legendary Pink Elephant diamond. Mine was possibly the largest pink diamond in the world.

I leaned back against the sofa and studied each tag, feeling the excitement build inside me. I opened all the bags and let handfuls of diamonds and emeralds drizzle through my fingers and fall across my face and neck and bosom, a brilliant shower of green and white stars. I was covered in them. I rolled the pink diamond in my fingers and laid the Lesser Stars over my eyes. They were so beautiful. They made me weak with desire.

They were all perfect. Perfect fakes, that is.

THIRTY-ONE

Intercoms evoke images of old movies for me—thick-lipped, cigar-chewing bosses angrily jabbing away at the buttons on the big gray box and shouting into the speaker loudly enough to be heard in the next county. It's like people who yell into the little mobile-phone bug micro-phones because they're so tiny they couldn't possibly carry the sound of anything of any import. Lack of size inspires a lack of confidence in the technology. So when I pushed the little button on my kitchen inter-com in an attempt to rustle up Barnhardt, it took a great deal of self-control for me not to shout.

"Barnhardt," I said as normally as I could.

"Your Highness?" The answer came instantly, as though he had been sitting next to the speaker awaiting the sound of my voice.

'Would you come over, please."

"Of course, Your Highness."

Moments later he appeared at the kitchen door.

"Do you know how to hook these things up?" I held up a pair of alu-minum snowshoes. "I'd like to give this a try."

"Certainly."

I had on a pair of tight coffee-bean-colored Bogner leggings, a light turtleneck sweater, a lightweight, mink-trimmed, semifitted Bogner jacket long enough to cover my rear end, and a pair of very snazzy spe-cial snowshoeing shoes. Big topaz-and-onyx earrings. And a couple of noisy charm bracelets. I stepped outside. Even bundled up as I was, I couldn't get over the cold.

"Just put your foot in here."

I did. He threw a couple of switches and there I was, legs inelegantly astraddle, already out of breath.

"Have you ever done this before?"

I shook my head.

"It's very good exercise—quite rigorous. The secret is to walk as steadily and normally as possible." He placed long poles in my hands. "Just go up the drive. You can't hurt yourself. If you fall, the shoes will come right off."

It was not possible to walk normally since the width of the shoes forced me into a sort of goofy, galumphy waddle, but I set out and aside from the fact that I had to stop every four or five steps to get my breath, it didn't take any what I would call skill. Now I no longer felt the cold. Instead, I thought I was going to roast to death.

"Thank you, Barnhardt," I called from the bend in the road. "I'll call you if I need you."

He gave me a little salute.

After about ten minutes, I made it to the top of my driveway, which makes it sound as though it was a long drive, but it wasn't. I was completely exhausted and had to stop and take a couple of little sections of the Toblerone chocolate bar I'd had the good sense to bring along. Some purists put down Toblerones as nothing more than overmarketed, overavailable, mass-produced, and thus inferior candy bars— after all the company is owned by Kraft Europe—but in my opinion, the combination of almond, dark chocolate, and little chips of almond, nougat and honey are the perfect answer when a little shot of energy is needed, especially if you're in the Swiss Alps in the snow. I mean, really, what could be more appropriate? Other than a St. Bernard with a cask of brandy. You wouldn't want to eat, say, a Snickers bar in such a setting. (Although I do admit I can always be tempted by a Milky Way.) And a Toblerone is just as effective and by far tastier than, say, Vitamin Water or electrolyte replacements, and it is after all, Swiss.

Nicely reinvigorated, I pretended to fiddle with something on my equipment while I peeled the paper off adhesive-ready strips on the backs of wafer-thin laser-beam transmitters and stuck them to the stone pillars on either side of the drive. I stood in their field and took out my cell phone and ran a test. The beams were properly aimed and operational. I stuck a small video transmitter next to one of them that took in not only a part of the road but also the width of the driveway entrance. It, too, was functioning.

At last, I started down the road, doing what I considered to be actual snowshoeing. Certainly, going downhill was much easier and I fell into a sort of comfortable amble. If all went according to plan, I wouldn't have to worry about how I was going to get back up the hill. But if all didn't go precisely according to plan, I'd just call Barnhardt and ask him to hook up the horse and drag me home.

It had stopped storming and the afternoon had cleared. The fresh snow shone like diamonds scattered across the mountainside and the sky was so blue and cloudless, it seemed as though I could see all the way into outer space. The sun was warm on my face and I hoped would put a little color in my cheeks. I'd really started to get the hang of this snowshoeing thing and was scooting along just fine. I'd just drawn abreast of the red mailbox at the entrance to Robert Constantin's chalet, where I planned to stage a Damsel in Distress incident—a helpless little tumble or some such thing—when, suddenly, something in my right snowshoe snapped and I fell hard, severely twisting my ankle and practically pulling the mailbox down with me. Not even slightly the graceful sort of wilt I'd had in mind.

I looked around for help. The road was silent and deserted. No one knew I was there. But, with the level of security around Constantin's house—really, it looked like a secret missile range or something there were so many cameras—I assumed my whole crack-up had been observed from beginning to end and I would be rescued before long. I was correct.

The biggest black man I'd ever seen in my life emerged from a door in Constantin's row of stables. He came toward me with the sort of muscle-bound gait typically associated with weight lifters, looking for all the world as if he were set on tearing me limb from limb.

THIRTY-TWO

"Are you all right?" he called. He had some sort of accent.

"I'm not sure," I answered. "I think I might have broken my ankle." I struggled to get up. The snow where I'd fallen was loose and deep.

"Stay still. Don't try to stand by yourself," he ordered. He spoke like a man accustomed to giving orders. He was enormous. I couldn't tell if he was Congolese or Ugandan, but he was from a part of Africa where the people have physical presence—he had none of the lithe, fine-boned grace of Ethiopians, Sudanese, or Kenyans. His hands looked as big as dinner plates and his shoulders were at least three feet wide. He had on black trousers that strained around thighs as big as oak trees, a white shirt and tie, and black leather lace-up boots with steel-capped toes and heavy treads on the soles. He had a cell phone clipped to his belt. He also had on a shoulder holster with a gun in it. He looked terrifying, like one of Idi Amin's thugs—an enforcer.

"Let me see." He knelt down and removed my snowshoes and straightened first my left leg, which was fine, and then my right. I would love to be able to say that he was as big as a giant and as gentle as a lamb, but in fact, his bedside manner, if you want to call it that, had all the gentleness and care of a man in the boxing ring swinging his way out from the ropes.

I couldn't help but scream. "Owww," I howled. "That hurts." And it did. It hurt like the dickens, not as much as I was acting as though it did, but even so, I'd very much overdone my phony fall. If I really had broken my ankle, I'd be in a terrible mess.

"I'm going to carry you into the house. Put your arm around my shoulder."

He smelled of strong, sweet cologne.

I must say, as a woman with my own physical presence, I have never in my entire life had a man carry me anywhere, or even attempt to carry me anywhere. But I had absolutely no compunction about letting this giant African pick me up. He and his muscles were so big, I think he could have picked up two of me and not experienced even a slight sciatic or lumbar twinge. He marched up the hill, knocked the door open with his foot, and carried me down a long hallway to an elevator, which I noted made four stops: basement, main, and two upper floors. We got off on the main floor. The door opened into a dark vestibule opposite a cloakroom. Then he backed us through a swinging door and we emerged into a blindingly bright commercial kitchen worthy of a three-star restaurant. The ching-chong sound of Asian rap music could be heard. A Chinese cook in a checked chef's cap looked up from a chopping board on the other side of the room, snapped off the radio with a flick of his hand that fell right in with his chopping rhythm, and returned to his task. A maid in a brown-and-white dirndl, green utility apron, and yellow rubber gloves was polishing silver candlesticks at a service sink. I could hear the water running in a slow steady stream.

The African settled me gently onto a high kitchen stool that had a padded back and arms, and lifted my legs onto a facing stool. Then he leaned over and removed my right shoe and sock, taking my foot in his giant black hand. The Cheery Cherry polish on my toes looked like pink sapphires against his skin.

"It's becoming swollen." He had an intriguing half-French/half-something-else accent. "I think I'd best call the doctor."

"I'm not sure," I said. "I'm beginning to think it's just badly twisted."
I gingerly moved my foot in a slow, painful circle. "It feels better than it
did a couple of minutes ago."

"I'll get an ice bag, that should help. You stay here."

I don't know where he thought I would go but I assumed with a boss
as high profile as Robert Constantin, he was on the job all the time. I
wondered if he was Constantin's security chief or personal bodyguard.
He seemed more the bodyguard type to me, but that was probably just
wishful thinking, just wishing that Constantin was back in town, here
in this house. More importantly, if he were, I hoped Tremaine and his
briefcase were with him.

While the African scooped crushed ice into a plastic bag on the other
side of the kitchen, I took advantage of the moment and pulled a small
radio transmitter out of my pocket and stuck it on the bottom of the
counter overhang. It was invisible—all its components made of clear
plastic—and was the size of a thin slice of a pencil eraser, or a round little transparent band-aid dot.

Honestly, I had so many gizmos and gadgets on me I could have
bugged the entire town.

He draped the ice bag over my injury. "Leave this here for a few minutes and if it's not better, I'll take you to hospital. Would you like a coffee or a water?" In themselves, his words were polite but his voice
lacked inflection or courtesy. The pupils of his eyes were as black as
coal and the whites were yellow with angry red corners. There was no
gentleness about him.

"Coffee, if it's not too much trouble, thank you."

"Cream, sugar?"

"Both, please."

"You want cappuccino?"

"That would be lovely."

He inclined his head slightly and walked over and delivered the order to the maid, who nodded. I could vaguely hear her assent. She immediately turned off the water, stripped off her gloves and apron, and went to a counter occupied by a sleek industrial espresso machine. He came back and stood at the end of the counter where I was, not too close, not too far. He was keeping an eye on me, as though I were in custody.

"What's your name?" I asked.

"Oscar." His expression had not changed since he gathered me up in the snow. It was flat as a mask.

"That's a nice name." I know that doesn't sound like much of a comeback, but it wasn't easy to gauge how to strike up a conversation with this man. For example, I knew weather wasn't going to work.

He grunted.

"Where are you from?"

"Kisangani, Congo."

"Umm. Lovely."

"You have visited?"

"No. But I've heard it's very beautiful."

"Very, very beautiful. Very dangerous."

"Lots of diamonds come from there, I think," I said. "And I know the natural resources are supposed to be sizable—gold, all manner of minerals actually, oil, gas." I could have given him at least an hour's worth of naming the alluvial diamond beds along the Congo River and the famous diamonds that had come from them—and still did—and that I knew Kisangani was one of the major ports along the river deep in the jungle. But I thought I'd wait until Oscar and I knew each other a little better before I expounded on the untapped wealth of the Democratic Republic of the Congo (which was a mess of a brutal dictatorship and not democratic at all) because I could tell he had virtually no interest in diamonds or natural resources. He seemed like the sort of man who was more interested in catching a lion bare-handed and ripping it apart and eating it for his dinner, raw.

"What do you do here?"

"Security."

"Whose house is this, anyway?"

This time he snorted impatiently, as though I were an idiot, and did not bother answer my question.

His cell phone must have vibrated because he put it to his ear. "Yes, boss." He listened and nodded. "Yes, sir. I will, sir. Yes, sir." He flipped the phone closed.

The maid brought my cappuccino and while I took a sip, Oscar removed the ice bag and examined my ankle. "Better," he said. "Move it around."

I twisted my foot in a circle. "Much better," I said. "I can tell it's going to be fine. Just a little sprain. Thank you so much for rescuing me."

"Okay. You can go home now."

"Do you mind calling Barnhardt and asking him to come get me? I don't think I can make it back up the hill and I'm not sure where to tell him I am."

"Number?" said Oscar.

I told him and he dialed while I pulled on my sock.

"Oscar here, Schloss Constantin. Your . . ." He looked at me. "Your name?"

"Princess Margaret," I answered.

I suppose when you work for a superstar like Robert Constantin, one princess more or less is neither here nor there. He didn't look even slightly impressed. "Your Princess lady is here and requires you to pick her up. She fell down on her ski shoes." He nodded. "When will you be at the gate? Okay. Fine. Come to the service door."

I needed to see much more than the elevator and kitchen on this first foray into Constantin's chalet. And, while I had no idea how long it would take Barnhardt to hook up the horse and sleigh, I assumed I had five or ten minutes at least to conduct some initial, critical reconnaissance.

"May I use your powder room?" I asked.

THIRTY-THREE

"Powder room?" Oscar looked blank. Evidently they don't have powder rooms in the Congo.

"Ladies' room. Toilet."

He nodded. "Come. I take you." He helped me down from the stool and while there was some pain in my ankle, there wasn't nearly as much as I pretended to have. He took one of my arms and put the other around my waist and guided me out into a wide, dark hallway as hulking and overbearing as Oscar himself. It was positively epic, operatic, nothing even remotely Swiss in sight.

The walls were paneled in rich, well-oiled black walnut. Persian rugs covered the hardwood floors and a wide staircase with newel posts as big as tree trunks ascended on the right. The posts were topped with carved walnut pineapples the size of basketballs. A black, wrought-iron chandelier, so tortured and ornate and dripping with candle wax it could have come from Zefferelli's opulent version of *La Traviata,* hung from a thick black chain in the stairwell. A stained-glass window, maybe eight feet wide and twelve feet tall, dominated the first landing. It appeared to be a portrayal of Robert Constantin as Radames in *Aida* standing on the banks of the Nile. He was dressed in an Egyptian officer's uniform, his sword at the ready in his hand, the river flowing just behind him, and a virtual Noah's Ark of animals spread out on the plains beyond.

"Women toilet here," Oscar announced when we reached a door set into the space beneath the stairs. He'd obviously brought his tribal view, his low opinion of the weaker sex, with him.

The dreary little powder room's walls were filled with framed covers of Playbills from around the world, proclaiming Constantin in concert or in one opera or another. A picture of Robert Constantin smiled from above the sink, straight down into your eyes while you did your business. It was most disconcerting.

When I emerged, Oscar was at the far end of the hall on the phone, so I hopped to the bottom of the stairs and sat on the second step and leaned against the post and rubbed my ankle and gave a little look-round. There was a miniature, high-performance security camera, not much bigger than a black cigarette butt up in the corner. Before leaving the ladies' room, I'd pulled the protective backing off the adhesive strip on another miniature transmitter, and as I stood up, I stuck it on the bottom of the banister, where it and the newel post joined.

"Your sled is here." Oscar came to get me. "Come."

We'd just reached the end of the hall when a voice echoed down the stairs. "Oscar!"

I recognized it immediately as Robert Constantin.

"Wait here," he told me, and planted my shoulder against the door-jamb as securely as I'd stuck the microstrip to the bottom of the banister. He went to the steps. "Sir?"

"What are you doing?"

"A woman hurt herself snowshoeing in front of our house and I am helping her to her sled."

"What do you mean, 'hurt herself'? Where?"

"At the mailbox. On the road."

"On the road or on my property?"

"Road, sir."

"Do you have it on film?"

"Yes, sir."

"We're in the clear? Not on my property?"

"No, boss."

"All right, then. When you've finished, please come up. I want to leave at four-thirty."

"I'll be there directly."

I was a little surprised. Didn't Constantin want to know if I was all right? What if I'd broken my leg? Or my neck? All he wanted to know was if I was going to sue him.

"Who was that?" I asked as Oscar hustled me through the kitchen. Evidently he'd decided my ankle was well enough that I didn't need the elevator. He didn't exactly drag me to my waiting sleigh, but there wasn't any dilly-dallying on the way, either. He also didn't answer my question.

"Thank you for the cappuccino," I called to the maid, who was back at her silver-polishing duties as we sped past.

A kitchen door I hadn't noticed flew open and another maid rushed out, almost running into us. "Oh!" She curtsied. "Pardon me."

Oscar frowned at her. Before she closed the door, I saw that it led to an upstairs staircase. Oscar bustled me down a separate long flight of stairs to the service door where we'd initially entered.

Barnhardt had my snowshoes and poles in the sleigh. "Are you all right, Your Highness?" he said with concern as he helped me aboard.

"Perfectly fine," I said, and pulled the fur rug over me for the 30-second ride home. I was better than all right. Robert Constantin was in the house. And the house had a full backstage operation—cooks, maids and service stairs. Oscar was his bodyguard and evidently performed personal, valet-type duties as well because Constantin had asked him to come upstairs. The place was under constant, extensive surveillance and I wondered where the security room was, how many people were in it, and if the same level of coverage included the upstairs. I was sure it didn't. I was sure the upper floor had nothing more than a couple of panic buttons.

"Thank you for rescuing me, Oscar," I said as we pulled away.

Oscar frowned and raised his hand in a little half wave before slamming the door closed behind him.

"Do you still want to go to town?" Barnhardt pulled Black Diamond to a gentle stop at my front door. He stepped down and helped me to the ground.

"I do. I'll be ready in about ten minutes."

"Are you sure you don't want me to take you to the hospital to have that examined?"

"No, thanks. I think I'll be fine." I hobbled through the door, thinking how damning it was to stage a fall, pretend to be sick, or lie about any illness. There was never a happy ending when you did.

THIRTY-FOUR

When Barnhardt and I left for the village, the afternoon shadows were already long and dark across the valley—it was just a little after four. I'd only taken the time to repair my hair and makeup. I kept my snowshoeing outfit on because I felt I'd earned the right to go to the square in outdoor athletic gear, like everyone else. And if someone asked me what I'd done today, I could say with all honesty, Oh, just a little snowshoeing. I leaned on a smart-looking black cane I'd found sitting at the front door because the Advil hadn't had any effect yet and my ankle was throbbing.

"Do you mind if I sit by you, Barnhardt?" I said. "I'd like you to teach me to drive."

"By all means. It will be my pleasure."

I began to climb up to the driver's seat, but he stopped me. "First you must become acquainted with your horse. Come up and say hello." He placed three sugar cubes in my hand. "Princess Margaret, this is Black Diamond. Black Diamond, this is Princess Margaret. She loves sugar. See, like this." He held his hand flat with his fingers straight, cubes resting in the center of his palm, and she moved her lips over them and then I heard the little dice-sized cubes crunching between her teeth.

I took off my gloves and stroked her glossy jaw and held my other hand flat while she gobbled up the sugar with her furry pink lips. I was amazed an animal so huge could be so delicate. Her teeth looked as big as piano keys and were slightly discolored. Her eyes shone into mine with what looked like humor and intelligence. Up close, she was absolutely huge—the biggest living thing I'd ever seen, actually. I would say she was approximately the size of an elephant. I stroked her neck. She was beautiful. She and I were going to get to be good friends because I'll tell you one thing, when it came time for me to leave this valley, I didn't know what my mode of transportation was going to be—snowshoes, train, sleigh, or horseback—but I knew what it wasn't going to be: helicopter.

"Now you are properly introduced." Barnhardt smiled. "We can mount to the bench."

I climbed up the opposite side.

"You hold the reins like so." He showed me how to wrap the thick, well-worn straps through my fingers. "And now give them a little shake."

I did and Black Diamond started us up the hill at a quick clip.

We crested the top of the drive and started down the road and she was picking up speed, going at what felt to me like an all-out racing trot. Our sleigh bells were out of control and I was afraid I was going to be catapulted right off the driver's box into the snow.

"Barnhardt!" I said as a panicky feeling began to burble up inside me and I grabbed the tiny rail along the edge of the bench with my right hand. "Help!"

He laughed and took the reins and talked to Black Diamond, reining her in gently until she'd reached a more suitable pace. "She's young and has a lot of energy. She needs a firm hand."

"I think I'll let you drive the rest of the way." I laughed. My heart was pounding a million beats a second.

"Don't worry. You'll learn—it takes practice."

The Place de Bonhomie was already filled with people and their horses and dogs. The sunlight had grown dim, the gas lamps were lit and warm light filled all the windows and doors of the establishments. Barnhardt dropped me at the café.

"I'll watch for you from over by Banc Naxos." He indicated the opposite side of the square where the bank and the real-estate office were located and where it was less congested.

I was lucky to get my same table outside by the railing. I put my injured foot up on a chair—there were a number of wounded warriors in the café, balming their sports injuries with strong spirits—ordered a Kahlua café, took out my book and waited.

It wasn't long before a beautiful restored antique Russian sleigh skidded around the corner into the square with Robert Constantin standing in command of a thundering troika of matching chestnuts. He wore a Cossack's bushy black bear hat and a full-length brown sable coat. Oscar sat implacably on the seat behind him, hands stretched to either side for balance, looking for all the world like a real Russian bear, angry and suspicious. Everyone turned to watch and smiled and some even clapped their hands together at Constantin's grand entrance. It seemed he lived his real life with all the drama of his pretend one.

Where was Sebastian Tremaine? Why wasn't he in the sleigh?

After letting the horses display lots of showy snorting and stamping and jumping around, Constantin reined them in and the doorman took hold of the bridle of the animal closest to him. The tenor stepped to the ground and greeted the fellow warmly, slapping him on the shoulder and exchanging pleasantries. Then, he strode into the café, leaving Oscar to sulk at the entrance.

Moments later he reappeared through the patio door and joined a noisy, crowded table of friends, a few tables away from mine. They were obviously ecstatic to see him, as though he'd been gone for a hundred years. His arrival juiced the entire place up a few notches, as if someone had plugged in an amplifier.

Even at midsixty-something, Robert Constantin looked the way he looked in all his pictures and performances, and I could see why he commanded the floor and made women scream. Even I, who was well inured to the charms of big shots, had a time of it not to gape. He was larger than life. He was about six four and his black hair waved back from his famous face, which exuded rugged, clean-edged masculinity, thanks no doubt to frequent tweaks and touch-ups. His tan made his dark eyes seem black and his teeth whiter than white. I wouldn't have been surprised to see a twinkle come from one of them. You could tell just by looking at him that he was a man of enormous appetites and passions. He squeezed himself in between a woman in a white fox hat and a slight, wiry man with gray, brush-cut hair. Although he looked completely different from the pictures Thomas had shown me, I realized the man was Sebastian Tremaine.

My eyes dropped immediately to the base of their table and searched for the briefcase among the ski boots and furry mukluks. It was nowhere to be seen, which meant he'd stashed it—or at least its contents—in a safe, either at the chalet or the bank. I wasn't surprised. Now that he was home, there would be no reason for him to keep the case and its contents in sight at all times if he could be assured the goods were well secured.

I had a good view of both of them. Tremaine's face was tanned and square jawed, very masculine and handsome. He had a closely cropped beard and mustache and wore wire-rimmed glasses. A red handkerchief was tied around his neck. He had an easy, genuine-seeming smile and gleaming white teeth that must have been replacements for the originals—no Englishman had ever had such beautiful teeth. He was obviously with what he considered to be friends because he appeared relaxed and an integral part of the group. But of course, that's one of the dangers and pitfalls of being the friend of the star, whether it's the star in show business, business business, or your own little bailiwick. You're part of the in crowd because you have the ear of the celebrity. Once the ear is gone, so are you. But after tending to the queen for decades, Tremaine was well accustomed to being second fiddle. And, from a strictly professional point of view, I'm certain that it would have been just as acceptable to him not to be the center of attention.

In short, he was exhibiting some of the signs of an accomplished criminal—the innate talent of dissembling, the smooth ability to fit in wherever you are, the easy lie or compliment always ready on the lips, the insinuation into the process.

I studied him as closely as I dared without attracting his, or Oscar's, attention. I wanted to hear his voice but there was too much noise. I knew that in spite of the joviality, he was always thinking, always watching for the next opportunity.

I called for my check and while I was talking to the waiter, I felt his eyes take me in in less than a blink, scanning my onyx-and-topaz earrings and my twelve-carat emerald-cut diamond ring. His glance was quick and his assessment smooth and thorough. I knew the look, I knew the scan, and it gave me goose bumps to be on the receiving end. I looked up and found myself looking straight into his eyes. He smiled at me, and then he winked!

It completely disarmed me, and as I finished my café and signed my tab, I felt the color flood into my face. What wonderful nerve. No wonder he'd been the queen's favorite and had won Constantin's heart. He was irrepressible, like a bad puppy.

On my way out, I gave the quickest glance at Oscar, who had not left his perch on the troika. His eyes stayed straight ahead and he pretended not to notice me. But I know he did because I could feel his eyes follow me all the way into Fannie's. I bought a wedge of soft Brie de Meaux and a thick slice of country pâté, a baguette, two dozen chocolate truffles of varying flavors, and all the ingredients necessary to bake and ice a devil's food cake: six ounces of unsweetened chocolate (of course I bought twelve), whole milk, light brown sugar, eggs, butter, cake flour, baking soda, regular sugar, and vanilla. Finally, I headed for the seafood counter with the idea that I'd have a few oysters for dinner as well, but thank God, I spotted Lucy Richardson having a conversation with the fishmonger before she saw me. I could do without oysters. I paid quickly and went to the wine and spirits shop next door and picked up a bottle of Glenmorangie single-malt scotch and two bottles of simply divine Romanée-Conti 2001 Echezeaux. Then I went home.

I sat in the back and let Barnhardt drive.

I was completely exhausted and starving to death, but I couldn't get Tremaine's face out of my mind. There was something very magnetic about him. Even from a distance, I could sense he had an enormous amount of charisma.

It was too late in the day to start working. I fixed myself a snack of cheese and pâté and a double scotch on the rocks and had a good soak in the tub.

Afterward, I was too drained to go out or cook—I didn't need any dinner. The pâté had been plenty. I just washed my face and went straight to bed. I was glad to be so tired. I was homesick. I missed Thomas and Bijou terribly and I didn't want to think about them. I turned off the light and was asleep immediately. I don't think I moved until morning.

THIRTY-FIVE

I was wakened by the sun coming straight into my eyes. I reached for the clock—it was after eight! I fell back into the featherbed and the down pillows. The sheets were the softest linen I'd ever felt—I couldn't even imagine how many times they'd been laundered to reach such a state. I strongly considered spending the rest of the day in bed. I'd accomplished a great deal yesterday between securing the house, setting up my manufacturing studio, snowshoeing, engineering a successful foray into the enemy camp, a driving lesson, and a firsthand look at the target.

Was Robert Constantin in on the job with Sebastian Tremaine? Too soon to know. But I couldn't come up with a single scenario that would make the world's greatest tenor jeopardize the adoration of his fans by stealing jewelry, unless he had a kleptomania problem, though I seriously doubted that—a tabloid would have revealed such a dirty little secret by now. Perhaps he had a constant need for presents, the more exotic and dangerous the better. Perhaps he needed constantly to be shown how much he was loved. That was often the case with artists and performers; they did what they did because they required the approbation, the constant adulation, to be able to live. Tremaine had certainly demonstrated he could provide gifts that were outrageous. What was their relationship? How long had they been together? Why was Tremaine already at the café, not at home and riding into town with his friend? Had they had a disagreement? No, that wasn't the case. It seemed that every time Tremaine opened his mouth to speak, Constantin laughed. I suspected Tremaine stole for the same reasons I did: to support his lifestyle. And, in fact, his success had landed him in a very lovely spot, as had mine.

There was one other possible scenario, of course: Tremaine wasn't the thief at all. He'd just been in the wrong place at the wrong time. Maybe this whole affair would prove to be a wild-goose chase. Maybe all the pieces were in Singapore, Shanghai, Teheran, or Damascus by now, or broken down, their settings smelted and the stones in a safe, waiting until the dust settled before being recut and coming back on the market. Maybe they were already sparkling from some sultan's or concubine's fingers or throat. Maybe they'd been stolen on their way from Buckingham Palace to the airport, not, as Thomas claimed, by Sebastian inside the palace.

I didn't have the answers to any of the questions, I could only surmise and have faith that the Windsor family's security personnel had completed an extensive investigation before lighting on Sebastian and enlisting Thomas. And, further, I knew what my plan was and I knew it was workable. Unfortunately, I also knew that if I didn't get out of bed and get to work, it was all just talk.

My video cell phone beeped. I picked it up and pushed a button. The screen came to life and showed Barnhardt shouldering his way through the kitchen door with a covered tray. He must have gone to the kitchen at the hotel and picked up what I liked for breakfast because he had with him a bowl of fruit, a small pitcher of what looked like grapefruit juice (one of my passions), a white cardboard pastry box tied with a green ribbon (which I prayed contained those cinnamon rolls), and the newspapers. He set a small covered pan on the stove and turned the burner on low—that would be the thick, soupy, almost chewy hot chocolate—and put a bowl of what I imagined was *Schlag*, that sinful sweetened whipped cream, in the refrigerator. No more Spa Super-

Fitness breakfast for me. They'd taken note of the uneaten eggs and yoghurt. Then he kindled the kitchen and living room fires and left.

I got out of bed, pulled on my robe, stepped into my powder puff mules, and headed for the breakfast table.

It had been almost two years since I'd sat at the jeweler's bench in the secret manufacturing studio in my London flat, and I was itching to get started, to see if I still had the touch. However, before I ventured in to reestablish my command of the craft, I adhered to the strict guideline I'd established for myself years and years ago and which, aside from yesterday's brief fashion lapse with the headband and the tool belt, I continue to apply to everything I undertake: I always look my best. I'm always ready for anything, and furthermore, if I look my best, I do my best. It's all part of my requisite ability to transit to another level, to vanish if need be, or to buy myself some time by my respectable appearance. I have always been ready to have my mug shot taken. Not that I expect that will happen, but particularly in an unknown environment such as this, any number of people—including, God forbid, Lucy Richardson—could drop in and welcome their new neighbor, and I needed to look as though I were having a leisurely, unpressured time of it working on my paintings, and invite them in for tea.

Chiffon is such a lovely, forgiving fabric. It should only be worn by the very young and the very old, certainly never by a woman my age with one big exception: work clothes. I have always preferred to work in what I suppose could be called chiffon hostess pajamas. They are extremely comfortable and so light and unencumbering they're almost not there. I'd found three pairs in Paris, all with tunic tops and floaty trousers, and decided to put on the melon set this morning. The color gave a little life to the snowstorm that had blown up again outside. I added matching lipstick, matching Jimmy Choo sling-backs, a torsade of natural pearls and pink coral beads, and went to work.

Once I accustomed myself to Tinka's desk chair, a comfortable, ergonometric affair with six wheels and the ability to pivot in every possible direction, I tightened the headband to which the magnification lenses were attached, and then, keeping my eyes on the work surface, I reached up and touched each one of my tools, one at a time. They were all racked within easy reach and it was important to refamiliarize myself with their specific individual locations without needing to raise my head.

I switched on the halogen lights and opened the thick manila envelope I'd prepared from my archives before leaving the farm. I withdrew a stack of photographs, blowups of the Cambridge and Delhi parure and the Lesser Stars of Africa brooch. The brooch would be the easiest to replicate, so I would do it last. I wanted to think that the only people who would need to be duped by the copies were the police, but that would be true only in the dénouement I'd written in my mind—I had no way to know how the real thing would play out. My copies had to be as perfect as I could make them, and the parure, in particular, would require every bit of my skill and concentration. Thank goodness Sebastian hadn't taken the tiara. Trying to replicate that on a tight time frame would have given me a nervous breakdown.

I decided to start with the necklace and slipped the other photos back into the envelope and set it aside. I placed four clear acrylic easels with clipboardlike clamps—two on either side of me—on the table's pop-up flaps. On one I put a photograph of the overall necklace, on another the clasp, on the other two I put sections of the links. Exact dimensions and carat weights of the stones ran down the sides for quick, easy reference.

Although the six cabochon emeralds—three on each side—which graduated in size from ten to fifteen carats from the clasp forward, looked at first glance as though they matched, nothing is ever a perfect match, especially in colored stones where it is the imperfections that give them their character. Each was a slightly different size, shape, color, and quality—some had a number of inclusions, some had almost none.

The 14-carat emerald at the clasp was diamond shaped and the 18-carat center stone was square. The six brilliant-cut diamonds that interspersed the emeralds ranged from 5.5 carats at the clasp to 6.5 toward the center. There were ninety-four .03-carat brilliant cut diamonds in the double rows that linked the stones. Each emerald was set in 14-karat gold and surrounded by a quarter-centimeter-wide border of pavé diamonds set in platinum. In the pendant, the fifteen-carat pear-shaped emerald was suspended from a petal-shaped, pavé diamond clasp attached to a chain of twelve .025-carat diamonds, while the other pendant—the 11.5-carat marquise-cut Cullinan VI—hung from a shorter chain of eleven diamonds.

While it sounds extremely complicated, in fact what made the piece particularly challenging to duplicate was its simplicity. With the exception of the pavés around the emeralds, each stone, no matter its size, made its own individual contribution to the whole, each had its own place and personality.

I began with the diamond chains that linked the larger stones. I sliced a sliver of platinum from an ingot and rolled it to two millimeters of thickness. Then I sliced off two five-millimeter-wide strips, making several steady passes rather than a single deep cut. I measured constantly, and when I was satisfied the shape and proportion were exact, I laid three of the small brilliant-cut diamonds in place. Once they were all properly positioned, I pressed them hard onto their platinum beds where the culet, or bottom point, of each diamond made its own distinctive imprint.

A jeweler's bench has dozens of implements, many of them appearing to be identical, but in fact each one is specialized to its task. There are buffs and burrs for finishing and polishing, pliers, tweezers and torches, and about fifty different gravers for cutting and shaping. My gravers were the finest available, made of the hardest Swiss steel, and therefore able to keep their blade longer on platinum, which was the metal I preferred to work in. Platinum is hard and light, as demanding to work with as it is rewarding. It requires patience, precision, and talent, and its beauties are manifold in the way it almost invisibly presents and holds stones.

The back of a piece of good jewelry should be as beautiful and interesting to look at as the front—this is where quality and workmanship of the construction reveal themselves. The visible area of the stones on the back should be almost as large as the front. The smaller the visible area, the poorer the craftsmanship, and generally the poorer the stones and the metals. Most top jewelers, when they cut through the metal to seat a stone, have a trademark shape—spades, hearts, diamonds, clubs, circles, squares, triangles, ovals, and so forth. Naturally, mine was a shamrock. By the time a piece is complete, the original cut-through shape is no longer viable. Some experts claim that if a piece is subjected to intense expert scrutiny, occasionally the signature can be identified. I don't believe it, particularly in the world of fine jewelry. If a design can be detected in the metal, then the workmanship is inferior and the piece is not worth studying or stealing in the first place.

I turned the first indented bed over and began to cut. The wooden knob handle of the scalpel-sharp graver was solid in my hand, but settling into the work after so long away was slow and frustrating. It took almost an hour before I began to feel my stride return, but I stayed on point and finally was rewarded with some of the most fluid, most skillful work I'd ever done. I completed the first series of cut-throughs, seated the stones, and then slightly heated the metal and softened and cajoled it into secure, silvery beds. On each diamond, I folded the sides up and cut off the excess platinum, tucking it down so it formed just the tiniest lip along the girdle, securing it in place. I soldered them onto miniscule platinum links so they were flexible and joined them together in short chains.

My concentration remained intense and I worked like a robot straight through lunch—I don't recall even stopping for a glass of water. By midafternoon, I'd seated 28 of the 117 stones and completed eight chains, four with three diamonds and four with four diamonds. It was an excellent start. I stood up and, for a minute, thought I was paralyzed I was so stiff. I pulled off the headband and massaged my forehead and reached my hands over my head, stretching one arm to the ceiling, then the other. I forced my arms back behind me and stretched and wiggled my fingers as though I were getting ready to play the piano. After a couple of minutes of motion, I felt much better.

Once the bench was tidied and in the closet, which I locked and armed, I turned on the steamer in the shower, fixed a pot of coffee and ate a little of the remaining cheese and pâté. The ingredients for the devil's food cake were still where I'd left them on the counter. Maybe later today. In the meantime, I took two dark chocolate truffles out of the bread box and ate them on my way to the bathroom, where I pulled off my clothes, went into the steam bath, and lay down on the bench, letting the eucalyptus clear my mind.

Barnhardt and I left for the square a little after four.

THIRTY-SIX

Every day I followed basically the same schedule, but with a much earlier, more disciplined start. I got up at five and worked from six until two, eight hours, without a break, leaving myself enough time for a little snowshoe adventure or a massage before going to the square.

The first afternoon, one of my cell phones beeped and I watched Lucy Richardson ski through my gate, done up like a ski bunny all in white Bogner with a big white fur ruff around her hood and glamour-girl dark glasses.

I got on the intercom immediately. "Barnhardt. Mrs. Richardson is just arriving. Would you please go tell her I'm working and can't be disturbed and I'll call her later."

"Of course, Your Highness."

He intercepted her before she was able to get her skis off. I watched him talk and her nod and smile, and then she walked up the hill doing what is called in skiing lingo a herringbone step. Lucy was in seriously good shape.

She left at least two messages for me every day. She was driving me crazy, she was like a meddling little magpie. One afternoon, I watched her come in in her sleigh, a little two-person rig Swissed up to a fare-thee-well, and she actually *peeked in the windows on either side of the front door!* before I could get Barnhardt out there to waylay her. Fortunately, for some marvelous reason, she did not go to après ski at the café, but I was constantly on my toes, dodging her in the market. No matter what time I went, she was there. Avoiding her had given me a headache and was starting to give me indigestion.

And then one afternoon, my luck ran out. I was in Fannie's picking up my dinner: a hanger steak and baby root vegetables to roast with olive oil and garlic. I was in the olive oil aisle when suddenly her head popped around the corner.

"Boo!" she peeped.

It took every ounce of my self-control to put a smile on my face and not slap hers. I was simply getting to hate her. "Lucy! How are you?"

"You're working too hard," she said. "You need to come out and play. Alma's going to think I'm not taking good care of you."

"I know—you're certainly doing your best. It's not your fault I have to be working. It's just what I need to do right now if I'm going to be able to make my deadlines."

"You still have to eat. Why don't you come to dinner tonight? We've got a couple of very, very attractive men coming. Single. Possibly straight."

I forced myself to laugh. "Thanks so much. For the moment, marketing is my only outing. Maybe in a couple of days."

"Poo."

Poo, my foot.

By the end of my first full week in Mont-St.-Anges, I had completed the necklace and was sufficiently up to speed that I knew I'd have the ear clips, brooch, and bracelet done in no time.

There was no question in my mind that by now Thomas had figured out where Robert Constantin lived and had been in contact with George Naxos, who would no doubt tell him that his agent was already embedded on the scene. I felt sure he knew where I was and wondered when, and if, he would try to contact me. I'd been keeping my eyes open for Thomas's assistant, David. But so far, unless he were very skill-fully disguised, I didn't think he was in Mont-St.-Anges.

To tell the truth, I liked the idea of Thomas knowing where I was. This was a huge caper. While the theft itself would not be impossible to pull off, once I'd been able to reconnoiter the Constantin chalet further, the locale was insurmountable, literally and figuratively, in many ways. Because of the location of the club, the fact that transportation in and out was only by helicopter or train, every escape route was basically controlled—there was no way to move spontaneously in or out of the valley. The knowledge that I had Thomas as a safety net if I found my-self in physical danger, or if the whole project went south in any num-ber of other ways, gave an extra oomph to my confidence.

In spite of the ever-present threat of the Terrible Lucy, I had easily fallen into the schedule of the place, arriving for my well-earned après ski at the café at a little after four every day. It had snowed on and off since I arrived. A couple of times there'd been an especially big snow-fall, and it made the skiers rhapsodize so euphorically about how the skiing had been, I considered taking it up. Other days the snow just danced about like little feathers. I'd even gotten somewhat accustomed to the cold. No matter the temperature, I always dressed up and made sure to wear noticeable jewelry, which was hard to do, bundled up as I was in outdoor gear. But at least I managed to wear largish earrings and rings and bracelets. I noticed that Constantin had some affinity for jew-elry as well. He seemed particularly partial to jeweled cuffs, sometimes he had three on each wrist. He also wore a large stud earring in his right ear, a different precious gem every day. He reminded me of a pirate.

Sebastian Tremaine, on the other hand, fascinated me more every time I saw him. The more I observed him, the less he seemed cut out for the high-wire life of a jewel thief, unless he was a complete reincarna-tion of the Scarlet Pimpernel—a bon vivant on the outside and a wor-thy adversary on the inside—which was certainly possible. He seemed open and accessible, and evidently had a wicked wit because often his words made his listeners open their eyes wide and drop their jaws.

I always sat at the same table, and Constantin and Tremaine and their circle of friends were always at theirs. I knew they were curious about me because I'd catch glances now and then and I was beginning to think they'd never make a move, when finally, on the sixth day, Tremaine got to his feet and headed my way.

My pulse kicked up a beat or two as the next step in my plan fell into place.

Tremaine typically wore a handkerchief around his neck; today's was yellow-and-blue calico. He stopped in front of me and after making a silly little schoolboy bow, he offered his right hand, and kept his left flat against his back, as though he were in the Prussian army.

I raised my eyes to meet his, but did not offer my hand in return. His eyes were grayish blue.

"Sebastian Tremaine," he announced. The eyes took in my ruby cabochon earrings and ruby-and-diamond brooch pinned to the neck of my pale pink turtleneck, just visible through the open top of my gray fox parka. All in all, it was a smashing getup, although rubies have never ranked very high on my list of favorites—however, I do love ruby cabochons.

I declined to offer my name. "Yes?"

I could tell he was injured by my attitude. Who did I think I was?

"I'm so sorry to interrupt. I told them you weren't going to be nice about it. I told them you didn't want to be disturbed because if you did you would have made it known to us but they disregarded me completely and made me come over to find out who you are. Well, at any rate." He looked over his shoulder at his friends. Constantin shooed his hands at Sebastian, instructing him to proceed with his inquiries. "We see you here every day reading by yourself and . . . what book are you reading? It must be positively gripping."

"Manchester's biography of Churchill."

"Ah. Wonderful man. Wonderful. How we could use more like him."

"Indeed." I nodded, trying not to laugh.

"Well," he began again. "Again, please accept my apologies for the interruption. I feel a perfect fool. My friends and I want to know if you'd like to join us for one more café before we all go on our way for the evening?"

"No, thank you. But please thank your friends for the invitation."

"Perhaps another time," he said.

"Perhaps."

I needed at least one more invitation before I'd accept. After all, we hadn't been properly introduced.

THIRTY-SEVEN

The following day, I was ready to move to the next stage. I had a fairly good fix on the social schedule for the week, thanks to the bugs I'd planted in Constantin's house. He and Tremaine were going to a dressy cocktail party that night with a number of friends. (I knew it was dressy because according to one of their maids, Sebastian planned to wear his kilt and she hadn't pressed it properly, the first or second time, and it had almost reduced him to tears.)

More importantly, just this morning, I'd learned that they were hosting a small, formal dinner dance at their chalet on Thursday. Today was Monday. They had to invite me.

I stopped working early enough to go for a walk on my snowshoes. My proficiency had increased dramatically since that first sortie when I thought I would die from the exertion. I was now able to make it to the top of my drive with only two stops for oxygen and then, instead of turning down the road toward the Naxos castle and Schloss Constantin, I turned uphill and pushed myself for what I think would be a city block or two. It was extremely hard, but very healthy work and there was a little turnout at the top where, if it weren't snowing too hard, I could see the entire valley from one end to the other. It was completely surrounded by mountains and every now and then you could hear the boom of dynamite echoing off the valley walls as the avalanche crews worked to keep the piste clear and safe. On the valley floor, I could see the train tracks come around a bend along the river at one end, and the heliport on its raised platform at the other. One day I watched a large, heavily loaded sledge drawn by four horses make its way slowly along a service road next to the tracks and then disappear from sight at the end of the valley.

Snowshoeing home downhill was my favorite part of this sport—I could almost run—and by the time I got there, I was out of breath and my cheeks were red with exertion. I was becoming extremely fit. Thomas would be so proud.

Thomas.

I left my snowshoes, poles, and boots at the kitchen door for Barnhardt to stow and padded in for a steam bath. By the time I was out, the Japanese masseuse, Yoshi, was set up and waiting, ready to give me a massage and an Energy Salt-Glow Rub, designed to invigorate even the most sluggish metabolism.

"This too hard, Highness?" she asked. She hardened her hands into sharp little hatchets and threw herself into a high-speed chop-chop of all the muscles from my neck to the soles of my feet as though she were a human jackhammer.

"Ow," I yelled.

"This good for princess. Almost finish." She started her third lap down my back, looking for a spot that didn't already have a hematoma. "Okay, that done."

She gently rubbed on a refreshing tonic from stem to stern and it made my skin come alive, as though she'd covered me with Alka-Seltzer.

"Very nice." I groaned and relaxed.

"You like?"

"Umm. Very nice."

"Now nice swishing."

"Swishing?" I mumbled. It sounded either slightly suspicious, a little illicit—as though she were going to take feathers and tickle me—or completely delicious. I was way off base. She delicately took a bundle of willow branches in each hand, and *thwack!* She started whipping me!

"Ow!" I yelled again.

She was such a tiny, pretty thing, how could she be so mean? And hit so hard?

"Swishing good for princess. Wake up nerves." The branches flailed down on my back, bottom, and thighs. "All done. Now Salt-Glow, then we done. Salt-Glow make skin beautiful. Soft."

"Un-huh." I pulled the sheet around me and started to get up. "You know what, Yoshi? I think my skin is fine—it's soft and beautiful enough."

She pushed me back down. "No. No. You see. Just a little rub. Then we all done."

Reluctantly, I lay back down and just surrendered myself to the pain as she scrubbed handfuls of grainy black sea salt over my entire body, ripping off my epidermis.

At least the whole procedure only lasted an hour.

"See tomorrow?" she asked brightly.

"Tomorrow," I moaned. "But much more gentle."

"You want seaweed mud wrap tomorrow? Very nutritional to skin."

"No. I want a regular massage with rosemary or lavender oil. Something gentle and fragrant."

She shrugged and nodded. "Okay. Seaweed better for you."

I'm a fast learner—I had a seaweed mud wrap once and it was terrific except that once the masseuse had gotten me all smeared with foul-smelling black goo, and bundled up in three sheets and covered with an electric blanket turned on high, she said, "Did they tell you you'll smell a little like seaweed for a couple of days?" I wouldn't fall into that trap again.

"Good-bye, Yoshi."

I hobbled into the bathroom, where I took a cool, needley shower that stung my poor skin and made me wail. Mind you, I didn't *like* the rough massage and cold shower, but if I were going to have the energy to make it through the afternoon and evening, I needed a wake-up call, not a warm-and-fuzzy. Finally, wrapped in a cozy white robe, I sat down at my dressing table with a small coupe de Champagne as a réstoratif and began my toilette.

Robert Constantin had been making his daily grand entrances. Today, it was my turn.

I swabbed my face with a cucumber refresher and patted cream around my eyes. I watched the news while I applied an antiwrinkle gel, after which I pinched my cheeks to give them some extra color and gave my whole face a vigorous rub.

My former nemesis, Giovanna MacDougal, had left her travels with the queen to cover a much juicier story back in London that had to do with a movie star who'd murdered her husband's lover. A different Sky-Word reporter, a middle-aged man, had been assigned to the queen and the royal entourage's world tour.

"We are here in Victoria, in the tiny island nation of the Seychelles, where Her Majesty has just arrived for a two-day visit en route to India."

She would wear the parure on Sunday at the Delhi Durbar.

I watched her get off her plane and greet the president and receive a bouquet of tropical flowers from a little girl in native dress. The queen had on what looked like a light cotton dress and a large straw hat. She smiled in her kind, genuine way and accepted the bouquet while her entourage assembled the required distance behind her. There was Prince Phillip, still, at eighty-three, one of the most handsome men in the world, and her ladies-in-waiting and . . . Thomas? What?

What was he doing in the Seychelles with Queen Elizabeth? He was supposed to be looking for me in the Swiss Alps. He was my backup in case anything went wrong. But there he was in his rumpled winter suit in that terrible heat, his white hair blowing in the island breeze, squinting into the sun, smiling and having a little tête-à-tête with one of the security men.

Oh, Thomas Curtis. Why did I let you talk me into this? "Goddamn it," I yelled at him. I threw my hairbrush as hard as I could at the television set but it bounced ineffectively off the edge of the tub and fell disappointingly to the floor.

What was all that business with the special cell phone and numbers? Call me and I'll be there in an instant, he'd said. He lied.

Men.

Did the absence of a safety net mean I was going to walk away from the heist? Not a chance. I'd never had a knight in shining armor before so it made no difference if Thomas were on hand to bolster me up or not. I'd worked my brain and my fingers to the bone preparing for this caper and I'd see it through. I didn't want to be a thief anymore and I didn't want Tremaine to be one either—if he was one in the first place. I intended to catch him, or whoever it was, red-handed and see him brought to justice. And furthermore, I intended to retrieve the queen's jewelry and return it to her personally because she was a nice person and didn't deserve to be a target for a greedy servant, even if he was a charmer like Sebastian Tremaine.

I had another glass of Champagne. I'd think about Thomas later. Right now, I had to get back to my own deal. I had some hills to climb.

"Hello, Black Diamond." I patted her neck and stroked her jaw. "Is it all right to feed her these? Does she like apples?" I asked Barnhardt.

"Very much."

She carefully removed them from my flattened hand.

"Would you like to start out again?" he said.

"I would." I climbed up next to him and picked up the reins and wrapped them expertly in my fingers. "So?"

"Very good. Soon you'll be driving yourself to town."

"All right, Black Diamond. Let's go." I gave the reins a little shake and she set off. By now I was accustomed to her energy and managed to keep her under control all the way to the square.

It started to snow.

I knew that Constantin and Tremaine had left for the café at four-ten and so we departed a few minutes after that. I'd put on what I considered my maximum outdoor princess clothes—the capacious full-length black mink cape with its hot pink satin lining, a cerise satin blouse with a matching camisole and cashmere slacks, kid gloves, lots of pearls and one of my very favorite pieces of jewelry, which I'd bought at an auction and paid almost 400,000 euros for—a large diamond bow pin— very similar to Queen Mary's Lover's Knot diamond brooch. I pinned it to the side of my black mink hat. Heads turned from every direction when we entered the square in our fancy red-and-gold sleigh drawn by our rare black Clydesdale.

"Kahlua café, Princesse?" the waiter asked, as he did every day.

"S'il vous plait." I picked up my book. I could feel Tremaine's eyes on my jewelry and Robert Constantin's eyes on my face. Constantin himself got up from his table and headed in my direction.

I sipped my drink. I was ready to be kind and gracious.

Suddenly, I heard a man's voice.

"Margaret!" he said. "I heard you were here!"

And then his arms circled me from behind the patio railing and gave me a huge hug around my neck and a kiss on my cheek.

I turned to see who it was.

It was George Naxos.

THIRTY-EIGHT

"George! Alma!" I jumped to my feet.

My arrival might have had the effect of turning heads, but the appearance of George and Alma Naxos had the effect of lighting a bonfire—the real king and queen of Mont-St.-Anges had arrived. Alma looked as regal as ever in a black mink hat and lap robe, a Tyrolean red melton jacket with gaily colored braid, a matching red cashmere scarf around her neck, and colorful peasant-style earrings almost the size of brooches, encrusted with multi colored precious and semiprecious stones. George led the way while their butler, Cookson, pushed her wheelchair through the café entrance and out onto the patio and up to my table. This was an incredible honor to have them come to me—way above and beyond their commitment to aid and abet my mission.

Constantin stopped in his tracks, and stretched out his arms in welcome, a huge smile on his face. He waited for them to get settled.

The waiter delivered the Naxoses' Kahlua cafés in record time. I was surprised Alma let George have anything so fattening. She lit a cigarette and leaned toward me, taking me in from top to bottom with those large almost almond-shaped, dark blue eyes.

"Impressive outfit," she whispered. "Any progress?"

"I believe so. When did you arrive?"

"This morning. Can you come to dinner tonight? I want to hear all about everything."

"Do you mind if I let you know in a while?" I answered. "I think Robert Constantin was just about to invite me to join them."

She smiled conspiratorially and raised her eyebrows slightly. "Oh, by all means—in any case, it will be just the three of us, if you come. I need an early night to recover from the trip."

"Did you fly in on your helicopter?" I couldn't help asking.

"Naturally."

I shook my head. "Too much."

Alma laughed. "Not for the fainthearted, but frankly, if I die, I die. I don't mind."

Well, I thought, that was definitely the right mind-set.

"Now," she continued in her regular voice, "with regard to tomorrow—"

Robert leaned down and kissed Alma. There was such affection in their greeting that I realized they were much better friends than Alma had indicated to me in Paris when she'd acknowledged she knew him but was noncommittal beyond that.

"My precious girl," he said. "Let me look at you—you are more beautiful than ever."

Her whole face lit up.

George and Robert shook hands warmly and embraced each other.

"Let me introduce you to one of our oldest friends," George said. "Margaret Romaniei. Incredibly this is her first visit to Mont-St.-Anges. Margaret, Robert Constantin."

"Margaret." He took my hand and kissed it. "Welcome."

"Thank you, Mr. Constantin."

He covered my hand with his and I felt as though I were surrounded by a soft, warm electronic field. He looked into my eyes and there was an amazing connection. I felt a zingy, tingling sensation as though Champagne bubbles were fizzing around me, tickling my nose and teasing my ears.

"Why haven't we met before?" he said. "I thought I'd met all the most beautiful women in the world. Why haven't I met you?"

I know my cheeks colored. "I don't know what to say. You're embarrassing me."

"I was just about to try to convince Margaret to come to our gin rummy party tomorrow night, Robert," said Alma guilelessly. "She says she can't but we need her. She's an excellent player, very competitive. Maybe you can talk her into it."

Alma was as good a liar as I was.

"I could certainly use you on my team—Sebastian's hopeless." He still had a hold of my hand. "You will come, won't you?"

I hesitated. I knew my expression was innocent. "I'm not sure—I have a lot of work to do and I've been staying in."

"That's practically a crime in Mont-St.-Anges," Constantin said. "Unless you're here to convalesce. Are you?"

I shook my head. "No, no. I'm a painter. I'm getting ready for a show, and I'm very far behind."

Out of the corner of my eye, I saw that George, who was still standing, was taking advantage of Alma's attention to our busy conversation to eat the flaky little chocolate-tipped almond tuille cookies that came with Kahlua cafés. He glanced sidelong at the waiter and a new batch materialized instantly.

"Well, if you're that far behind," Robert said to me, "you might as well come to dinner with Sebastian and me tonight. We're going to the Shaw's for an early supper. Of course everything's insanely early here because practically everyone, except for Alma and I, gets up at the crack of dawn to ski. Are you a skier?"

I shook my head.

"Good. So a late night shouldn't bother you at all. Have you been to the disco yet?"

"No."

He frowned. "This is outrageous. Do you like to dance?"

"I love to dance."

"Okay, it's done. After dinner, we'll go to the Rialto. Alma, are you and George going to the Shaw's?"

I figured out that Robert and George had an understanding: He kept Alma occupied to give George a chance to eat as many cookies as he wanted without getting yelled at.

"Not tonight, my darling boy. But we'll see you tomorrow evening at eight."

"We'll be there. It was an honor to meet you, Margaret, and I'll call for you at seven tonight. Where are you staying?"

"I've rented Schloss Alexander next door to the Naxoses for a couple of months," I answered.

"No! That's right up the hill from my house."

"It is?"

"Yes. You know the chalet across the road from George and Alma's? The one with the red mailbox?"

I nodded.

"That's mine."

"Small world," I said.

"See you tomorrow, George," Constantin said, and winked at him. "Are we still on for lunch?"

"Noon. Main dining room."

Robert nodded, slapped him on the shoulder, and returned to Sebastian Tremaine and their table of friends.

For the next hour, our corner of the terrace was mobbed with members and guests wanting to welcome George and Alma back to Mont-St.-Anges. I smiled and participated as best I could but the fact was, no one was really interested in me or who I was or what I did, they were just being nice because they wanted to get close to Alma and George.

The whole time, Alma took little swipes at George, who'd ordered a

Napoleon. Poor George. He was the richest man in the world but nevertheless was completely tyrannized by his invalid chain-smoking wife. What a horrible way to live, to have someone after you about your weight all the time. Didn't she get it? The more she harped at him the more upset he got and the more he ate.

As we were leaving, once George and the butler had gone through the ballet of lifting Alma into her sleigh, she leaned down and whispered to me, "Look out for Robert Constantin. He swings both ways with equal enthusiasm."

I couldn't help but laugh out loud. "Thanks for the tip. I'll keep my eyes on his hands. But frankly, Alma, it doesn't make any difference if he swings ten ways to Sunday, with all the groupies and opera junkies around him all the time, he's not going to spend his time on a woman my age."

Alma shook her head. "I wouldn't count on it. He has no discretion. He's as bad as a dog."

Well. Excuse me? I watched their sleigh pull away and worked to keep my jaw shut when all it really wanted to do was drop open. That wasn't very nice, was it? I might be a certain age and I might be wholesome but that doesn't necessarily mean that a man would need to put a bag over my head in order to make a pass at me.

That Alma. She was a liar and she had a mean streak. I wasn't sure if I wanted her on my team or not. She'd better not start making cracks about my weight or I'd . . . what? I'd what? Slap her silly? Don't be ridiculous.

THIRTY-NINE

"Oscar," Robert called. I heard him via the staircase transmitter in Schloss Constantin. "All ready?" His feet thundered down the carpeted stairs.

"Ready, sir," Oscar responded. "Big sled ready to go."

"Sebastian, did you call the Shaws and let them know we're bringing a guest?"

"Indeed I did. You know she's a princess." Sebastian sounded a little put out, a little pissy. Was he having a tantrum because Robert had invited me to come along? I hoped not. Maybe the jewelry I had on would soothe him.

I was wearing a fairly simple chartreuse satin cocktail dress with art deco Cartier diamond clips pinned at my waist, an unbelievably fanciful, noisy necklace of diamond, tourmaline, and peridot beads, diamond-and-tourmaline earrings, three jeweled bangle bracelets, satin sling-back pumps, and a spray of yellow Cymbidium orchids tucked in one of my matching diamond combs. I looked sensational, if I do say so myself.

"What kind of princess?" Robert was now passing through the kitchen.

"Romanian."

"Isn't that nice." From the tone of his voice, Romania clearly didn't rank very high on Robert's list.

"I know," Sebastian replied. "The Romanians are as desperate as they come. But she does have beautiful jewelry. Did you see that brooch this afternoon?"

"Umm." Robert was evidently also uninterested in women's jewelry. "Very nice. Are you ready?"

"I am."

A few minutes later, my cell phone buzzed and I watched the big, brightly painted antique sled, its lanterns aglow, come through the laser beams at the gate, the three horses moving at a fast clip, their hooves throwing clods of snow into the air. Oscar was perched up behind in the higher of the two benches. Every time I saw him, I wondered what was going through his mind. If he was wondering how he, a man from the tropical jungles of the Congo, ended up in snow country, riding in a fancy horse-drawn sleigh driven by an opera singer. I loved the incongruity, but I had no interest in getting any closer to Oscar than I had to.

I put my cell phone on silent and slipped it into my dress pocket. Moments later there was a knock on the front door.

"Margaret!" Robert's voice boomed. "We are here to take you away."

I opened the door and felt that same intense, intimate, immediate warmth of his personality that I experienced at the café. I'd never met anyone with such an indomitable persona—it was as though a giant had entered my house.

"Come in."

He bent forward—I am a tall woman and he was at least five inches taller than I was—and kissed my cheek. His lips were like velvet and he smelled of spice.

Silly as it sounds, I was almost breathless. Here was one of the greatest superstars on the planet picking me up to take me to dinner. Don't, for a second, get the impression I was getting starstruck. Not a chance. My brain was instantly full of visions of Owen Brace, a famous man with a famous line that I'd fallen for in a very big way, who'd tried to steal my money and break my heart. He failed spectacularly, due to my wiliness, and I learned a lesson—a humbling lesson. In spite of what Alma had said about Robert's promiscuity, I knew who I was and what I was, and what I looked like, and no big superstar who wanted sex was going to go after me to get it. No, it simply wasn't going to happen. Which was fine. I was immune to superstars, but still, it was flattering to have him make such a to-do over me.

"What a beautiful, beautiful woman you are." He looked in my eyes.

My mouth went slightly dry. I swallowed.

"What is that perfume?"

"Opium."

"Appropriate—delicious and addictive."

I handed him my sable coat and he held it while I slipped my arms in, and then he placed his hands on my shoulders, not in a suggestive way but almost as though he were trying to reassure me. I pulled on my gloves and tucked a cut-velvet scarf around my neck. I picked up my purse. "Ready."

"Come." He tucked my arm through his. "Your sleigh awaits. Have you met my companion, Sebastian Tremaine?"

"Only briefly." I offered my hand, which Sebastian took and helped me climb into the sleigh. "I'm glad to meet you—glad to be properly introduced."

He smiled, a little defensively, as though he were expecting me to hurt his feelings again. "Indeed. I'm glad you could join us. No one should sit at home every night in Mont-St.-Anges. Robert told me you haven't been out at all."

I nodded. "It's true."

"That's disgraceful!"

"It's been by choice, not for want of invitations." Inwardly I cringed at the grandeur in my voice but I wanted to put some pressure on Tremaine, see just how impermeable he was. I suspected his skin was no thicker than a frozen glaze on a pond.

"Oh, my." He raised his eyebrows. "You are quite grand, aren't you? You might possibly be the most important person I've ever met."

Okay. I'd pushed and he'd pushed back and I knew what I needed to know—he was not a cream puff, there was a little starch in his spine. I put my hand on his. "Forgive me," I said. "That was completely unwarranted. I've been on the phone all day with my lawyers and the gallery owner and they've just about worn me out."

He nodded. "I understand—I talk to Robert's promoters all the time."

Well, that was interesting. Tremaine hadn't struck me as the business type.

Robert called an unintelligible command to the horses and off we went.

"Russian," explained Sebastian. "These are Russian horses specially bred for centuries to pull a troika. They're called Orlov trotters."

"They're magnificent," I said.

"The breed was almost lost during the 1900s thanks to the dictatorships but it's coming back now. It takes someone who really knows horses to appreciate them. Are you a horse person?"

"I'm certainly becoming one."

Robert maneuvered the sled expertly around my drive and let the team accelerate slowly. It was fascinating to watch them, and him. We absolutely flew along the road.

"This team has been working together for seven years," Sebastian said. "You'll notice that the center horse is in a fixed harness—that large ornate bowed frame above his back is called a Duga—and has two reins while the outside horses only have one rein each. Quite interestingly, the duga horse trots at a very high speed while the two outside horses gallop. It's quite remarkable."

"You really are a little jabber box, aren't you?" I said, but by then our sleigh bells were making such a racket, he couldn't hear me. But I caught Oscar's expression out of the corner of my eye and I could tell he had heard because his eyes squeezed shut and his shoulders shook.

And the fact was, Sebastian never stopped talking as we raced through the center of town. He was just being polite, telling me all about this and that since I was a newcomer to the valley, but I stopped listening. We thundered into an enclave similar to ours and pulled up to a large, brightly lit chalet. A number of sleighs were already there, but none as fancy as Robert's.

Because I was with Robert, I was near the center of attention, but mostly I kept my eye on Sebastian, watched what he watched. There was some amazing jewelry in the big jovial living room, easily snatched, but I knew he wasn't interested in ripping off his friends. Instead, he stayed close enough to keep an eye on Robert and me, and unbeknownst to him, within my earshot. I have excellent hearing, finely honed by decades of keeping all my senses tuned in to the almost imperceptible sluggish hesitations and ticks that occurred in spin locks on safes. I listened to him gossip about me.

"I did some checking," he said to one of the semiregulars from their daily café table. "She's in the market for a husband but I think she's going to have some trouble finding one here—she has a reputation as a gold digger."

The woman rolled her eyes. "Heaven help us," she said. "That's what we're supposed to be protected from in Mont-St.-Anges."

Sebastian pursed his lips. "Well, that wouldn't get to me as much, I mean we all do what we must to survive, but she's so arrogant, it's unbelievable. What on earth would a Romanian have to be arrogant about?"

"How did she get into the valley?"

"She's a friend of Alma and George."

The woman's expression changed. "I'd be careful what I said about her, then."

"Indeed I am." He looked slightly miffed. "I can't imagine you'd think I'd say it to anyone but you."

And so it went.

Sebastian was jealous of me. He thought I was after Robert when in fact it was he whom I had in my sights.

"Ooooooh," Lucy Richardson whispered in my ear. "You have the most beautiful jewelry I've ever seen in my life. I'd almost kill to get my hands on that necklace."

"Thank you." I smiled.

"You've certainly hit the jackpot, haven't you?" Her bee-stung lips had curled into a mean little smile.

"What do you mean?"

"I heard George and Alma made over you like crazy this afternoon and now here you are with Constantin. Nothing like starting at the top—makes my little invitations look like nothing." She patted my arm. "I have a feeling you're up to something, *Princess* Margaret. And I'm going to find out what it is. By the way, look out for Robert—he's all hands."

"Lucy—" I began.

"Just make sure you keep *your* hands off *my* husband," she cooed, "or I'll scratch your eyes out." And then she walked off.

I was beginning to understand the attraction between her and Alma—they were both just plain vicious.

The party ended at eleven-thirty and it had been the kind of party that would go all night if the host and hostess had agreed to it. But, they explained very good-naturedly, they wanted to get up and go skiing in the morning, so their guests would have to find somewhere else to carry on. Consequently, there was a mass exodus of revelers. We all stood outside in the snow while our sleighs were retrieved and brought round. Everyone was a little tipsy and enjoying the flurries, talking about what they had planned for tomorrow.

The temperature had plunged, and Sebastian and I huddled as close to each other as possible, while Robert commanded the team and Oscar stifled a yawn from his perch.

Back we raced toward town and into the square, which was now illuminated by a big, bright neon sign. It wasn't anything you'd notice during the daytime unless you knew it was there, especially because it was over the café.

Disco Rialto, it read.

We pulled up to the door. Inside, I could see a wide, curving staircase, carpeted in faux zebra skin, descending to the basement.

FORTY

When was the last time I'd gone to a disco? Never. I have never in my life been to a night club or a discotheque. I've never cared for noise or revelry and the deeper we wound down those zebra-skin steps, which were banked with big bronze braziers filled with red flowers, the louder and louder and dimmer and dimmer it got. Finally we entered a huge room with a dance floor in the center. A stage with a disc jockey and two dancing girls in sequined hot pants and white go-go boots was opposite the entrance. A large U-shaped bar sat off to one side. Aside from its '70s music, the room reminded me of pictures I'd seen of a glamorous pre–World War II nightclub. There was an elevated section with tables for four and six. Leopard- and tiger-skin-upholstered banquettes and little cocktail tables for two or four, with white cloths and silver Champagne buckets, circled the dance floor.

The ceiling was black and sparkly and the place was absolutely packed. Except for the clothes—which, like mine, were beautiful and expensive cocktail clothes—the dancing was exactly like a disco in the movies. Another noticeable difference (with the exception of a handful of young and shapely trophy wives), most of the people were what is known as age-appropriate to the vintage of the music, so we all knew all the words.

Fun has never been a major factor in my life. I have, instead, directed all my energy and attention to providing for myself. Sir Cramner and I had what he considered fun, so I did, too. For him, fun consisted of an evening at my flat, sipping scotch and eating a cheese soufflé and some tomato soup, watching the news and perhaps a BBC mystery on TV, possibly followed by a little comfortable lovemaking if he were still awake and if there was time before he had to get home to Lady Ballantine. Thomas and I have what we consider fun—going to lunch, shopping for antiques, discovering new wines, followed by a little comfortable lovemaking, for which we are generally awake, more or less.

But when it comes to what most people consider fun, such as going to an all-night dance hall? This was a new one for me.

I took to the disco life like a duck to water. We danced without a break. I knew all the music by heart—it was what we'd played at the reform school back in Oklahoma: the Beatles, Bee Gees, Beach Boys, Linda Ronstadt, Chubby Checker and Fats Domino, with a little Zorba the Greek and Shirley Bassey singing "Goldfinger" thrown in for atmosphere.

At some point I realized Sebastian had disappeared from the scene and it made my senses sharpen. If he were going to make a move, now would certainly be a good time to do it.

I never knew Zorba could be so sexy, until—this was at three-thirty in the morning after who knows how many glasses of Champagne— Robert and I started clapping our hands and snapping our fingers, circling each other and looking into each other's eyes. The music was more erotic than "Bolero." If he'd asked me to take all my clothes off at that very moment, I would have.

But like a bucket of ice water over my head, or a slap in the face, my cell phone vibrated in my pocket and I was forced to excuse myself to go to the ladies' room. I went into a compartment—this club had the most fabulous powder room, all private cabins and enough wonderful makeup and toiletries to do a complete makeover—and locked the door. I slipped my video phone from my pocket and watched Sebastian Tremaine break into my house.

FORTY-ONE

At least, I think it was Sebastian. But on second thought, with the night-vision goggles and the tight black clothing and high turtleneck pulled up over his chin, it could have been anybody. It could have even been Lucy Richardson. She and Sebastian were exactly the same size, and when you get right down to it, from what I knew of Sebastian and what I knew of Lucy, I realized it could absolutely be her. Did that mean I thought she'd stolen the queen's jewelry? Not at all. She hadn't. But I was 99 percent positive she was in my house looking to steal my jewelry.

I'd spotted the blind spots in the existing security system and the thief had, too. But he or she'd made the mistake of not checking to see if any modifications had been made since I'd moved into Tinka Alexander's house.

Although I'd left a few lights turned on low, with the night-vision goggles, the burglar looked like someone from outer space. He'd scaled the side of the porch off my bedroom and entered through that door, setting off the silent alarm of the pressure pad under the door mat. He crept quickly, catlike, to the front of the house and searched the living room, dining room, kitchen, and then back to the master bedroom— moving paintings, sorting through bookcases, pulling up rugs, looking for a safe. Whoever it was, was extremely thorough, but not particularly efficient or savvy. For example, he—or she—moved and opened things before checking to see if there were any telltale booby-traps, such as pieces of thread or paper that only the victim would know if they had been moved. He entered my sitting room and rifled through papers on top of the desk, evidently looking for something incriminating. There was a small wall safe in the bookcases, easily discovered. He pulled an electronic scanner from his back pocket and opened it. Inside were a few pieces of Tinka's jewelry, nothing spectacular, certainly nothing worth stealing.

Unfortunately, the intruder lifted the cloth covering the canvas on the easel and saw a completely white spread. He let go of the cloth and let it flutter back down and shook his head and then flipped through the blank canvases leaning against the bookcase. I knew there was a contemptuous look on his face and I felt a little embarrassed that my lie about working so hard had been caught out. Well, so what? I'm sure painters get painter's block, the same way writers get writer's block. I was having trouble getting started.

Then he went to the closet that contained my workbench and Tinka's big safe, and found it locked. A locked door is no obstacle for a good thief, or even a semicompetent one. He flipped his lock picks into his gloved hand—he seemed to have them on some sort of instant spring-loaded affair on his wrist, something I would definitely look into—and after studying the lock for a second, selected the proper pick and inserted it.

Although I couldn't hear it, I knew at that moment, the alarm had gone off. He jumped almost ten feet in the air. It was a horrible alarm, many, many decibels above the norm. A screaming, wailing, high-pitched sound that could deafen you for days in no time. I watched him open his mouth and yell and put his hands over his ears and then I watched him hightail it out of the house and leap over the balcony rail like an Olympic hurdler and vanish from sight into the deep snow below.

Poor Barnhardt. It took a minute for him to get himself together, and by then, the burglar was long gone—he'd sprinted up the hill and was on his way home. Barnhardt ran out of his quarters, barefoot, trying to tie his bathrobe around himself one-handed. He carried a shotgun with the other. Once inside the kitchen, he stood there, an agonizing grimace on his face, trying to figure out where the sound was coming from. The blare was so horrific, its source was untraceable. I turned it off and I watched his shoulders slump. He closed his eyes and took a long, deep breath and then conducted a good, thorough search of the house. He checked all the window latches and door locks and after leaving me a note on the kitchen counter, he returned to the stable. Shortly after that, his light went out.

I went back to the dance, but the evening's sparkle had dulled. I was perplexed and preoccupied by the break-in. Thankfully, the party was wrapping up. Donna Summer's "Last Dance" was just ending.

"Margaret," Robert said. "I wanted to dance with you to this. It is so romantic."

"Sorry, Robert," I said. "Maybe next time."

If I were going to dance to that song with anybody—which I never had—it would be my husband, once I'd forgiven him. What was wrong with him, running off with the queen like that?

Thank God for fresh, cold air.

I was tired. I'd never been up this late. Although Sebastian had departed earlier, Oscar had remained, ever-present in the background, silently keeping his eyes on his boss and watching the crowd as though he were protecting the president of the United States or the Bank of England. We glided back to Schloss Alexander, with Robert singing *"Addio, fiorita asil"* from *Madam Butterfly,* singing out his heart to me. As we drew abreast of Schloss Constantin, he slowed down just enough for Oscar to jump out and then spurred the horses on up the hill to my house.

"Oh, Robert," I said, as we jingled to a stop. "Thank you so much. What a wonderful, wonderful evening."

He jumped from his side of the sleigh and came around and helped me down. "Tonight—disco dancing. Tomorrow—gin rummy!"

I laughed and shook my head. "It already is tomorrow." I put my arm through his as we negotiated the icy path to my front door.

"Thank you again," I said. I was ready for a move of some sort and curious what form it would take.

"How about a little cognac for your Robert?" He pushed his way past.

Before I knew it he had his arms around me and was kissing me—a very aggressive, very French, very leaned-over-backward opera kiss.

Oh, for heaven's sake.

FORTY-TWO

The invention of Viagra has turned mature men into complete idiots. And ruined more good relationships and marriages than outright cheating. Viagra has made them all think that they're irresistible, that every woman on the planet has been mourning the fact that her husband has had other things on his mind for the last twenty years besides sex. He thinks that she's just been waiting, waiting, waiting, praying for the day when she could be attacked while she's trying to get a glass of wine inside herself to give herself some relief from the stress of her responsibilities and get dinner on the table and sit down for a few minutes and catch her breath because she's spent the whole day shuttling between the nursing home and her job, trying to arrange in-home care for her mother, and a major real-estate deal for her partners, and her back is absolutely killing her, she has business problems on her mind, and she hasn't had a good night's sleep without a sleeping pill in a month because of hot flashes or chills or because of his snoring. And now while she's trying to lift the roast out of the oven, here he comes across the kitchen, all juiced up on sexual-aid pills wanting to play goddamn kissy face. It really is a miracle more older men haven't been found murdered on their kitchen floors, dead of carving-knife wounds.

I read an article not long ago about an elderly man, ninety years old, who was tossed out of his retirement home because he was taking Viagra and mauling all the ladies. What was he thinking?

What was Robert Constantin thinking? Where was his finesse?

Where was his refinement? What had happened to the concept of just getting to know each other a little? Roles had completely reversed. Men of a certain age had started using Viagra instead of their brains. And the women had started using their brains instead of their bodies. Where would it all lead?

Well, I knew what he was thinking, but more to the point was what was I going to do about it?

"Robert." I pushed him away and sat down on the edge of the sofa. "You have to stop."

He looked completely floored. "Why?"

I put my hand on my chest. "Because I have a serious heart condition. I can't take this sort of excitement."

That worked.

"Oh, my God, forgive me." He fell to his knees. And then his eyes searched mine. No matter how great an actor he was and no matter how hard he tried, he couldn't hide his confusion. "Are you sure?" he said. "The way we were dancing . . ."

"That was exercise. Sexual excitement is something very, very different, very stressful and I've already suffered one major heart attack." I had a terrible time keeping a straight face. "That's why I've come here, actually—to have a very quiet, safe, secure place close to the finest medical care in the world while I finish my collection."

"Oh, my God. How frightening. I'm so, so sorry. I had no idea."

"It's all right. I should have told you sooner."

"But"—he frowned—"you were drinking tonight. Should you be drinking? Isn't it dangerous?"

"Only wine and Champagne. My doctor categorizes wine as food, not alcohol."

He nodded. "Very progressive. I agree." He struggled to his feet. "Please forgive my behavior. I am so ashamed. Oh, Madonna."

"Robert, no one knows about this. Not even George and Alma."

He shook his head vehemently and crossed himself extravagantly. "Never a word from me."

"Thank you. Well, it's late. I need to go to bed."

"Yes. Yes. Let me help you up." He took my hand and very gently helped me to me feet. "You'll be at the gin rummy party won't you?"

"I wouldn't miss it for the world."

"Shall we pick you up?"

"I'll take my own sleigh. I'll probably come home earlier than the rest of you."

He kissed my cheeks. *"Bonne nuit, ma belle princesse.* Sweet dreams."

"Bonne nuit, Robert. *A domain."*

When the door was closed I put my hands over my face and started laughing. Now Robert could go get all Viagra-ed up with whoever he wanted but at least I was out of the running.

I poured myself a double scotch and went to bed.

FORTY-THREE

I slept until almost noon, an act I consider dissipated beyond all redemption, and worked for just a couple of hours. But my brain wasn't fully engaged. The events of the day before impinged on my concentration, most especially the barmy scene with Robert. Robert was a big baby. He was not a buffoon and he was not to be taken lightly, but he was an artist—full of love and passion, bluff and bravado, and as easily swatted down and crushed as a fly. I'd seen through him, seen what a child he was. He lived completely in his own made-up fantasy world. Robert was insecure, harmless, and probably very kind.

Sebastian was an entirely different animal. He seemed genuinely kind and sensitive and irresistible on one hand, but on the other, if he was in fact the thief I suspected him to be, was he also the sort of person who could be comfortable in a knife fight? Would the tactics that successfully foiled his attempted theft at my house stop him? I didn't know. I know if it were me—and since no earplugs on the planet can block the sound of that alarm—I'd find someone else to rob. Had Robert known what Sebastian was up to? I didn't think so. I didn't think Robert ever knew what anybody was up to, including himself, unless he was onstage and pretending to be someone else. He needed direction.

Lucy continued to nettle and unsettle me. I tried to put aside the fact that I simply didn't like her and focus on her behavior and what she said: "I think you're up to something . . . and I'm going to find out what it is." She'd thrown a monkey wrench into my strategy—nothing I couldn't handle, but still. Personality-wise, I had her pegged—mostly. But there was something darker there, a need to manipulate. A need to know everything. Was she Alma's eyes and ears? Was that her particular power and currency? From my point of view, she was an uncontrollable wild card, and short of shooting her, there was nothing I could do to take her out of the mix. The more I thought about it, the more I believed she was the one who had broken in to my house.

Thomas's abandonment continued to annoy me, although he hadn't appeared on the noon news, so who knew where he was now. Aside from my own insecurities—oh how I hated to admit that I actually had any, but the fact is I'm so inexperienced and suspicious when it comes to love, I'm always ready to jump ship, get there before the other person, beat him to the punch, hurt him before he hurts me—I knew deep down that Thomas wouldn't ditch me unless there were good reason. He was a man of his word. What was up? Where was he now? What had happened that he would need to go meet with the queen?

And what about George Naxos? Hard to believe, to say I was sorry for the richest man in the world, but I was. In spite of my initial impression of his dedication to Alma when I'd been in their apartment in Paris, yesterday at the café I'd seen something else. She wasn't nice to him. Was he blind with love for her? She exuded an undeniable influence that her beauty only intensified. Was he under her spell? Or was she an aspect of his life, a responsibility he simply assumed along with all the others? Perhaps he had her in complete perspective and allotted her the same amount of time and attention he gave to his other projects. Or was it because she was his wife and he had promised to care for her no matter what?

I also couldn't help but think about how much fun the disco had been. What a treat it would be to go someplace like that with Thomas. Robert was a fabulous dancer. I tried to recall if Thomas and I had ever danced together. Come to think of it, I don't believe we had. Oh, well, there was that one time in Portofino at the gala, but that was just for a couple of seconds and I'd been so angry with him I'd stepped on his shoes on purpose to scuff up the shine he was always so overweeningly proud of.

At about three o'clock in the afternoon, I gave up trying to work—I was just going through the motions. The snow was falling so hard it looked like a Christmas card blizzard. The world outside my windows no longer existed—everything was white. It was time to make the cake.

"Barnhardt," I said over the intercom. The smoke from his chimney was blowing sideways.

"Yes, Your Highness."

"I don't think we'll go to the square today, it's too cold."

I sensed his relief. "Very good."

"And Barnhardt."

"Yes?"

"I'm going to a party at the Naxoses' tonight. Do you think—if it's not snowing this hard—I'm ready to take Black Diamond by myself? It's not far."

"Yes," he answered. "I think that would be a good first solo to stay here in the neighborhood. But if the weather is like this, I will insist on driving you myself."

"Agreed."

"Would you like me to come over and stoke the fires?"

"Please."

In minutes, Barnhardt had the fires in the kitchen, living room, and master bedroom roaring. I handed him a covered mug of hot chocolate on his way out the door. *"Mit Schlag,"* I said.

"Danke." He tipped his hat and shouldered his way into the storm. I knew he was grateful for an afternoon off.

I draped a white chef's apron over my head and tied it around my waist, then flipped through Tinka's CDs and found a copy of Tchaikovsky's *Sleeping Beauty* and put it on full blast. Did the sleeping princess like devil's food cake? I'm sure she would have if it had been invented at that time. The music was romantic and beautiful. I sang along.

I turned the oven to 350 and measured and arranged all the ingredients on the counter; buttered and floured three eight-inch pans, which as usual I put into the freezer until it was time to put them in the oven. Many cooks don't take this step but in my opinion, when the frozen, batter-filled tin hits the hot oven, it seals a wonderful smooth crust onto the cake.

While the dark chocolate melted in a double boiler, I sifted cake flour, baking powder and a pinch of salt, creamed butter and sugar, added an egg, a teaspoon of vanilla, then starting with the flour mixture, I alternated it with the liquefied chocolate and beat the batter until there was not a hint of a granule of sugar or a dot of unblended flour to be seen. I filled the pans evenly, lifted them carefully into the oven, and set the timer for thirty minutes.

I washed and dried the dishes and laid out the ingredients for the icing on the counter—four more ounces of unsweetened chocolate, a cup of sugar, two cups of water, and vanilla. I wouldn't begin to prepare the icing until the cakes were out of the oven. That way there was no danger of frosting them while they were still warm and sacrificing the whole project for the sake of the gratification of needing to taste the cake right now, a common pitfall. Successful cake making requires equal parts self-control and talent.

Icing a cake properly is terribly complicated, as well. To some, it comes as easily and naturally as breathing, but for me, it is more challenging than making a soufflé, which I can practically do blindfolded.

Proper utensils are essential. Of course, Tinka had every utensil ever invented to make every dessert under the sun.

I boiled the sugar and water until it reached the proper temperature on the candy thermometer and also dripped heavily enough from the spoon to leave a filament that broke and curled back up on itself. I whipped two egg whites until they were frothy and added them, and then, with the motor running the whole time, poured in the melted chocolate and vanilla and kept beating until the frosting reached the perfect consistency—it resembled dark, dark brown satin.

It was close to four-thirty when I placed the first layer on the revolving stand and scooped out a good big spoonful of icing and plopped it into the center of the cake. I heard the lasers up at the gate beep but by the time I got to my monitor, whoever it was, was already well down the drive to my house.

Moments later there was a knock on the door.

"Come in," I called. "It's open."

"Margaret?" he called back.

"Yes?" I stuck my head around the kitchen door. It was George Naxos. "Oh, George. Come in. I'm just icing a cake and can't stop!"

He left his snow-covered hat, parka, and boots in the entry hall and entered the kitchen in an endearing sort of way. Ice was frozen to his mustache, and the warm air made his glasses fog. "Sorry to disturb you."

"No, no. You aren't disturbing me at all. It's just that when you're icing a cake, you really can't stop or you'll lose the rhythm and the icing will set too much to spread easily."

"You made that?"

"I did."

I could tell that no matter what George Naxos had thought of me before, he now thought I was positively glorious. A goddess.

"We were all concerned when you didn't come to the square this afternoon. So I'm here to make sure you're all right."

"I'm fine." I laughed. "To tell you the truth, George, I stayed out so late with Robert, I never did get myself together today. Come in and have a seat. I'll be done in a couple of minutes."

He perched himself on the stool opposite where I was working and watched, a rapt expression on his face.

"Done." I performed the final fillip in the center and it relaxed into a gentle glossy curl. "Isn't it beautiful?"

George swallowed.

"Would you like a slice?"

He nodded.

"With a glass of milk?"

He nodded again.

"Me, too." I took two tall glasses out of the cupboard and filled them with cold milk. Then I picked up the cake knife and began to cut. I paused and looked at him. "You aren't by any chance on Viagra, are you?"

For a second, George looked as though he hadn't heard me right—he'd heard something but it couldn't possibly have been what I said. He got a perplexed expression and then he burst out laughing. "Don't tell me," he said. "Constantin?"

All I could do was roll my eyes.

George stayed for an hour and we had an absolutely delightful time. We also ate half the cake.

"Alma's going to kill me," he said.

"Don't tell her."

He looked at me as though I'd lost my mind.

By the time George left, I'd learned a number of things: he didn't know I was an undercover policewoman, which meant that even though he might tell Alma everything, she didn't reciprocate. George also didn't know I had a heart condition, which meant Robert had kept his mouth closed, which was good information to have, because if he'd told Sebastian, Sebastian would have told everyone by now. I also learned that George loved his business and he loved his life. We never got around to discussing his wife, and I purposely avoided bringing up the subject of the Richardsons. I didn't want to tip my hand that I had any particular interest in them.

FORTY-FOUR

There was no time left for a nap after George left, so I cleaned up the kitchen, took a leisurely bath, and put myself together at a sensible pace.

Among my other extravagant purchases on my Parisian shopping spree, I'd found a gorgeous dinner suit that would be perfect for Alma's gin rummy party. The jacket was brownish bronze bouclé wool with a leopardskin collar and cuffs and the long skirt was comfortable wool jersey. The plain ecru silk blouse was vaguely sheer so I put on a bronze-colored French-cut bra with rust-colored satin ribbon binding. Every now and then Sir Cramner's Pasha would catch the light and glitter enticingly from its hiding place behind the ribbon trim.

I added a necklace—three strands of rare sixteen-millimeter golden pearls, ear clips of golden pearls set in diamond clusters, and an unusual Cartier estate brooch of a tall trumpet vase of yellow pavé diamonds overflowing with a lavish bouquet of precious and semiprecious stones. I finished up by tucking rusty red roses into my hair. I'd finally gotten accustomed to my darker hair and darker eyes and thought I looked quite well. I slipped my cell phone into my skirt pocket.

I also took the added precaution of turning the volume on the closet alarm up even higher. It would be so loud I wouldn't be surprised if it were audible from the Naxos castle.

"Are you ready, Barnhardt?" I said through the intercom. It was eight o'clock sharp and the storm had faded to intermittent flurries from a broken sky.

"Black Diamond and I are ready, Your Highness. But more to the point, are you ready to drive yourself?"

"Yes, I believe I am." I laughed. I pulled on a fur jacket, tight kid gloves, and wrapped a warm cashmere scarf around my neck and went outside.

Black Diamond looked so beautiful, all decked out in her ribbons and bells, and Barnhardt had lit the lanterns on the sides of the little red-and-gold sleigh. But now that I was standing there, planning to set out on my own with this giant horse and little sleigh, my heart started to pound and I felt my nerve begin to leave me.

"Did you bring your sugar and apples?" Barnhardt asked.

"Oh, I forgot. I'll be right back." I dashed into the house. The familiar act of getting sugar and apples for my horse, something I gave her every day when we said hello, had the effect of calming me down. She eagerly lapped them from my outstretched hand and I patted her and kissed her on the jaw and hugged her neck and drank in her scent. I'd begun to understand and appreciate how people could be so attached to their animals since I'd gotten my little Bijou, my first pet, a little over a year ago. I missed her terribly and in some ways, Black Diamond had filled up that aching corner of my heart. Not only was she majestic and powerful, she was also trusting and dependable. When I got home, I decided, I was going to buy horses for Thomas and me and we'd ride them around the farm and inspect our apples and our lettuce crop.

I climbed into the sleigh and picked up the reins.

"The gatekeeper, Hugo, is expecting you. If you are having any problems, let him know and he will drive you the rest of the way in." Barnhardt's words came out with puffs of cold air.

"I'm fine. It's just next door."

Barnhardt nodded. "Yes, you will do just fine. She won't give you any trouble at all."

"Let's go, Black Diamond," I said, and gave the reins a little shake.

She started along the drive at a nice pace. I looked up at the black starry sky above the puffy clouds and the towering snow-covered trees. The air was sharp and cold. I looked over my shoulder and there was Barnhardt, jogging slowly behind, just like a mother sending a child off to school for the first time. It made me feel very secure and it also made me laugh. I didn't want to embarrass him, so I pretended I didn't see him as he shadowed me all the way to the Naxoses' gate, a miniature fortress of its own, behind which a long drive disappeared into the woods. But I think he probably knew I knew he was there.

"Would you like for me to drive you the rest of the way in, Princesse?" Hugo the gatekeeper asked.

I shook my head. "I think I'm all set, Hugo, thank you."

As Black Diamond trotted through the gate, I turned and waved good-bye. "Thank you, Barnhardt," I called. He gave me two thumbs-up and a wave before turning for home.

The castle was unreal. I came around a corner through the forest, and there it was, white and turreted with a blue slate roof, just like in the fairy tales. Golden light streamed from the windows.

George greeted me at the front door, kissing both my cheeks. He was dressed elegantly in a black cashmere sport coat, charcoal slacks, and a light gray open-necked shirt with a yellow ascot.

"Thank you again for the chocolate treat this afternoon. I don't think I've ever had such a delicious cake." He patted his stomach. "I'd like to be able to say I'm so full I don't think I'll be able to eat any dinner, but regrettably, I've never been too full to have another meal."

"Neither have I. Unfortunately. It's a good thing we're both so good-looking." I smiled and he laughed. "George, the castle is incredible. How long has it been here?"

"We built it about twenty years ago. It's actually a replica of Neuschwanstein," he explained, referring to Mad King Ludwig's land-mark monument in Bavaria. "Only slightly larger."

"Of course it is." I laughed. "Neuschwanstein is way too small."

"We have a ballroom *and* a media room—what did we do before media and media rooms? And, of course, we have an indoor swimming pool for Alma and lots of proper bathrooms and running water. And"—he smiled—"I could go on and on."

"It's extraordinary." I handed my coat and gloves to the footman. "Thank you for including me."

"Alma's in the library. You're the first to arrive."

The opulence of the castle's furnishings was in stark contrast to the severity of their Paris apartment. Did that mean there would be more food and wine on the table for dinner? I wasn't optimistic.

The library with its massive bookshelves, painted ceiling, shields and standards was a grand affair that looked as though it had been in place for centuries, a room where treaties had been signed in blood and war had been declared and armies ordered onto the field of battle. Its contemporary life was given away by the presence of a number of Impressionist paintings by well-known artists such as Monet and Renoir and Van Gogh, a flat-screen TV and a flat computer monitor on the desk. A large portrait of Alma with layers of white tulle wrapped romantically around her snow white shoulders hung above the mantle. A gigantic Oriental rug covered the floor.

Alma sat in front of the fire in a tight, silvery, long-sleeved top that was encrusted with crystals. A silvery gray blanket covered her lap. She looked like a queen. All her jewelry—actually she would have been wearing a complete parure if she'd had on a tiara—her necklace, earrings, bracelets, and brooch—was rubies of every color, shape, and size. It was a breathtaking suite and complemented her coloring perfectly.

I recognized them immediately. They were the copies I'd made of Mrs. Lucien Marks's set of fine ruby jewelry! The real stones—of course I'd melted down the platinum settings within seconds of getting the originals home—were still in their separate briefkes in my vault in

Geneva. The suite was auctioned at Ballantine's Magnificent Jewelry Auction two years ago. I'd swapped my counterfeit pieces with the originals at the last minute when they were bought by an anonymous buyer, not a dealer who might, on serious scrutiny, have spotted them as fakes.

Cookson, the tidy little butler I'd met in Paris, stood in the background.

I took her crippled hand gently and kissed her on the cheek. She looked extremely fragile and her eyes seemed flat, distant. "How are you?"

"*Comme ci comme ça.*" She took a deep drag of her cigarette. "Better than earlier. I haven't been out of bed all day. George told me the two of you ate an entire cake this afternoon." There was disapproval in her tone.

I felt myself blush. "Well, that's not entirely true. We ate *half* a cake."

Alma shook her head. "He is incorrigible. If I didn't keep an eye on his diet, he'd weigh five hundred pounds."

"Your jewelry is amazing—are those all rubies?"

She nodded. "George bought them for me at auction in your hometown."

"Oh?" I said.

She laid her fingers across the necklace. "At Ballantine and Company in London—surely you've heard of them. They have the finest jewelry auctions in the world."

"I'll have to go there sometime if I'm ever in the market for fine jewelry. An inspector's salary doesn't really leave much room for pieces like that," I said with a sense of humor. "Maybe I'll meet a rich husband."

"That's always a very workable and realistic solution." She smiled. "But you must be doing something right. You've been wearing some beautiful pieces."

"You think this is all mine?" I said. "Oh, how I wish it were. But in fact, it's part of my cover, provided to me by the Crown. I don't know what most of it is but it must be very good because they practically made me sign my life away before they'd let me take it out of the vault."

"From what I've seen so far," Alma said, "they outfitted you with very, very good pieces. I'm surprised our resident jewel thief, Sebastian, hasn't tried to steal it."

"I'm sure he will."

Alma nodded and ground out the cigarette and Cookson immediately stepped forward and held a lighter so she could fire up another. "Let's not waste this minute or two alone. Tell me what's going on. Have you made any progress?"

I shook my head. "A little—it's going to take some time. Without your support and help, Alma, it would be impossible. But I've got to tell you"—I couldn't help but start laughing—"the fact that Robert seems to be a Viagra devotee adds a little unexpected challenge."

She got tickled, as well. I'd never seen her really smile, and now to see and hear her laugh was wonderful. "Isn't he awful? He's even tried to seduce me! An invalid in a wheelchair! I told you—he's worse than a dog." She was laughing so hard she was almost crying. "Oh, the stories I could tell. But he's so precious and so talented and means so well, everyone gives him a lot of latitude."

"He is all those things, in addition to being oversexed. But I think I've got him neutralized, for now at least."

She dabbed the corner of her eyes. "I'm not sure how authentic his passes are, if you want to know the truth. I think the number of times he's actually succeeded in getting someone into bed are minimal. It's all a show—he's always after women our age and older, because he knows we have so many other things going on in our lives we aren't going to take him seriously. I mean, really—at this point, who needs a fling? Now"—she gazed at me through the curl of smoke—"tell me, is there anything I can do for you?"

"In Paris, when I asked you about Robert and Sebastian, you were very closemouthed about them, and naturally, I respect that. But now that I'm on the scene, I see they're good friends of yours. What do you know about Sebastian? Any information you can give me is important to cracking the case." I was trying to sound like a Scotland Yard detective, give some official gravitas to the situation, but as the words came out, I realized how silly they sounded. Alma, on the other hand, didn't seem the least bit amused. Maybe detectives really do talk that way.

"Sebastian," Alma said, as though she'd bitten into a lemon. "I can't bear him. He's a complete phony. But Robert adores him and makes it quite clear that if we want to see him, Sebastian is part of the package."

"How long have they been together?"

"Over a year, I'd say."

"Where did they meet?"

"I have no idea, he simply appeared on the scene. He's become Robert's 'business manager.'" She put quotes around the words with her fingers and raised her eyebrows in an expression of skepticism. "If he's a business manager then I'm a brain surgeon." She turned her eyes toward the doors. "Here they come now."

FORTY-FIVE

I heard him before I saw him. He was singing. Not an aria but "The Happy Wanderer," and "Val-de-ree, val-de-rah," boomed throughout the house as though it were an echo chamber. It sounded wonderful and ridiculous at the same time, totally unexpected.

Robert burst into the room with the same immensity with which he strode into everything in life. He paused in the arched doorway, arms outstretched, mouth wide open. The upbeat reprise reverberated from the walls. I wouldn't have been at all surprised if he'd sailed a hat across the room and flung a velvet cape to the ground for his squire, Sebastian, to collect. Instead, he was wearing a Tyrolean jacket and a red vest and looked as if he'd just escaped from the set of *The Sound of Music*.

"My God! I am so happy to be here tonight. Alma!" he declared as though he hadn't seen her for a hundred years. He kept his arms thrown wide and marched to her side and engulfed her and her wheelchair and spun her around. "You are the most beautiful woman in the world."

She laughed like a child, just like Clara in *Heidi* when her father came to visit. She laughed and giggled and banged her fists on his massive chest as though he were King Kong and she was being kidnapped. This was too much, too corny, too over-the-top, and then it dawned on me that, of course, these were two of the greatest performers of the twentieth century (I feared they would be eclipsed in the twenty-first). Their lives revolved around drama, around the grand gesture that could be appreciated from the third balcony, around being the centers of attention.

"You look like a princess who needs to be rescued—to be taken away from all this. Run away with me, Alma. I can make you so much happier than old George."

He timed this perfectly and purposely to coincide with George's arrival, as well as that of their other guests.

"Hush, Robert," Alma said sotto voce. "I don't want my husband to hear."

Robert turned to me and gave me a similar bear hug and twirled me around. "My dancing partner," he said. "You dance like a feather. When shall we go again?"

"Anytime," I answered.

Sebastian was no less effusive in his greeting of Alma and me. He would be on his best behavior tonight. His eyes took in our jewelry, performing a quick assessment. I could tell he was particularly captivated by Alma's rubies, and I must admit I felt a proprietary sense of pride as well as a little resentful that my golden pearls and lovely brooch didn't get more play. They might not have been as showy as Alma's but at least they were real. I was interested that he gave not even a tiny indication that he could tell the difference.

The other guests were, no surprise, Lucy and Al Richardson—she had on a black velvet evening suit with silver trim—and Allegra Cimino, a nice and very trim lady from Turino who had on a simple bright red wool sheath cocktail dress and stunning diamonds.

Cookson took cocktail orders. I was longing for a scotch but Robert took the liberty of ordering for me.

"The Princesse will have the Riesling." He put his hand on my upper arm and gave it a little squeeze. "I am looking out for you tonight," he whispered.

"Lucky me," I said. I shuddered a bit—I didn't need looking out for and I'm not wild about German wines. Most of them are too fruity for my palate. For me, they are generally like a headache in a glass. And sugary sweet, grapy rich Riesling was at the top of my list for least favorites. But it was thoughtful of Robert to be so considerate of a fragile woman with a potentially fatal heart condition. It had been a desperate declaration on my part but one that I knew would derail him permanently. Now I wished I'd been able to come up with something else.

Once we all had cocktails and a maid passed a silver tray that had exactly enough caviar canapés that we could each have one—George and I caught each other's eye and I knew we were both thinking the same thing: thank God for the cake—Alma led the way into the card room, a wonderful chamber with painted mural walls, Dresden chandeliers, and a Dresden hearth crackling with a cheery fire. Four card tables with green felt cloths decorated on their corners with colorful appliquéd-felt playing cards were lined up approximately ten feet from each other down the center of the room. Each table had a library lamp with a green glass shade, putting it in its own little pool of light like an island; two chairs; two new packs of cards; a score pad with a pencil; a bowl of cashews; and a little library-type bell. If I hadn't known we were to play cards, I might have thought we were there to take a final examination.

We gathered around while George read the teams aloud—again, there were no surprises: Lucy and Al; Robert and me; Sebastian and Allegra; George and Alma. He indicated where the ladies should sit and Cookson held our chairs. And then, with great flourish, he took a folded sheet of paper out of his breast pocket.

"The rules," George announced importantly. "Please pay attention. We will be playing regular gin rummy—Hollywood rules—before and after dinner. We play for forty francs a point, all tonight's winnings will be donated to the hospital's Albert Richardson Fund for Heart Disease Research. This will not be in lieu of anyone's current pledges or annual gift." He gave Al a hard look.

Everyone, especially Al Richardson, laughed, and I surmised he had endowed the fund—it was named for him, after all—by making a major financial commitment. Forty francs a point was a lot of money, the equivalent of ten Euros. This was a high-stakes party.

"And the losers must match the winnings."

No one batted an eye.

George continued. "The ladies will remain seated on the far side of the tables and the gentlemen will exchange places after each game. As I have already mentioned, we are using Hollywood rules: Each game has three bouts and each bout is to one hundred twenty-five points."

I did some quick math. If the losers matched the winners, that meant each game would render a minimum of 7,500 Euros, times three (there were four couples but partners wouldn't play against each other) equaled 22,500 Euros, and if we played before and after dinner, that meant a net of 45,000 Euros or 11,250 Euros per couple. That was pocket change to this group.

Alma indicated to me that she had something to say. I leaned down. "Don't worry, Margaret," she whispered. "We'll pick up your share."

"Thanks," I whispered back. "I was getting nervous."

"No whispering!" George barked, and everyone laughed. "Now, if I have your attention." He rattled his paper. "At the end of each hand, you will count up and record your points and then ring your bell and Cookson will confirm the scores. This is a new rule because, as we all know based on our last party, counting and addition are not Robert's strong points." Everyone clapped. "This is for your protection, Robert. And ours."

My first match was against George. We both played quickly and efficiently and he won, but not by much. We were the only ones to finish our bowl of cashews.

"How are you doing, Robert?" I called down the way. He was a very slow player—I could tell he studied every single card and move end-lessly, and even then, still had no idea what to do. He was playing against Lucy, who was looking frustrated. She was drumming her fin-gernails on the table.

"Robert." She tapped his arm with her folded-up hand. "Please. You know you're going to lose anyway. Just put down a card."

"All right. All right." He discarded.

She picked it up. "Gin! Finally, this game is over."

Next, I played against Al, but there was really no match there. He completely walloped me. And the whole time we played, I felt the burn of Lucy's anger on me.

"Wow," I said. "I didn't get a single point."

Al beamed. "I 'Schneidered' you, which means"—he picked up his pencil and drew long Xes through my sections—"you get zero and I get double points." He blew me a kiss.

I caught Lucy's eye. If looks could kill, I'd be dead.

The fact that I didn't get any more cashews made it worse.

Next, I played against Sebastian. The skin on his hands looked soft and pampered. His nails were short and well manicured. He was slightly prissy and effeminate in his movements but I felt it was an act, except he did have on a little mascara.

"I'm the best gin rummy player in this room," he declared as he dealt our first hand. "And I'm going to clobber you."

"Really." I arranged my cards.

"Really," he replied, and after only two draws, he said, "Gin!"

"Now," he said, once he'd shuffled and dealt our next hand and we'd exchanged a couple of cards, "tell me everything about yourself."

I was trying to figure out what to do in my next play.

"You're far too beautiful to actually be from Romania—I mean the young girls there are very, very pretty but when they get to be our age—

look out. They lose their waistlines and the hair on their heads moves to their faces! Oh, my God. They look like trolls. And their shoes. The worst."

"Sebastian." I laughed. "I'm trying to think."

"I think it's a lack of vitamins and proper skin care. Don't you just want to go to Bucharest and give everyone a facial? And a good waxing? I'll tell you, Jimmy Choo could make a killing there."

"Sebastian. Shut up." I finally discarded.

He picked it up. "Gin!"

"You're going to be sorry for that."

He won the first bout and it looked as though he were on his way to winning the second.

I picked up my cards and sorted through them.

"Let's move along," Sebastian said. "We haven't got all night."

"Hmmm," I said as I casually discarded. "How's this for a move: What were you doing in my house last night?"

His eyes widened and stared into mine. "What do you mean?" He drew a card and his hand trembled slightly. He put the card on the discard pile without really looking at it.

"I mean"—I picked it up—"what were you doing in my house last night sorting through my things and trying to pick the lock on my closet while I was at the disco with Robert?" And discarded.

He licked his lips and then pursed them together. "I don't know what you're talking about." He drew. He discarded.

I picked it up. "Would you like to see the video?" I discarded.

I could tell his mouth had gone dry. He drew. He discarded.

I picked it up and sorted languidly through my hand. "I said, would you like to see the video, Sebastian?"

His eyes met mine. "Yes, actually. I would."

I leaned toward him. "Gin."

I snapped my cards down on the table and he laid his down carefully. He looked as if he were about to throw up.

"Let me see." I began to count. "I get twenty-five, plus . . ." I sorted through his cards. "Oh, my, Sebastian, you didn't really have anything at all, did you?"

Cookson came over and verified the score. I picked up the deck and shuffled. I placed the cards in front of him to cut. I began to deal.

"Who are you?" he asked.

"More to the point, Sebastian, is who are you? Does Robert know you're a thief? Does Alma?"

I saw a tinge of fear in his eyes. He stared straight at me.

I met his eyes. "Don't worry. I'm not going to be the one to tell them. As to me? I am who I say I am—Margaret of Romania—and I am an extremely cautious person. Stay out of my house and we'll do just fine."

"I was never in your house. I swear it."

I glanced down at Lucy. Had it been her after all? "Well, then, who was?"

"I truly have no idea."

Unfortunately, the more I thought about it, the more I believed him. I was, it seemed, in a war with two fronts.

"I believe it's your discard," I heard him say.

FORTY-SIX

By the time we went in to dinner, Robert and I were trailing significantly, in spite of my decimation—my "Schneidering" in two out of three bouts—of Sebastian and the resulting point count. I wasn't a pro at this game, but at least I knew how to play, had some card sense. Robert was hopeless. Sebastian was a superb player, but I was glad to note he had come slightly unhinged, a complete no-no in a profession—stealing jewelry—where nerves of steel were the first order of business. Would he take the time or make the effort to try and see if there was a connection between my ramped-up security system and the fact that his secret life could be exposed? No. He'd become too sure of himself in his new life and was beginning to commit the sin of pride. And that would, somehow or other, be his downfall. His ego was such that I was sure he would completely recover his composure by the end of the meal.

When we got to the dining room, I saw with chagrin that I was seated between Al and George—more grist for Lucy's mill. Well, that was her problem. She was seated directly opposite me on George's left side, next to Sebastian.

In spite of Lucy's growing bile, I could tell it was going to be one of the most delightful, hysterical dinners I'd ever been to. All the people, except for me, and to some extent Sebastian, were very close, longtime friends but they made me feel completely part of the crowd. I'd never had friends in my earlier life. I couldn't afford to. Now I had Thomas, who was surely somewhere in the vicinity by now, and my little Bijou. And our friends, the Balfours, in Les Baux. It was a start.

"I'm starving to death, aren't you?" George said to me under his breath.

I nodded, praying there would be a proper meal served, not those scanty tidbits Alma had served in Paris.

"I'm so hungry I could eat a bear," Robert announced, shaking out his napkin and spreading it across his lap.

Sebastian and Al nodded in agreement.

When the appetizer, slices of rare tuna and a little dab of wasabi, served with an exquisite Chasselas appeared, I glanced at George. We had, it seemed, little hope. But I was wrong. The moment the first-course plates were cleared away, the kitchen door swung open and in came a footman carrying a large silver tray with a boned roast of braised beef surrounded by parsley and what looked like cherries, a dish I'd read about for years but never tasted and certainly never prepared. It required a minimum of a week's marinating of the roast.

"Aargauer Suure Mocke," he beamed.

"Bravo! Bravo!" Robert cried.

It was, indeed, a rare treat.

We all fixed our eyes on the parade of assistants that had followed the footman with domed silver bowls of side dishes, which they arranged on the long sideboard.

The head footman picked up his razor-sharp, bone-handled carving knife and fork and began to carve. The heady scent of the cherries and peppery denseness of the roasted meat wafted over us. He layered three slices of perfectly cooked roast onto the antique ecru plates bordered with wide green-and-gold rims, as carefully as he would place a filament of gold leaf over a cake, and then with the sharp point of the knife and one prong of the fork, picked up a bouquet of six or seven roasted cherries—tied together with a cherry stem—and tucked the bow just beneath the serving of beef. It was beautiful to watch him. An assistant then settled a heaping spoonful of a creamy purée of potato, celeriac, and turnip and julienned strips of braised carrots and parsnips around the roast. Another footman served the plate while a fourth followed him with a boat of a dense savory sauce, surely the result of a week's worth of marinating and final deglazing. The plate wasn't a precious work of art, the way some grand cuisine dishes are—arranged so artistically it almost seems a crime to touch them—but it was a beautiful, colorful, fragrant creation that beckoned you to begin. The aroma of each element was distinct and complementary. It was hard to wait, but we all persevered until the entire table had been served.

In the meantime, Cookson had wasted not a second in getting to the wine. He wheeled in a cart with a half-dozen bottles of uncorked 1975 Château Mouton-Rothschild Pauillac. He held up one of the bottles for George to examine, and once George tasted and approved, Cookson nodded to his assistant, who moved quickly to fill the glasses. The party was on.

George raised his glass. "To friendship," he said.

"To friendship," we agreed, and clinked all round.

The cherries with the braised beef gave a wonderful sweet contrast to the tangy sauce, and the purée with its combination of root vegetables was positively decadent. The carrots and parsnips were carrots and parsnips. There's just so much one can do with them.

Alma didn't scold George a single time—I'm sure it was because she was at the far end of the table and too well mannered to shout at him. She did shoot him a few looks that he ignored, but they were nothing compared to the ones I was getting from Lucy. Hers were positively lethal, as though she were planning some way to get even with me. The people who knew her were right: she was nuts.

Dessert was white chocolate mousse, butter almond cookies, and demitasses of dark Colombian coffee.

By the end of dinner, in spite of the strong coffee, everyone was stifling yawns.

"Shall we postpone the retribution round until next time?" Alma asked.

We all began to nod assent.

"Absolutely not!" Robert declared. "Margaret and I demand a chance to redeem ourselves."

I looked at him as though he'd lost his mind.

"Don't we?" He challenged.

"Absolutely," I said, and nodded adamantly. "We demand a rematch."

Sebastian and I played each other first. He had himself completely under control—his eyes hid his thoughts—and his mouth went nonstop about absolutely nothing the whole time we played, which amused me.

"Sebastian," I said. "Please be quiet just for two seconds."

He leaned toward me. "No. And I want you to know, I was never in your house. I would never do anything so reckless."

Was that a confession of his skill as a thief? I looked in his eyes. They were open and honest, completely without guile. He was calling my bluff. At that moment, I knew he was the Palace Thief, and I also knew he had not been in my house the night before.

At one o'clock in the morning, we all stumbled home, completely sated with beautiful food, wine, friendship, and gin rummy. All of us except Lucy, who took the opportunity to whisper to me as she was kissing my cheek.

"I thought I told you to stay away from my husband."

And then she walked out the door.

For the first time in my life, I went to sleep with a gun under my pillow, the big handgun I'd bought in Zurich. The dealer said it could stop an elephant. He'd given me a course on how to use it and let me fire off a couple of shots in the basement range. The recoil was so strong, it almost knocked me down.

"Take charge!" he'd ordered. "Lean into it."

I did and the next two were better.

I don't know if I actually could or would use it to shoot anyone, but having it close by gave me a certain peace of mind.

FORTY·SEVEN

The booming echoes of crews dynamiting avalanches up and down the valley started with the first hint of gray morning light. The sky was low and more snow was in the forecast. I was getting awfully tired of this weather. I ate my breakfast and then, comfortably decked out in citrine chiffon pajamas, coppery kid sling-backed pumps and a torsade of topaz beads, I settled in to my workbench to wrap up the little that remained of my projects.

The countdown was on.

Thomas was on my mind. I expected that the next time the phone or doorbell rang it would be him.

Sebastian had had the night to think about our conversation. It was possible, but extremely unlikely, that he would take his booty and run before I could make my own well-plotted attempt to discover where it was and steal it. I also couldn't shake the feeling that I was in peril, that I was walking close to the edge of a sheer dropoff, that Lucy was going to do something crazy. She was as unpredictable as nitro and to someone as meticulous as I, unpredictability was one thing I loathed. I also appreciated that she was an element I couldn't control. However, there were certain other elements that I could manipulate. I picked up the phone.

"Schloss Constantin," a woman answered.

"Good morning, is Mr. Constantin in? It's Margaret Romaniei calling."

"One moment."

"Good morning, Margaret," he said seconds later, his voice robust and enthusiastic. "Did you sleep well?"

"Very well, thank you. And you?"

"Always. I think it must be the brandy and fresh air—lots of each."

"I'm calling to see if you and Sebastian can come to dinner tonight. I know you're getting ready for your dinner dance tomorrow, so thought maybe you'd enjoy a quiet evening."

"We would love to. What time?"

"Seven-thirty. Just a casual supper. I thought we could play whist or canasta. Or Parcheesi—do you play Parcheesi?"

"It is my most favorite game—I always win. Sometimes even without cheating. We'll see you at seven-thirty. May I bring the wine?"

"Just yourselves."

I disassembled my studio, packing everything—everything but my unused easel and paints and draped canvas—neatly back into the boxes they came in, sealed them up, and called the shipping company to come pick them up. I shredded all my work documents—close-up photographs, descriptions of the pieces, receipts for the supplies and shipping information—and stowed my personal documents such as passports and identifications and personal jewelry (except for what I planned to wear for the next few days) into the false bottoms of my Hermès travel satchels, which I placed in my clothes closet with the rest of my things.

I laid out the replicas of the queen's jewels on the bathroom counter and carefully tucked each piece of the parure and the Lesser Stars of Africa brooch into individual Velcro-fastened pockets stitched all round the inside of a specially padded corset. Years ago, I'd designed and constructed a number of these foundations—bras, waist-cinchers that resembled back braces, girdles, and corsets—and they had served me well. I'd used them successfully to carry gems and currency between my vaults in London and Zurich, Provence, and Geneva. I'd never try to pass through airport security wearing finished pieces, but loose stones were undetectable and the undergarments were so ingeniously constructed and padded, a thorough body search would not give them away. In addition to which, they were comfortable. They added bulk to my figure, to be sure, but what possible difference could a few more pounds make at this point?

I cinched on the lacy black strapless affair. I'd wear it from now on.

"Kahlua café, Princesse?" the waiter asked.

"Please." I wanted to ask for a double I was so exhilarated from driving myself into town, by myself, for the first time. I'd called Barnhardt to tell him I'd made it without a hitch. Black Diamond performed like a dream.

"Naturally. Call me if you want a ride home."

I was at the café before the rest of Robert's group and took my regular table. I made my marketing list for dinner—smoked salmon canapés, noisettes de veau, rösti with shallot sauce, fresh spinach, and burgundy. And the rest of the cake. I pulled out my book, which I'd become very tired of—I was ready for some sort of a grand adventure story—and sipped my café, which I'd become addicted to. Robert and Sebastian thundered into the square in their troika a quarter of an hour later.

Robert came directly to my table. "Please come join us," he said. "You can't sit and read your silly book all the time. It's too boring."

"It's not boring at all and besides, I was just leaving for the market. I'm cooking tonight, remember?"

"You mean *you're* going to do the cooking? Not your cook?"

"I don't have a cook."

"That's insane. Come to my house for dinner."

"No. Absolutely not. You don't understand, Robert. I *like* to cook."

"No, no. You need to take care of yourself. You must stay off your feet. I insist."

"Robert . . ."

"That's the final word on the subject. I will call for you at seven-thirty."

"All right. If you insist. But I'll drive myself."

I wandered next door into the predinner bustle at Fannie's. I wouldn't have many more opportunities to visit this gastronomic wonderland and I wanted to remember every inch of it.

The charcuterie counter alone was worth the trip, with sausages and cheeses available only in Switzerland. I was trying to decide which combination to purchase when, right on cue, Lucy sidled up next to me.

"Aren't these sausages gorgeous? I'll take that schnitzel, please," she said to the fellow.

We both watched him wrap it in white butcher paper and tie it with string. He handed it across the counter.

"I figured it out," Lucy said, holding the sausage.

"Figured what out?"

"Where I know you from."

"Back at that again?"

"Have you ever been to Portofino?"

My throat tightened a bit. "Dozens of times."

"I knew it! You were at the gala last June with that movie star . . . oh, what's his name?" The sausage wagged back and forth like a pendulum.

I shook my head. "I don't know. I've been invited to the gala a number of times, but I've never been able to attend. Was this the one where the diamond was stolen?"

Lucy nodded. "Yes, the Millennium Star. Oh, darn. What's that actor's name? It's right on the tip of my tongue. *Michael Douglas*."

I started to laugh. "You think I was there with Michael Douglas? What about his wife? Catherine Zeta-Jones."

"Oh! My God, you're right." Lucy's mouth formed a perfect O.

"That's who I've had you confused with all this time. Catherine Zeta-Jones. I am so embarrassed. You look exactly like her."

"Like her mother, maybe."

"No, no. You're what Al calls a dish."

"Lucy, may I tell you something? I'm not interested in Al."

"Don't be ridiculous. All women are interested in Al Richardson. He's one of the richest men in the world. And I've heard that you're down to your last centime and you're in the market for a husband." She wiggled her schnitzel at me. "Just stay out of my Al's pockets and his pants." And with that she jammed the sausage into her basket, turned on her heel, and left.

She was a case. But unfortunately, she was a smart case. She'd somehow come up with me and Portofino in the same sentence and that was not a good thing.

Tomorrow night couldn't come fast enough.

FORTY-EIGHT

That evening, as Black Diamond trotted up the main drive to the porte cochere, I studied the carriage entrance to Schloss Constantin more carefully than I had when I'd been on foot. This was a new perspective. Before, Oscar had carried me in through the ground-floor service entrance. Tonight, a footman at the front door held my horse's bridle while I dismounted.

"Where are you going to put her?" I asked, concerned. "I've grown so attached to this gorgeous beast, I'd like to take her inside with me. She is a very special girl." I patted her shoulder.

"She'll be right here at the front, madam. Did you bring her blanket?"

"It's in the box."

He lifted the top of the storage box that ran the width of the back of the sleigh and pulled out Black Diamond's travel coat, a snappy black wool affair trimmed with red braid.

"What do you do when it's a big party?"

"They go down into the stable yard. It's covered and heated." He smiled kindly. "Believe me, they are very comfortable."

"Are you sure?"

He nodded. "Very sure. We should all be so well taken care of."

Oscar greeted me—well, the words "greeted" and "Oscar" don't really fit in the same phrase, except we were warming up to each other slightly. When he opened the door, I was practically knocked backward by a wave of music—Robert and a soprano singing some duet or other—that was so loud it was almost deafening. Evidently there were speakers hidden in all the walls of the house, and it was almost as though Robert were standing right next to me screaming in my ear at the top of his lungs. I love music, but this would give me a nervous breakdown.

"Good evening, Oscar," I called over the noise. "Did you have a good day?"

"Okay." He took my coat and I followed him toward the cloakroom but he caught the toe of his boot on the corner of the rug and tripped. He fell with such a thud, it sounded as though a bomb had gone off.

"Oscar!" I said, and helped him to his feet. "Are you all right?"

He frowned and nodded. "Why are you thinking about me? You're the only one who's thinking about me."

"I'm sorry to hear that. All of us need thinking about and looking after."

"This way," he said.

I followed him past the dining room—so Gothic, so packed with heavy, oppressive furniture I almost felt like crawling—and down the wide hallway into a library with dark wood paneling and bookshelves jammed with leather-bound volumes, an ornate carved stone fireplace and more overly large, overly carved, overly dark, dreary furniture. Thick, weighty brocade curtains were drawn across the windows. The drapes strained at their loops as though they, too, wanted to fall to their knees and collapse. A flat-screen television showed a performance of Constantin in Puccini's *Tosca*.

Sebastian pressed the mute when I entered the room and the house fell wonderfully silent. He smiled and stepped toward me.

"Princesse," he said and kissed me on either cheek.

"Good evening, Sebastian." Just knowing he was the Palace Thief and that the queen's jewels were, hopefully, somewhere in this house, made shivers of excitement ripple up my spine.

He was a very worthy adversary. There was no way he would let my accusation about his entering my home, and my calling him a thief, run him out of town. After all, I'm sure he reasoned, they were just lucky guesses. Sebastian might have looked and acted like a nancy boy, but he was as intrepid and brazen as I was. His smile contained assurance and possibly even a challenge.

Robert put his hands on my shoulders and kissed me with gusto. "Welcome. You look magnificent tonight, like a movie star," he said. "If your sapphires were just slightly darker, they would be the same color as your eyes." In fact, if I hadn't had the contact lenses in, they would have been the same color as my eyes.

He was dressed in a red velvet smoking jacket with satin lapels and looked every inch the grandest of grand tenors. "What can I offer you to drink? Red wine? White wine? Champagne?"

I looked at his vodka martini longingly.

"Champagne, please." It couldn't possibly be as bad as the sweet Riesling the night before.

Robert went to the drinks table and held up a bottle of Dom Perignon. "Will this do?"

"Perfectly."

The three of us sat in front of the fire, each man in his own easy chair at either side and me on the sofa in the center. I don't care how pretty sofas look, or how they complete furniture arrangements, they are pure hell to sit on, particularly if you're wearing a tight corset or, more importantly, if you want to participate in a conversation with any energy or credibility. A slouching person cannot make a point. The only time a sofa is of any use is when you're sick and have on soft, warm pajamas, a lush cashmere blanket, a stack of fashion magazines, and can lie down for a nap. I sat as far toward the front edge of Robert's sofa as I could without sliding off onto the floor.

"Tell me about your painting," Sebastian said. "How are you coming along?" There was that look again—humor and defiance all in one. "Making lots of progress?"

Oh, dear. Maybe he *was* the one who broke in and saw that I hadn't cracked a single tube of oil paint. Or maybe I was just becoming paranoid, seeing a burglar around every corner.

"Some. Thank you for asking."

"What exactly do you paint?" asked Robert.

"Landscapes are what I'm most known for. I do the occasional portrait. I'm rather stuck at the moment, rather uninspired. I think it's all the snow. The snow is white. The canvas is white." I shrugged. "I'm sure the sun will come out one of these days. You have such an interesting face, Sebastian, perhaps you'd consider sitting for me? Tinka's study is a perfect studio for painting. Have you ever been there?" I kept my eyes on his. Touché.

"We've been to her house a number of times. Do you remember that fondue party, Robert? Cheese fondue for dinner and chocolate for dessert. I thought we would explode. But I've never been in her study or bedroom. Have you, Robert?"

Robert shook his head. "It's not that I haven't tried."

We all laughed.

A maid came in and passed a tray with hot cheese puffs. I put one on my plate and considered a second.

"Please help yourself," Robert said. "You can tell from looking at me, this house is nothing like Alma's. And there are many, many more where those came from."

"Thank you." I added two more. "Tell me, how long have you lived here?"

"Since the club opened twenty years ago," Constantin answered. "I was one of the first members. My residence of record is in Milan—I keep a big house there and that's where the world thinks I live. There are photographers and fans outside the gates all the time. God knows what they think they're going to see, all the cars have blacked-out windows. In reality, I haven't been inside my Milan house in years, my mother and my sister live there. I live full-time here in Mont-St.-Anges. It's the only place on the planet I've been able to find that allows me to live a somewhat normal life. It's amazing that George has been able to keep it such a secret all these years. But then, that's the power of Naxos."

"He is amazing." I bit into the cheese puff, one of my favorite hors d'oeuvre. Ubiquitous and so simple to make, just a little circle of buttered toast, topped with a mixture of mayonnaise, grated onion, and shredded cheese, either Parmesan or Gruyère, and a sprinkle of salt. Tonight it was Gruyère, of course. A little dusting of paprika and then put in the broiler until bubbling and golden.

"And now that Sebastian's here," Robert continued, "it's made my time at home all the more relaxing and healthful—he's taken a lot of the day-to-day business-management burdens off my shoulders. I used to have to spend hours on the phone with my agent and my business manager and now Sebastian does a lot of that for me. I don't know what I did without you."

The men smiled at each other. It would be easy to leap to the obvious conclusion that they were lovers. But frankly, I wasn't so sure, and to be perfectly honest, I didn't care. I was fascinated at how Sebastian had insinuated himself into such an insider caretaker role. He was after more than jewelry. He clearly intended to gain—or possibly already had gained—control over Robert's significant assets. I just hoped he wasn't putting ground-up glass in Robert's food. And I realized that was a major difference between Sebastian and me. He was a thief who had happened to steal jewels and had now moved on to a different target. I was a jewel thief. In my opinion, that put him at the bottom of the food chain, ethics-wise.

"That's wonderful," I said. "I can imagine what a help that is." I wanted to say to Robert, Have you lost your mind? Don't you read the papers. Don't you know people like you are sitting ducks for rip-off artists like him? You read about actors and singers and dancers every day who've been duped by their managers.

As I regarded Sebastian, I recalled Bernard Lafferty, the obsequious butler who had insinuated himself into every aspect of Doris Duke's sorry life and ended up by killing her through benign neglect and then inheriting her entire estate. Lots of people felt sorry for her because that's what she wanted. Poor Doris, so unhappy and so taken advantage of because she was so rich. I'm sorry, but we all make choices and make our own lives and it's just so much easier not to be accountable, blame our sorry mess on someone else. Well, Robert was a grown-up and if he wanted to hand over financial control of his portfolio and business, that was his business.

"What is your background, Sebastian?" I leaned forward in anticipation.

I knew whatever he was going to answer, it was going to be good.

FORTY-NINE

"Law and finance."

If I'd had an olive in my mouth, I would have shot it across the room.

"I was director of international banking for Barclay's for a number of years. And I read law at Oxford, years ago, of course. I retired from the bank, let me see, how long has it been, Robert? Almost two years now. But I consulted for them for a long time after that—I only retired completely a couple of weeks ago."

His expression was so innocent and sincere, if I didn't know his background was domestic service and thievery, I would have believed him, too.

"I imagine assisting Robert is much more exciting than banking."

"Indeed." He smiled.

"Do you travel a lot?" I asked Robert.

"Less and less these days," he answered. "It's getting harder and harder for me to keep my voice in shape. The older I get the more vulnerable I become to colds and sore throats. But I still do one or two major productions a year—always one at the Met and one at La Scala—and a number of concert dates. And I still record, of course. It's extremely hard work. People don't realize how heavy the performance burden is. They only know they've had their tickets for months and the tickets are extremely costly and hard to get. They aren't interested that I've been on tour and I'm exhausted—and in fact, they shouldn't have to be aware of that. They've paid for a show and I'm there to give it to them so every time I walk onto the stage, I am committed to giving the performance of my life. It's just that sometimes it takes so much out of me, I think it may just be the last performance of my life."

I smiled at him. "That's why you are where you are."

"You're so very right. I've worked hard my entire career—I've always given a hundred and ten percent and I've made an effort not to be temperamental, although I don't always succeed. But I love what I do. And no matter how exhausted I am, the second I fly over the ridge into this valley, it all falls away. I can put the whole world behind me and no one knows where I am. And more importantly, no one cares *who* I am."

Oscar refreshed our drinks, and the girl with the cheese puffs returned. Robert and I each put three more on our plates. Sebastian took one.

"Robert," he said, "you know what your doctor said."

Robert waved him off. "*Basta*. You're not my mother. I'll eat what I want."

Sebastian pursed his lips and looked away archly. I could tell he was biting his tongue not to give Robert a speech, or else he was working up to a big pout or throwing a big tantrum.

"I imagine that privacy is your greatest luxury," I said, ignoring the little kerfuffle and putting another canapé in my own mouth.

"It is as underrated as fame is overrated. I'm grateful to my fans, God love them, but sometimes fame reaches a point where it takes on a life of its own. There are a few of us who draw crowds that need entire police forces to manage them. It's ridiculous. I'm a *singer,* for heaven's sake. I haven't discovered a cure for cancer or performed any miracles. Do you ever watch golf on television?"

"Occasionally," I lied. I've never watched golf on television or anywhere else in my life.

"When Tiger Woods is playing, if you look in the long shots, there are literally thousands of people around him. They're perfectly well mannered but every single one of them wants to get close, to touch him, get a little piece. My fans are the same, they press in. It's unnerving. I don't mean to sound sacrilegious, but sometimes I know how Jesus must have felt. One of him and millions of them following him everywhere he went—the man could get no rest."

"Robert!" Sebastian said. "That is just over the line."

I burst out laughing.

"Forgive me." He looked at the ceiling and crossed himself and his cheeks colored. "But you know what I mean."

"I think I understand."

"I'm always so relieved to get home and let my hair down. There are a number of us here in Mont-St.-Anges who are victims of our success."

Oscar appeared in the door.

"Ah," Robert said. "Dinner's ready."

The dinner was in a small dining room, not the large one I'd passed on the way in, and the decor wasn't quite as heavy-handed. The meal itself was quintessentially Swiss and perfectly prepared. The first course was *capuns,* which are cubes of sausage in *spätzli* batter, wrapped in Swiss chard leaves, tossed in butter, simmered, and served with a cream sauce; and the entrée was a gorgeous, bubbling, gooey, pungent cheese fondue with cubes of crusty bread and a wonderful snappy Chablis. Dessert was classic apple strudel with pastry so feathery and light if you'd thrown it in the air, it would have floated away.

The three of us had a very harmonious time. We enjoyed each other's company tremendously. Robert regaled us with stories of living on the road as an international superstar, and Sebastian added his own adventures as a fancy international financier. He had an unbelievable imagination.

"I had no idea banking could be so thrilling," I said.

"Extraordinary, isn't it?" he answered straight-faced.

I asked him a few pertinent questions and could tell by his answers, he knew what he was talking about.

I looked at my watch. "It's getting late. I should go."

"Let's have one more glass of wine. I want to show you my house. Would you like a tour?"

"I'd love one."

We took the elevator to the second floor and I saw everything I needed to see. Robert's room was predictably Robert, a completely overdone, messy affair with a huge bed with old-fashioned bed curtains. A painting of him, in a smoking jacket similar to tonight's with a pipe in his hand, leaning on a mantel and looking regal, hung over the fireplace. His bathroom had a large Jacuzzi and an old-fashioned exercise bike that had a tall stack of magazines piled on its seat, giving the impression it was little used.

Sebastian's bedroom was a little slice of English countryside— loaded with bright yellow-and-green chintz, comfortable chairs, and piles of books. Off his bath was a serious gym with weights, a treadmill, a StairMaster, and a rowing machine.

Their bedrooms connected through a large central study with an oversized antique partners' desk that the two men shared. Flat computer screens sat on credenzas that extended out from the desk on either side in the shape of an L. On the wall above Sebastian's credenza was a Richard Jack painting of Buckingham Palace in the rain, the red jackets and black bear hats of the Coldstream Guards fuzzy in the mist. The painting stood fractionally away from the wall—so slightly that no one would ever notice, unless that someone were a thief looking for a wall safe. Tucked neatly in the darkness of the cubby hole under Sebastian's desk, I spotted the black briefcase. Ready to hand at the drop of a hat. I realized he must have his emergency exit strategies as well, and I wondered what they were. Like the Naxos apartment in Paris, there was no easy way out of Mont-St.-Anges.

"We'll see you tomorrow evening," Robert said when we were back downstairs.

"I'm looking forward to it."

I'd already told Sebastian good night and Robert walked me to my sleigh. "Let me take you home," he said. "It's no trouble."

"No, thanks. I'll be fine."

He kissed me on either cheek. His beard felt silky against my skin. "You are so calming for me to be with, Margaret. So down-to-earth and peaceful. I could spend the rest of my life with someone like you."

I smiled at him. "Robert. Are you proposing to me?"

"Not yet. But I'm considering it."

"Keep me informed." I climbed into the sleigh and shook the reins. "See you tomorrow."

I would be lying if I said I wasn't hugely flattered by Robert's affections, but I had a feeling he said basically the same thing to everyone he was fond of—men and women alike. He needed more attention than anyone I'd ever met.

Before I went to bed, I double-checked all the doors and windows and cross-checked my security system.

Something wakened me at three-thirty. I checked the video screens and nothing was out of order. It must have been the wind, but I couldn't shake the feeling that I was vulnerable. I went back to bed but wasn't able to sleep, so finally, at about five, I gave up, got up and made myself a cup of hot chocolate, and sat in the dark living room and ran through my plan for the dinner dance.

That was where I'd make the switch. Just smooth and easy during dinner, and Thomas would show up at some point, make a discreet arrest, recover the (fake) jewels—the real ones would be in my pocket by then—and once Sebastian was securely on his way back to London, escorted by Thomas's adjutant, Thomas and I would spend a few more days here in Mont-St.-Anges, eating fondue and drinking wine and having a little winter holiday. Maybe I'd even get those monkey gland shots. And I would have the queen's jewels in my possession and I would give them to Thomas once we were safely out of the valley.

That was somewhat the plan. I would make the switch during dinner, but the part with Thomas and me relaxing in Mont-St.-Anges? Pure fantasy.

I sorted through my cache of one-time-use identifications and then, a little after eight, picked up the phone.

"Heliport. Jurgen speaking."

"This is Mrs. Rogers calling and I'd like to book a helicopter to take me to Geneva later this evening."

"Very good, Mrs. Rogers. Approximately what time, do you know?"

"I'm not sure. If it could be ready to go from nine on, that would be fine."

"Nine o'clock it is. Your crew will be ready at that time and on-duty for you for twelve hours, until nine o'clock tomorrow morning. Come whenever it's convenient."

"What if it's snowing?"

"We use heavy cargo craft when the weather's bad—no need to worry."

I gritted my teeth.

I called the Hôtel d'Angleterre in Geneva and reserved a suite.

FIFTY

I fixed breakfast, sipped my chocolate, read the morning papers, and watched the news—there wasn't a sign of Thomas—called the spa and made a number of appointments. This would be a day of total relaxation—I was ready. I didn't even care if I saw Lucy, because I was set. I wasn't so immature or naive to think I was invincible, but at this point I was impermeable. On cruise control, as though I were watching events unroll from some point in the sky.

The morning was a sybaritic extravaganza—steam, massage, facial, shampoo, nails. I even had the low-calorie, spa fitness lunch and when I bundled myself back into my outdoor gear, I was relaxed and focused.

The doorman had Black Diamond harnessed and ready to go when I emerged.

"We have a little bit of sun, maybe, Princesse," he said, indicating the dark blue sky showing through broken clouds.

In fact, it was so bright I had to put on my dark glasses. I felt as though I hadn't seen the sun in months. I needed to satisfy my curiosity about something before I went back to Schloss Alexander. Black Diamond seemed happy for the exercise as we sailed through the valley at top speed. We went from one end to the other, all the way to where I'd watched the horse-drawn sledge disappear around a distant corner alongside the train tracks. The road ended with a solid metal gate. There was a small security camera in the trees and the gate was controlled by a high-end remote-operated electronic system, similar to an upgraded electric garage door. The area was cold and remote, tree branches drooped with their burdens of snow and it was totally silent. I couldn't help but shiver.

Much as I loathed the thought of getting back on a helicopter, this was not a valid means of egress. I didn't know what was on the other side of the gate and the area was avalanche prone. Between the trees, rocky, ice-clogged chutes plunged straight down a thousand feet from the high peak.

I turned the horse around as efficiently as possible and we got out of there and went home.

Barnhardt was occupied huffing and puffing as he shoveled the porches, so I drove straight into the barn, just as I'd watched him do so many times, unharnessed Black Diamond from the sleigh, led her into her box stall, and poured a scoop of molasses-oats into the small wooden tray attached to the wall. Then I went into the house—waved at Barnhardt through the living room windows, he still had a long way to go to get that porch done—and grabbed some carrots and apples and my Hermès travel bags. The little stable was warm and cozy and Black Diamond eagerly gobbled up the treats. She watched over the door of her stall with interest as I lifted the top of the storage box on the back of the sleigh and dropped my travel bags into the compartment and covered them with her blanket.

It was time to contact Thomas.

His voice mail picked up immediately. "This is Special Chief Inspector Thomas Curtis, New Scotland Yard," his voice intoned on the recording. "You've reached my voice mail. Please leave your name and phone number and I'll return your call as quickly as possible."

Wasn't that just like Thomas to leave a long message, giving his esteemed title and stating the obvious?

"Thomas," I said. "It's me. I have things ready to go and am just checking in to see where you are. Will you be at Robert Constantin's dinner dance? Call me at this number."

Moments later, my phone beeped.

"Kick." Thomas said. "Are you all right?"

"Of course I'm all right."

"Where have you been? What number is this? Where are you?"

"I've been taking my horse for a drive."

"What are you talking about?"

"I'm in Mont-St.-Anges where they don't allow cars, so I'm taking my horse, Black Diamond, for a drive."

"Mont-Saint-What? Where's that?"

"You don't know where it is?"

"No."

"It's in Switzerland."

"Where in Switzerland?"

"I don't know, Thomas. Where are you?"

"Milan," he said. "At Robert Constantin's estate."

"Oh, dear. You mean you really don't know about Mont-St.-Anges?"

"No." He sounded testy. "I really don't."

I explained to him about George and Alma Naxos and their super-private hideaway for the superelite. I told him I'd known about Mont-St.-Anges for a long time and that Robert Constantin lived there and not in Milan.

"Why in the hell didn't you tell me?" he asked angrily.

"I'm sorry but I honestly thought that since you're a detective, you'd find out fairly easily."

"Well, that's fine, Kick. Do you intend to arrest Sebastian Tremaine and return him to England? Should I just go on back home?"

"Of course not. I thought you'd be here by now. I know where the jewelry is—it's in a wall safe behind the Richard Jack in Tremaine's and Constantin's shared study at Constantin's chalet."

"Are you positive?"

"Ninety percent."

"And exactly where is this town?"

"That's the thing, Thomas. I'm not sure."

"Where do you *think* it is?"

I told him how long I thought I'd flown from Sion in the helicopter and approximately what direction we'd gone, "But frankly, that's a guess, I was so scared out of my wits the whole time. My God, Thomas, I feel like this is Shangri-La or something. I can't believe you don't know about it."

"What else don't I know?"

"Nothing." I couldn't bring myself to tell him that I was pretending to be a Scotland Yard inspector pretending to be a Romanian princess—that would have sent him straight off the roof.

"Call George Naxos." I gave him the phone number at the Naxos castle. "And tell him you have it on good authority that there is a world-famous jewel thief in Mont-St.-Anges and you're expecting him to make a move at a party at Robert Constantin's tonight. He'll tell you how to get here."

"All right. I don't want you to make any sort of a move in any direction until I'm on the scene."

I didn't answer.

"I'm telling you, Kick. Stay where you are. You've done what I asked you to do, now let me take it from here."

"We'll see," I said, and hung up.

This was good. Thomas would get here, just not quite in time.

I put on the artist's smock and messed around with the paints, but it really wasn't my field. I hung the smock back on the edge of the canvas and took a nap.

FIFTY-ONE

At six-thirty, I poured a glass of Champagne, and filled the big tub with steaming water and carnation-scented bubbles. I lay in the warm bath—the room was so quiet, the only sound was the buzz of silence—and reviewed my plan. The Pasha flashed prisms of light on the ceiling. I went over and over every step until the bath cooled, and then, wrapped up in one of my silk robes, I settled myself at the dressing table and set about preparing for my evening.

The machine in me had taken over, as though I were a general preparing for battle, a surgeon preparing for a major operation, or a soprano for an important aria. I smoothed back my hair with unusual art deco combs that had four rows of baguettes in a herringbone pattern and tucked a white gardenia and a small spray of shamrocks behind one ear. I took particular care with my makeup.

As soon as I looked just right, I laid the black corset on the dressing table and opened each of the pockets and removed the queen's replicated jewels and laid them out, side by side. Then I began to dress.

The corset, without its secret booty, gave me a very lovely, almost sinfully voluptuous hourglass figure. I hooked my black stockings to the garters and stepped into my dress, a black satin strapless ball gown with a skirt so voluminous it looked as though it would weigh a ton but was actually as light as a cloud. I clipped on white diamond earrings, and around my neck, I hung my pièce de résistance—originally intended to flush out Sebastian, if need be, but no longer necessary, of course—my own very good necklace made of sixty five-carat, emerald-cut diamonds. It made my neck look as though it were circled by a ring of fire. I'd bought the piece at auction in Geneva several years ago and was glad for the opportunity to wear it, since there are very few private white-tie dinner dances in Provence. From the necklace, I suspended the synthetic forty-carat teardrop-shaped pink diamond I'd gotten in Zurich. It sparkled on my décolletage like a frozen drop of pink Champagne. I clasped a wide diamond cuff over my black satin full-length gloves and arranged my satin evening shawl.

I looked in the mirror—I was positively majestic. Queen Mary would have been proud.

Finally, I scooped the queen's jewelry off the counter and dropped it into the deep pocket on the right side of my gown. I turned off my cell phone and dropped it in the left.

Drop into the left, take out of the right.

Time to go. I slipped the full-length black mink cape from its hanger and it whirled around me so it rippled like wings and settled gently on my shoulders. I buzzed Barnhardt to let him know I was ready.

"Your Highness," he said. "If I may tell you—you look magnificent."

I inclined my head. "Thank you, Barnhardt." I held my hand out with sugar cubes for Black Diamond, whose bright ribbons had been replaced with elegant black satin tassels. I kissed her cheek and then accepted Barnhardt's arm as he assisted me into the red-and-gold sleigh. I felt rather like Catherine the Great or the dowager empress of Russia as I set out through the frigid, snowy night to the ball.

FIFTY-TWO

I wasn't sure what to expect at Robert Constantin's dinner dance. I've been to a number of very grand gala charity affairs where the guests are garbed and gowned in glorious dresses and wearing sensational jewelry—most of it borrowed from jewelers in exchange for publicity—and the men have on obligatory black-tie evening attire. The opening nights of our semiannual Magnificent Jewelry Auctions at Ballantine's were always filled with such people.

But this was different—this was a private white-tie ball, the sort of affair only found in private homes, and most certainly hidden from the eyes of the paparazzi. I was dazzled from the moment my sleigh turned into the drive. Torchères lit the way and when Black Diamond stopped under the porte cochère, two formally dressed footmen helped me to the ground.

Inside the front door, a maid in a black uniform and white lacy apron lifted the cape from my shoulders and helped me rearrange my shawl.

"Mr. Constantin and his guests are in the salon." She indicated with her hand. I watched her take the cape to the same cloakroom Oscar had used the night before, the one opposite the elevator, around the corner in the hall leading to the kitchen.

Electrified torchères jutted dramatically out from the walls about ten feet above the floor and illuminated the corridor to the salon with golden light. It reflected off the gilt frames and mirrors. Mammoth, well-polished black walnut sideboards seemed to sag beneath the weight of gigantic Della Robbia-like arrangements of fruit and dried flowers. Everything was larger than life, just the way Robert saw it. The setting was grand opera at its grandest.

"Princesse." Robert took my hands. "You are so beautiful." He kissed my cheeks. "I was getting worried about you."

"I'm sorry to be late—don't tell me I'm the last to arrive."

"Not a problem at all. Here, let me get you a glass of Champagne." He removed one from a tray.

I felt Sebastian's eyes on me from across the room. He was visiting with Alma and Lucy Richardson. He was too far away for me to read his expression, but at that moment, I wondered if he sensed the threat, if he knew it was now all-out war, and I was going to win. He smiled at me affectionately, as did I at him. I don't think he had a clue.

I looked around. It was a small group of only forty or fifty. I've never seen more beautiful women in more beautiful gowns or with more stunning jewelry—gorgeous, enormous new designs as well as estate pieces that had been around in family vaults for decades, even centuries—only brought out for family weddings or occasions such as tonight's. It reminded me of a documentary I saw of a private dinner held by the queen and all the guests had on their best things. Jewels far too opulent and valuable to wear in public. Jewels that only a handful of insiders—royalty, old money and discreet superrich—were ever permitted to see. It was an inside look few get to take.

A small chamber orchestra played in the background. Oscar was nowhere in sight, which was probably a good thing—he would be a wet blanket at such a gala occasion.

"Margaret." George appeared, looking very distinguished in his white tie. The silver cross of the Order of the British Empire hung around his neck from its distinctive dark pink ribbon. A number of men had on such official awards and decorations, sashes and medals. If

George had had a monocle around his neck, he would have looked like a nineteenth-century diplomat. "You must have one of these." He handed me a twist of crispy bacon. "The girl told me it's brushed with maple syrup and then baked until all the fat is out of it. Have you ever had anything so delicious?"

I took a bite. "Never. But believe me, George, all the fat isn't out of it."

He laughed. "You're my partner in crime. Let's have one more and then go see Alma. She was asking about you."

Alma looked much stronger than she had two days ago and I wondered if she'd gone to the hospital and had those monkey gland shots herself. Her skin had good color, her nails shone with bright red polish, and her eyes were clear and sparkling. She had diamond combs in her hair and a necklace of diamond, sapphire, and emerald beads that was so extravagant it was outrageous. It almost could make the Cambridge and Delhi Durbar parure in my pocket look like trinkets from a toy box. She and I greeted each other warmly. Her eyes fell on the pink diamond pendant. "Is that real?" she whispered, holding up a cigarette for her little butler aide-de-camp, Cookson, to light.

"I think so," I said. "It's beautiful, isn't it?"

"Sensational."

Sebastian kissed my hand. "Princesse. So glad you could make it—we were about to call."

"I've got it!" Lucy said. "I just remembered where we met."

"Give it a rest, Lucy," Al said sharply. "You've never met her, all right? Don't bring it up again."

I almost burst out laughing at the expression on Lucy's face. It seemed the honeymoon might be nearing its conclusion.

At the far end of the room, tall double doors opened and a footman in a red satin waistcoat appeared. He rang a small chime. Dinner was served.

"Shall we?" Robert said, and offered me his arm.

The ballroom was too small to be called a ballroom and too large to be called a music room. It was the perfect size for this group. The walls were mirrored and blazed with the light from multitiered crystal chandeliers. Six round tables of eight covered with cloth of gold, votive candles in golden orbs, gleaming silver and crystal, and low arrangements of dark red roses were in a horseshoe around one end of the dance floor. A fifteen-piece orchestra was on a low stage at the other.

I sat with our gin rummy group—except for Sebastian, who was hosting a table of his own—between Al Richardson, who also wore an OBE medal, and George. I ignored Lucy. Whether or not she'd been the one to break in to my house, she had no role in this evening's caper. She flirted with every man who got anywhere near our table, presumably in an effort to make Al jealous or get him back for his reprimand.

The first course was served, and no sooner had I taken a bite than Robert asked me to dance. Then George. Then Al. Then Robert again. And so it went. Our wineglasses were never empty and there were constant smiles on all our faces. It was a fairy tale evening and if I didn't have a duty before me, it was the sort of night one would wish would never end. I kept checking for a sign of Thomas, but there was none.

Before dessert was served, I joined the exodus of ladies going to powder our noses. The small powder room under the stairs was in use with two women waiting, so I went up. Lights were on in the guest rooms, and I could hear ladies in both of them chatting, repairing their lipstick and waiting their turn. The opposite end of the hall where Robert and Sebastian's rooms were located was in darkness and their doors were closed. I lifted my black satin shawl fully around my shoulders and neck so from the back I had no skin showing at all, making myself as close to invisible as I could, and disappeared into the shadows.

I went to the door of their shared study, put my hand on the knob, took a deep breath and turned. The door opened soundlessly. I closed and locked it behind me. The room was in deep shadows except for dim light that glowed from a green shaded lamp on top of the desk and from the picture light above the painting that covered the safe.

I stepped quickly to the painting and gave it a little pull. It didn't budge. I ran my fingers up the sides—a long hinge ran along the left. A small spring latch at the top right kept it closed. I pushed the latch and the painting swung away, revealing the safe. I was surprised it wasn't more sophisticated. It was a simple electronic lock—simple if you had the proper equipment, which I did, but impossible if you didn't. I pulled my cell phone/scanner out of my left pocket, keyed in a series of commands, and within seconds, the safe was open. Navy blue leather cases with the queen's jewelry were stacked neatly inside. I ripped each one open and thrust the pieces into my left pocket as fast as I could, then I pulled the fake suite out of my right and began replacing them.

"What do you think you're doing?" a voice said behind me.

I spun around. It was Alma.

She was holding a gun.

FIFTY-THREE

"Alma!" I said. "My God, you scared me to death."

The fake Cambridge and Delhi Durbar parure necklace dangled from my hand like booty scooped from a trunk in Ali Baba's cave.

"Give them to me, Margaret."

"Excuse me?"

"I said give them to me."

I don't know what kind of gun she was holding, but it was big—almost as big as mine, the elephant stopper—and was made even larger by the presence of a silencer. Her hand was as steady as a rock.

"What do you mean? This is the evidence I needed, Alma. Look." I held out my hand. "I found them, the queen's jewels, right here in Sebastian's safe. And now they can be returned, and he can be brought to justice." I continued to lay the fake pieces in their cases. "You know, none of this would have happened without your help. I imagine the queen will even give you a medal for your assistance." My breath and hands were steady in spite of having a gun pointed at my head for the first time in my life.

"I already have lots of medals," she said. "Put the jewels down. I spoke with an Inspector Thomas Curtis this afternoon. I told him his agent was here on the scene, I even described you to him and he didn't know what I was talking about."

"What do you mean?"

"I mean, he said he had no inspector on the scene."

"That's not true."

"You'll have to take that up with him. He wanted to know where Mont-St.-Anges was and I told him, but I'm afraid I left out a couple of key coordinates. We don't need any police help here. We handle our own affairs."

I felt an icy presence behind me, as though a grave had opened. Sebastian. He stepped silently up beside me.

"Sebastian," she ordered. "Please be so kind as to take the parure from Margaret Whoever-she-is and remove that pink diamond pendant from her necklace while you're at it."

"Alma." He licked his lips. "Please put that gun away. It's not necessary."

Alma's eyes were dark and cold and I suddenly realized with complete certainty that she actually intended to kill me.

I opened my mouth to speak, but for a second, no words would come out. "Wait a minute," I finally blurted. "Are you telling me you're in this together?"

"Sebastian," she warned.

"Alma," I said, "why are you doing this? For heaven's sake, you're the richest woman in the world. The jewelry you have on tonight is far superior to these pieces."

"What do you know about jewelry? What do you know about being crippled and spending your life in a wheelchair?"

"Nothing. But I know you could be making a difference in the world." The whole time I was talking I was trying to figure out what to do, but kept drawing a blank. "Instead you have some silly little butler steal things for you?"

"I am not a silly little butler," Sebastian snapped.

"Alma," I said. "Just put down the gun. Let me take Sebastian into custody and let's forget this happened."

"Sebastian. The diamond, please."

"Now, Alma . . ." He stepped in front of me and held his hand out for the gun. His fear was palpable and I was impressed by his courage.

"Now," she ordered.

He turned to face me and his hands shook as he unhooked the pink diamond.

I had nothing to lose. I leaned toward him.

"You're breaking one of the first rules, Sebastian," I whispered. "You're trembling. I overestimated you. Forgive me for this." With that, I jammed my knee into his groin as hard as I could and shoved on his shoulder, making him fall back toward Alma. At the same time, I threw the necklace in her face with all the force I could muster and dove for the floor just as the gun went off.

"Oof," Sebastian groaned.

I scrambled to my feet and started running. Out of the corner of my eye, I saw Sebastian crumpled on the floor and then, across from him in a dark corner, behind Alma, I caught a glimpse of Oscar's unmistakeable silhouette in the dim glow. He'd seen the whole thing and wasn't making a move to stop it.

"Oh, my God," Alma cried. "Sebastian. Sebastian, are you all right?"

Out the door I flew. Down the hall. I tore open the door that I prayed led to the back stairs, and I was right. I closed it behind me and ran down the steps as fast as I could. When I got to the bottom I put my ear against the door and listened—only regular kitchen sounds. I took a breath to calm myself, went into the unattended cloakroom and found my cape. Then I walked through the busy kitchen as though I owned the place and down the service stairs to the stable yard.

All the grooms were in the tack room, watching television and playing cards. I slipped past, undetected, and went out the door. The stable yard was dark, filled with sleighs and surrounded by stalls. Black Diamond stuck her head out of her stall and whinnied softly.

"Thank you, you beautiful girl," I whispered. I crossed the yard and opened the stall door and took her by the bridle. Thank God she still had her harness on, otherwise I'd be in a terrible mess. All I had to do was find our sleigh and hitch her up. Since we'd been the last to arrive, ours was the closest to the entrance.

I worked frantically to get her hitched. It was too dark to be able to see everything I needed to see on the complicated harness. Without warning, the door opened, throwing a wedge of light across the yard. I froze and ducked behind Black Diamond and peeked around her. My heart was beating so hard, if I didn't know any better, I would have thought it could give me away. A groom came out, went to one of the stalls, and spoke softly to his horse, and then went back inside.

Finally, I got all the buckles buckled correctly and all the hooks hooked. I climbed in and off we went into the dark, snowy night—without benefit of headlamps—toward the center of town and the distant heliport.

I wanted to go faster, but neither Black Diamond nor I could see much, so I kept her to a medium trot. All of a sudden, flashing lights appeared through the snow. An ambulance. It must have been for Sebastian. I wondered if Alma had killed him. Wouldn't that be ironic? And fitting. And grand.

The emergency lights whirled closer. I knew it was an ambulance, but as far as my horse was concerned it might as well have been the Monster from the Black Lagoon or Godzilla coming to eat her up. She'd been raised in this valley and had never seen nor heard a motorized vehicle, and certainly never seen flashing red and blue and white lights, nor heard a siren. She went completely crazy. As the ambulance passed us, she screamed and reared, and then bolted down the road in a dead run. She was uncontrollable. I held on to the reins and the front edge of the sleigh for dear life as it swayed wildly behind her, frightening her even more. I knew there was a sharp corner coming up, so I tightened my grip. She never slowed her stride. We galloped full speed into the corner in a total panic. The harness snapped and the sleigh was instantly airborne. I sailed into the air like a doll.

FIFTY-FOUR

The landing knocked the wind out of me and I lay, deep in the snow, trying to get my breath and make sure I was still alive. The sleigh lay on its side a few meters away. Black Diamond was nowhere to be seen and I supposed she was probably back home by now. I tried to move but a searing pain shot up my leg.

"Ow," I yelled into the wind. This was a legitimate ow, not my pretend one from my fall in front of Robert Constantin's house. Something was seriously wrong.

I made myself as comfortable as I could. Someone would find me sooner or later, and while I waited, I tried to figure out exactly what had happened and how the hell I was going to get out of here now.

I'd overestimated Sebastian and underestimated Alma. How incredibly bizarre—the richest woman in the world needing to possess stolen jewelry. Money does terrible things to people and she'd let the bitterness and resentment at being an invalid consume her. What a total waste of life. Once I'd gotten over my little bout of being somewhat starstruck when I'd first met her in Paris and realized that she had a bitter, angry, unkind side to her, I forgave her that because of her life in pain and in a wheelchair. Never in a million years would I have imagined anything like this. And, she'd completely outmaneuvered me. She'd planned to get rid of me from the moment I mentioned Prince Frederick, Sebastian, and the jewelry. She'd set me up. Gone out of her way to befriend and assist me. To bring me to Mont-St.-Anges so she could control and eliminate me. I shivered. It was just too bizarre to comprehend.

And where did George figure in this? I couldn't even imagine.

"I bet this has gone on for years," I said out loud into the empty silence of the night. I wondered if some of the pieces she'd been wearing like that incredible, unforgettable diamond bead necklace tonight, had been stolen for her by Sebastian.

Poor Sebastian. He'd made a deal with the devil and gotten in over his head. I wondered if he was all right. I hoped Alma hadn't killed him.

In spite of my long fur wrap, it was getting very cold sitting there in the snow and still, not a single sleigh had gone by. Finally, down the way, I saw the ambulance's headlights, and as they drew closer, I started to yell and wave my arms.

"Help! Help!" I screamed at the top of my lungs.

Thankfully, the lights hit on the overturned sleigh and then me in the distance.

The paramedics waded through the snow. Once the formalities were over—Was I all right? No, something's happened to my leg—they retrieved a stretcher. After much whimpering from me—I've never handled pain well at all—they laid me on it and carried me to the open doors of the van where Sebastian Tremaine lay on a stretcher, a thick dressing on his left shoulder. He was bawling like a baby.

"Oh, good heavens," I said as they slid my stretcher in and locked it into place. "What have we here?"

"Sorry, madam," the man said. "But there's only a short way to go."

I nodded and tried not to burst out laughing. Before we left, they salvaged my two travel satchels from the storage box on the back of my broken sleigh and placed them inside the bay door before slamming it shut and leaving Sebastian and me alone.

"Well, well, well," I said. "Look at you, all shot up. Rather overplayed your hand, I'd say."

"Oh, shut up." He sniffled and tried to get himself under control.

"I'm afraid your brilliant career is over, Bradford."

He looked at me wide-eyed.

"That is your correct name, isn't it? Bradford Quittle, most recently of the queen's service? I think your next stop will be Wormwood Scrubs. I bet they have a lovely cell all ready with your name on it."

"I'd die before I'd go to that hellhole. And you're wrong. Alma will protect me—she has to. I know too much. And besides, I'm the only one who can get her what she wants."

"So it was you who broke into my chalet."

"Of course it was me—she was longing for that bow pin in your fur hat."

"Does Robert know about this?" I asked.

"Good heavens, no. Robert lives on the moon." Sebastian moaned. "My shoulder is killing me. I can't believe she actually shot me."

"Why does she do it?"

Sebastian looked at me as though I'd just asked the most ridiculous question in the world. "Because she's insane. Literally. Why do you think George keeps her out of the spotlight? She's mad as a hatter. You think Cookson the butler is there to serve her? He's her attendant. She really should be institutionalized. She certainly was off her dope tonight—Cookson will have hell to pay for that. As far as I know, she's never done anything like this before. I can't image how she got her hands on a gun. I wonder if it was mine. Owwww," he whined again. "This hurts so much. They should have given me more morphine."

In my opinion, he'd had plenty. He was starting to slur his words.

"How would she get your gun?"

"Out of my bedside table, I guess. I have a few of them in there. Self-protection only, of course," he added quickly. "I haven't ever shot anyone."

"Of course. How long has Alma been this way?"

"Forever. George doesn't want a hint of her condition getting out to the public, so they keep her heavily medicated and restricted to a very, very tight circle of friends. Even her close friends think she's just a little zooey because of her arthritis medication. They don't know she takes about ten Fluanxols a day for schizophrenia. Lucy Richardson knows, but she's just as crazy as Alma."

"You can say that again," I said.

"This is all a game to Alma, something to keep her entertained, and she just happens to own the ball and the playing field."

"Does George know everything?" I asked, praying he didn't.

"You mean about the jewelry?" Sebastian shook his head. "No. He hasn't a clue. He works all the time and then they get together for meals. If she turns up with a new bauble and she's happy, he's happy."

"Why are you doing this, Sebastian?"

"For the money, of course. I've got a couple of questions for you."

"Oh?"

"Well, for starters, who are you?"

But we'd arrived at the hospital and just at that moment, the back doors of the ambulance were opened and Sebastian and I were taken in opposite directions at the emergency room.

"Good-bye, Sebastian," I called as I was wheeled into a treatment room. "Good luck."

FIFTY-FIVE

A doctor and a nurse appeared, followed immediately by a portable X-ray machine. Pictures were taken.

"What's your name?" the doctor asked as he hung the films over light boxes.

What to say. I opened my mouth and nothing came out. What on earth was the name I'd used to reserve the helicopter?

He turned to look at me. "Are you all right?" he asked. "You didn't hit your head, did you?"

"No, no. I'm fine." I laughed. "Except for my leg, of course."

"Your name."

"Millicent Rogers."

The nurse made a note.

"Mrs. Rogers, you have sprained your ankle, not broken your leg."

"Aha. I might as well have broken it, it hurts so much."

"You're lucky. It's quite a minor sprain, actually. Should heal quite easily and quickly."

He gently lifted my shin and ankle and laid a stretchy socklike bandage beneath them. Then he tightened the sock around and carefully pressed the Velcro into place.

"I'd like for you to spend the night so we can keep you under observation in case you have any problems."

"No. I'm fine, really." In fact, all I wanted to do was lie down, my ankle was killing me. If this was a minor sprain I'd hate to experience a severe one. But I was on a march and I had to stay the course. "It's late and I'd like to sleep in my own bed."

"I understand. I would do the same."

He gave me a bottle of painkillers and his cell phone number. "Call me if you need anything. May we call a sleigh to take you home?"

"Please."

He helped me to my feet and handed me a pair of crutches. "Have you ever used these before?"

I shook my head.

"There's not much to it, once you get the rhythm. Try crossing the room and back."

After a couple of unsure steps, I easily got the hang of it. The jewelry in my pocket swung back and forth beneath my skirt and banged into my thigh like a bag of sand.

"They look quite smart with your gown."

"The latest thing." I smiled.

He draped my cape over my shoulders and carried my satchels to the waiting sleigh. "I'd like to see you again tomorrow afternoon. Four o'clock."

I nodded. "I'll be here."

"Have a good sleep." He waved and went back inside.

"Heliport, please," I told the driver, and swallowed one of the pills without any water.

The helicopter was about five times larger than the little one I'd flown in on, which made me feel much better, as did the weather, which was still clear. They put me in a special wheelchair sort of affair to get me up the steps, and helped me into my seat and fastened my seat belt as though I were a hundred years old. I let them.

The passenger cabin was warm and comfortably fitted out with soft navy blue leather seats and all the communications and entertainment bells and whistles that important people and executives require. I put my wounded leg on the seat opposite me and closed my eyes. I was almost safely out of Mont-St.-Anges, only moments to go. The engine came to life and seconds later we shuddered off the ground like a big ungainly bug.

I sat up and looked out the window. I wasn't even slightly afraid. In my pocket, the queen's jewels—the real Cambridge and Delhi Durbar parure and the Lesser Stars of Africa—poked into my leg, reminding me they were there. We gained altitude quickly as we flew down the valley and passed far above the Naxoses' castle and Robert Constantin's chalet, both of which were still brightly lit. I could only imagine what had happened when Alma had finally summoned help, once she'd pocketed the phony parure, the Lesser Stars, and my pink diamond.

What would she tell George and Robert? It didn't take a genius to figure it out. Here's what she would say: She and Sebastian had caught Princess Margaret trying to rob Sebastian's safe. Alma had accidentally shot Sebastian, and Princess Margaret had escaped.

I wondered if Oscar had moved from his dark corner.

I wondered if any of the guests would grow curious why there would be no investigation of a missing Princess Margaret, no all-points bulletin, no hot pursuit. But there wouldn't be. George would smell something awry, he would instruct Cookson to take Alma home and give her an injection immediately, and the entire affair would be swept under the rug. It either never happened. Or it was a lark.

Moonlight peeked through the broken clouds and hit the steep cliffs as we made our way through them. They looked beautiful and mysterious and while I couldn't see what was ahead, I knew the pilots could, and tonight, that was enough for me.

The pain pill took hold and I nodded off as we zipped our way to Geneva.

FIFTY-SIX

I must admit, I felt a little silly walking into the lobby of the d'Angleterre in an evening gown, mink cape, and crutches as day was beginning to break. But if I received any stares, which I'm sure I didn't, I ignored them. I love the Swiss. They never ask any questions about anything.

"Would you like a wheelchair, madam?" the front desk clerk asked.

"No, I think I'm fine, thank you." The pill had worked wonders.

"This way, please. We have one of our lady's suites for you."

There are certain fine hotels around the world that have gone out of their way to make sure their female guests who are traveling alone feel safe and secure. The Hôtel d'Angleterre is one of these enlightened institutions and has a special set of rooms reserved exclusively for unescorted women—they have extra security locks on the doors and hallway video systems. The bathrooms have extra space for toiletries, the bathrobes and slippers are more feminine, and there are so many beauty amenities on the bath and dressing room counters, you can practically open a store of your own.

I followed him into the elevator and to a warm pink-and-yellow suite on the third floor. The bed had a cornice with fat, regal swags of yellow satin held back with satin cords. Arrangements of pink and yellow roses were everywhere. The balcony opened out onto the frozen lake and the first rays of morning sun sparkled through the Jet d'Eau. He set my travel cases on the rack in the dressing room.

Once he was gone, I called room service and ordered grapefruit juice, croissants, and a pot of coffee. "I'm getting in the shower," I told the room service woman. "Please just come in and set it up in the living room."

"Very good, madam."

I closed and locked my bedroom door and then removed my gown and laid it on the bed, leaving the jewels in the pocket. I pulled the wilted shamrocks and gardenia out of my hair and then the combs. I balanced on my good leg and stretched my arms toward the ceiling as far as I could. I started to smile.

I'd done it, and no one knew who I was or where I was. The question was, would I leave it that way?

After a hot shower, I dried my hair, put on the soft terry-cloth hotel robe, and took the parure and the diamond brooch into the living room. I laid them in a semicircle around my butter and marmalade and croissants. I couldn't believe my eyes, they were absolutely magnificent.

The copy I'd made was technically perfect, and the synthetics exact as well, but up close, it was like the difference between new and old sterling silver: nothing could come close to matching the inner glow, the luster and patina that can come only from age and experience.

I hopped over to the full-length mirror on the bedroom door and put on the necklace. I pinned the Lesser Stars brooch to one side of my bodice and the emerald brooch to the other. I clipped on the earrings and bracelet. They looked so well on me—emeralds were much better with my coloring than with Alma's. The Lesser Stars—the Cullinans III and IV—particularly enchanted me. They weren't perfect diamonds, nor were they the largest I'd ever seen by any means, but they lay there, one on top of the other, with the incredible power and mystique of their African heritage, smoldering with their long and complicated history. I could almost feel them daring me to keep them, to add another chapter.

It would be incredibly easy to do. I still owned the little place in Portofino. I could go there. I could go anywhere.

I sat down, poured a café au lait, ate the croissants, and read the papers. All the while, the morning sun made the jewelry sparkle, sending little beams off the silver pots and flatware. I swear, it was almost as though this jewelry was talking to me and after breakfast, I was sorry to have to tuck it into the pockets on my corset. But this was no time to get lazy or casual about my haul. I turned on my cell phone.

I had six messages from Thomas. I called him.

"Where are you?" he answered immediately.

"I'm in Zurich," I lied. I still hadn't decided what I was going to do. "Where are you?"

"Mont-St.-Anges. I had a hell of a time finding this place. Are you all right?"

"I'm fine," I said. "Are you all right?"

"Well, this is quite a little setup they've got for themselves here, Mr. and Mrs. Naxos. I'm just leaving their castle, where they've fed me what would be a delicious breakfast if I were a bird. I'm on my way to the hotel to get something to eat and charge my phone—the battery's almost gone. It's snowing like hell—I've never seen so much snow." His words faded in and out.

"What?" I yelled.

"So, Kick, I'm very grateful you did as I asked and got out of here before the shooting started."

"Shooting?"

"It's been quite a night. Alma Naxos shot holes in Robert's study, trying to shoot a thief who was robbing his safe. Would you know anything about that?"

"Really," I said.

"Alma is certainly a brave woman. Sitting in that wheelchair, totally vulnerable, and having the presence of mind to shoot, even if she missed. I'm terribly impressed. And may I add, grateful she missed."

I rolled my eyes. She was as helpless as a cobra. "She only told part of the story, Thomas. She shot Sebastian. He's in the hospital. Well, actually, he's probably home by now, his wound didn't look that serious. Aren't you the slightest bit curious what Alma was doing with a gun in the first place?"

"She said she found it in a drawer."

"Sebastian's drawer. What happens next?"

"After breakfast, I'm going to investigate the scene of the crime, although I don't really expect to find anything. Alma said the safe was emptied."

"That's not true, Thomas. Alma and Sebastian are in this together."

The connection grew weaker.

"Say again."

"Thomas," I shouted. "Don't go to Constantin's house. Sebastian will be there. I'm sure Alma arranged for him to be picked up and taken home. He has guns. I'm afraid he'll try to kill you."

"What?" Thomas shouted as his phone went dead.

Oh, hell.

Love, duty, and conscience are terrible things, especially if you're having to choose between keeping the queen of England's best pieces of jewelry or rescuing your husband.

FIFTY-SEVEN

"Heliport, Piers speaking."

"Piers, this is Mrs. Rogers."

"Yes, Mrs. Rogers. Did you have a good flight to Geneva?"

"Yes, thank you," I said. "I've gotten my business done more quickly than I thought. Do you know if the crew that flew me in is still here?"

"Yes. They are taking off in about fifteen minutes."

"Would you ask them to wait for me?"

"If you get there quickly, the weather is closing in—it's supposed to get very bad here. Otherwise, I'll arrange transportation for you as soon as it lifts."

"No. Please ask them to wait—I'll get there as soon as I can. I'm leaving right now."

"Very well."

I pulled on slacks and a sweater and the black Bogner parka with the black fox trim, which I couldn't bear to leave behind in Mont-St.-Anges, and my Russian-style black mink hat. I checked to make sure my big gun and all my gizmos were in my tote bag. On my way out of the hotel I left my travel satchels, which had my jewelry in their false bottoms—I still had the queen's pieces in my corset—with the porter to put in his locked storage closet, and when I arrived at the private air terminal, I left my crutches in the car. I wasn't in that much pain anymore and they would just get in the way.

The flight to Mont-St.-Anges was a total nightmare, far worse than the first one, but I couldn't afford to let it get to me. I kept my eyes focused on the closed cockpit door and thought about Thomas.

Half an hour later, we shuddered to the ground in white-out conditions.

I hoped after today, I would never see snow or a helicopter again as long as I lived.

Piers helped me into a sleigh at the bottom of the stairs. "Gluhwein?" he asked once he'd covered me with warm blankets.

"No, thank you."

"Very well." He stepped back and saluted as we pulled away.

"Schloss Constantin," I said to the driver.

Off we went through the storm.

"Just turn in the service entrance," I instructed my driver when we rounded the corner into the enclave. I climbed out at the service door and watched the sleigh pull off. Robert must have been planning to go somewhere because the three big Orlov trotters were in their harness and ready to go. The door opened. It was Oscar.

"Is Sebastian here?"

He nodded. "In his bed."

"And Chief Inspector Curtis?" I started up the stairs to the kitchen.

"Just arrived. I took him to the upstairs study."

"Come on, Oscar." I limped as fast as I could through the kitchen and threw open the door to the back stairs. "Sebastian's got all those guns."

"What guns?"

"His bed table." I started up the steps. "He has a whole drawer full of them." I pulled my own gun out as I climbed. Oscar's eyes got wide. "Don't worry," I said. "I'm not going to shoot it."

We reached the second floor and raced to the open study door. I heard Sebastian's voice and when I rounded the corner, I saw Thomas standing in the middle of the room with his arms raised above his head. Sebastian, in his dressing gown, his left arm in a sling, stood in his bedroom door with a weapon pointed at Thomas.

"Sebastian." I pointed my gun, which was larger than his, right at his face. "Don't shoot him. Are you crazy?"

"Margaret!" He frowned. "Where did you come from?"

"Don't shoot him."

"Of course I'm going to shoot him—he wants to take me to prison."

"I said"—Thomas's voice was calm—"I wanted you to show me the inside of your safe and to ask you some questions."

"I'm not going back to England," Sebastian threatened. He cocked the gun and took aim.

I had no choice. I "leaned in," as the man in Zurich had instructed me, and pulled the trigger and fired. I shot Sebastian in the foot.

"Owww," he yelled, and fell to the floor.

"Run," I said. "Follow me."

Two shots from Sebastian's gun shattered the doorframe just as we rounded it into the hall.

We raced for the back stairs, but by now my ankle had gone all mushy on me again and I was having to hop. Oscar, God bless him, swept me into his arms and led the way down, through the kitchen and down to the stable yard. I heard the elevator bell ding as he put me into the front of the troika and then tossed Thomas into the passenger seat like a sack of groceries.

"You go," Oscar ordered. "You know how."

I pulled my yellow ski goggles over my eyes and picked up the reins.

Robert, all done up in his fur coat and Russian hat, bounded into sight. "Margaret! You look magnificent. Wait! Where are you going? Where are you taking my horses?"

My last sight of Schloss Constantin was of Robert running after us.

He couldn't believe what he was seeing. His prized Russian horses and antique sleigh were vanishing right before his eyes. "Oscar!" he yelled. "Stop them."

Oscar joined him in a few halfhearted steps in pursuit, but of course we got away.

As we turned onto the road, and began to pick up speed, Thomas struggled to his feet and leaned over the driver's brace. He put his face close to mine. "Who are you?" he called into the wind.

"Sit down and be quiet and hold on." I pushed him back with my elbow. "This is dangerous."

To my surprise the team was a dream to drive, easy and responsive, and we quickly disappeared into the blizzard. I guided them down the hill and out onto the main road, but I turned right instead of left, which would lead us back to town. Minutes later we flew across the train tracks and veered onto the service road and headed into the woods to freedom.

"You have to turn around," Thomas shouted, when the gate loomed into sight. "The road's blocked."

I pulled the scanner out of my pocket and seconds later the heavy metal barrier lifted and we tore through. As the gate came down behind us, I pulled my gun out of my other pocket and fired two shots into the air. Thank God, it didn't faze the horses a bit and they continued at their fast pace. After a couple of minutes, I let them slow and we could hear the sounds of avalanches thundering down and closing the road behind us. The woods on the outside of the gate looked exactly the same as those in Mont-St.-Anges, and I had no idea where we were or how long we'd need to keep going. Fifteen minutes later we crested a ridge and there was a small town, twinkling through the snow.

"Excuse me," Thomas said, and started to get to his feet.

"Please just be quiet. I'm trying to think."

He sat back and crossed his arms over his chest.

I stopped at a small farm on the edge of the village and climbed down from the driver's box.

"A gentleman, a rather large, black gentleman, will be coming to collect the horses and sleigh," I explained to the perplexed farmer, as I handed him several hundred francs. "Their coats are in the trunk. Will you care for them until he arrives?" He nodded. "Is there a train station?"

He pointed.

Thank God.

"Wait here," I said to Thomas when we got inside the small depot. "I'll get our tickets. Order us something warm to drink."

When I got to the small café-bar, Thomas was sitting at a table with two steaming mugs of gluhwein. I sat down with a whoosh. My legs had almost turned to jelly from the drive. It had taken an incredible amount of balance, strength, and concentration to drive that team.

Thomas slid a mug across the table to me. "Thank you for the rescue, Margaret. Whoever you are."

I stared at him blankly. I'd forgotten I still had on my mink hat and ski goggles. "Thomas," I said, and pulled them off and removed the dark contacts from my eyes. "It's me."

It took a couple of seconds for him to realize it was true.

"I'll be damned," he said. "You did it to me again."

I smiled and nodded.

"What about the jewelry?"

I patted my bosom. "Safe and sound."

Thomas leaned across the table and kissed me. "You are one in a million, Kick Keswick. And I adore you."

"I adore you, too. Thomas. Let's go home."

EPILOGUE

Thomas came into the kitchen late one afternoon with the mail. We'd been home from Switzerland for two weeks, and life, as it was, had resumed its normal, unruffled pace. Bijou was asleep on her cushion next to the stove, and I was making a ginger cake that would go perfectly with the Kahlua café we'd taken to drinking for our afternoon tea. The cafés weren't completely the same of course. The Swiss have a knack for that sweet whipped cream, the *Schlag,* some secret ingredient or technique that I think you need to grow up with. But my effort was perfectly acceptable.

Among the various flyers and bills Thomas carried in was a large ecru envelope with the words Buckingham Palace engraved in the upper corner.

"Look at this," he said.

"Open it up." The cream cheese icing had reached just the right consistency and I started to frost the first layer, the most crucial point in cake making, the point of no return when you cannot stop.

He took a paring knife from my rack to use as a letter opener, something that drives me right out of my mind, and slit the top of the envelope and pulled out a letter written on a heavy sheet embossed with the royal crest. He read it. He scratched his head. "Huh." He read it again and his cheeks began to color. "Amazing."

"What is it, Thomas?" I spun the cake stand and laid the shiny icing down like creamy satin.

He shook his head. "Well. I can't quite believe my eyes."

"Thomas."

"It's from Her Majesty. She's going to make me a knight."

I dropped the spatula. "No!"

He nodded.

"What does it say? Read it to me." I wiped my hands on a damp tea towel.

Dear Inspector Emeritus Curtis,

With profound gratitude for your years of service to the Crown and to Her Majesty, personally, and in recognition of your recent selfless, daring, secret service to the Crown, Her Majesty requests the pleasure of your, and Mrs. Curtis's, company to join her on Wednesday, 20 March, at six-thirty in the evening, for a private ceremony at Buckingham Palace, whereupon she will declare you a Knight of the Realm and invest you with the Order of the Garter. Immediately following the ceremony, there will be a small dinner dance with select guests and members of the royal family.

Yours very truly,

Bosworth Christiansen

Secretary

"Oh, Thomas." I threw my arms around him. "I am so proud of you."

"I don't deserve it," he said humbly. "I couldn't have done it without you. You did almost the whole thing."

Why quibble? I did the whole thing.

"I'm thrilled for you to get all the credit," I said. "Let's celebrate."

Thomas opened a special bottle of Dom Perignon 1993 while I finished frosting the cake. Then we went into the living room and sat in front of the fire and wholly consumed the cake, the Champagne, and each other.

Two weeks later, on March 20, the first day of spring, we left Claridge's in a black sedan sent by the palace, and drove the along the park, around Hyde Park Corner and through the private gates on Constitution Hill where we were subjected to a thorough, unsmiling, but very polite security search. I hadn't been in London since my escape to Provence almost two years ago and I was unprepared for how much I would feel its tug. It had been my home for over thirty years and the cool, misty evening, the daffodils blanketing the park, the bustle of the traffic, caused a slight pang.

And of course there was the extraordinary irony that I, the most notorious jewel thief in the history of London, was going for a private dinner with the queen of England to celebrate the knighting of my husband. According to the briefing we'd received that afternoon, unlike typical investitures, when as many as one hundred individuals were awarded in one large ceremony, this was to be a private investiture since Thomas's services had been top secret and personal. Tonight, there would be no other honorees and no outside witnesses.

We went up the grand staircase and entered the same small reception room that had been in the documentary about the queen's dinner party, the one where all the ladies wore their Family Orders, medals, and best jewelry. New Family Orders are established at the start of each reign and the list of who the monarch gives them to is never published. The Orders themselves—small, jewel-framed pictures attached to wide bands of fringed gros-grain ribbons—are seldom seen by outsiders. A number of family members were there and greeted us as though we were one of them. I tried not to stare at who had on which Family Orders, who was a Court favorite.

A very distinguished man in black knee pants, black silk stockings, a short black jacket, and white ruffled blouse appeared at Thomas's side. "Sir," he said. "If I may escort you and Mrs. Curtis."

He took my arm and we went through a pair of doors into an extremely ornate gold-and-white room. There was a long red runner and at the end of it, in front of two gold-and-red thrones, stood the queen, in a white satin ball gown. She wore the entire Cambridge and Delhi Durbar parure, including the tiara. I thought I would faint with joy.

It was quite a sight to see my beloved Thomas—so handsome in his white tie and tails—on the kneeler before the queen, her sword lying gently on his shoulders, investing him with the Order of the Garter, the oldest and most prestigious order, given only for the highest levels of service and to immediate members of the royal family.

When he rose to his feet, they shared some private words before he escorted her over to join me, where I curtsied deeply.

"You have a very special husband, Mrs. Curtis. I hope you don't mind my asking him to come out of retirement occasionally. No one could have ever figured out how to find and rescue my jewels but him."

"I don't mind a bit, Your Majesty."

"I still don't know how you did it or where you found them," she said to Thomas. "And I don't want any details, it's better that I not know. But I was hugely relieved when you said Bradford wasn't involved. He seemed far too loyal and kind to do such a thing."

"I don't believe we'll ever know who the real thief was unless you ask Scotland Yard to take it up officially."

She shook her head. "I'm glad to leave it where it is."

"I hope you've improved and tightened your procedures, Your Majesty," Thomas said.

"Indeed we have. No thief on the earth could make his way through our new maze of signatures and seals."

I kept the smile on my face and my thoughts to myself but felt the sidelong don't-even-think-about-it glance from Thomas. As though I'd try to rob Buckingham Palace. Really.

Once Thomas had seen Mont-St.-Anges and met the Naxoses, he appreciated the complete futility of trying to bring the case to any sort of closure as far as justice was concerned. While the long arm of the law could reach into Mont-St.-Anges, no one would welcome the media circus, starting with the queen. Better to leave it alone. He and I both knew that Sebastian was no longer a threat to Her Majesty's possessions. I was also confident that George Naxos had no idea of the games his wife paid Sebastian to play, nor that any of the queen's jewels had ever been involved in any aspect of his life. But then, no one knew everything that had gone on: not Thomas, not Alma, not Robert, not Sebastian. They all knew a little. I was the only one who knew the whole story.

She removed the tiara and handed it to her aide, presumably a more trustworthy fellow than Sebastian had turned out to be. "We have quite an interesting group this evening—more business oriented than usual. Very international."

We went into another reception room, also gold and white, where about thirty guests awaited the monarch's arrival. It was an incredible thrill to enter a room in the queen's entourage, to follow her and look at the expressions on people's faces when they saw her. A mix of awe and excitement. Except for on one person's face, where there was sheer bewilderment.

I almost burst out laughing when I saw Alma Naxos's perplexed expression when she saw that the queen had on the Cambridge and Delhi Durbar parure. I didn't know what was going on in that muddled, medicated brain but I'm sure it ran along the lines of *Where did those come from? They're in my safe at home.*

She was, however, wearing my large pink diamond pendant (fake), and I recalled what Sebastian had said about George and Alma: "If she's happy, he's happy." I wonder where she told him she'd gotten it, or if he'd even asked.

The Richardsons were there, as well.

After the queen had greeted each of her guests, Thomas introduced me to George and Alma. I could tell they had no idea we'd met. George introduced us to Lucy and Al.

"Oh," said Lucy, "I'm just sure we've met before. You look so familiar to me."

"I can't imagine where we would have met," I answered.

A maid with a tray of beluga canapés materialized next to me, as did George Naxos.

"Ignore her, Mrs. Curtis," George said. "She says that to everyone." He and I each took one of the tidbits.

"It was the strangest thing, Chief Inspector," I heard Alma saying to Thomas. "You know the woman who was trying to break in to Robert Constantin's safe? The phony Romanian princess?"

"Yes," Thomas nodded.

"I told you there was something funny about her, Alma," Lucy said. "Actually"—she turned to me—"if you had short black hair, you would look just like her."

"Really?"

George rolled his eyes at me and we laughed and then we each helped ourselves to another hors d'oeuvre.

"In any event, if you don't mind, George," Alma scolded, "I'm trying to tell Chief Inspector Curtis the end of the story."

"You have my full attention, Mrs. Naxos," Thomas said. He gave me a look.

"Well, she had rented Tinka Alexander's house and told everyone she was a painter—landscapes, I think. She actually had the temerity to tell me she was an undercover police officer."

Thomas frowned. "You're not serious."

Alma shook her head. "She was nothing but a con artist and a thief. But, the most amazing thing, when our police chief went into Schloss Alexander to see if the woman was by any chance hiding there, all was *comme il faut*. Except for one thing."

"What?" we all said.

"There was a painting—just a single one. And it was quite good, actually. It was a bouquet of shamrocks tied with an ivory ribbon. And, written across the bottom it said:

> *With my compliments.*
> *the Shamrock Burglar.*

Turn the Page for an Exclusive Sneak Peek
at Marne Davis Kellogg's Next Novel

FRIENDS
IN
HIGH PLACES

Coming Soon in Hardcover from
St. Martin's Press

CHAPTER 1

Éygalières, Provence

"You're looking particularly elegant this evening, Kick," Thomas said as we turned onto the road from Éygalières to St. Rémy on our way to a dinner party at the Balfours' farm in Les Baux. "Very calm. Serene, in fact."

"What a lovely compliment," I smiled over at my husband. "You know, in the last few months, since we got home from that extraordinary trip to Switzerland and I retired for good, I have been feeling secure. It's silly, I know, because the statute on my crimes doesn't expire for who knows how many years and, to my knowledge, Interpol hasn't suspended the international dragnet for me."

"No. But at least I can keep you out of their sights."

"And, there isn't a bounty?"

Thomas laughed. "No. No bounty. And listen, if worse came to worst, and you were somehow identified and apprehended, you've done such outstanding service to the crown over the past couple of years, I'm sure Her Majesty's courts would look upon you with compassion."

"Oh, wonderful—you mean only ten years' hard labor instead of life?"

"Something like that,"Thomas teased. "But I'll come visit you every day." He turned serious. "Kick, believe me, you're in no danger. I'd tell you if you were. I love seeing a contented smile on your face—you've earned a little peace in your life, a little serenity. Enjoy it."

Maybe Thomas was right. Maybe it was time for me to let up a bit, move down from my normal state of high-alert. But I've never been relaxed or complacent—after all, you don't get to be the most elusive and successful jewel thief in history by being, to use the vernacular, laid-back. My journey from an impoverished girl born to a destitute mother on the fringes of the Oklahoma oil fields to the sunlit existence of a millionairess well-settled in the legendary lavender fields of Provence had been arduous, dangerous, and meticulously planned.

And when I decided it was time to leave the game, I simply disappeared, and immersed myself in the luxury gleaned from decades of solitary, anonymous work. I vanished into the gauzy fairy tale world of the super rich who spend their days bathed in golden light and Premier Cru Burgundy. And, as if that weren't enough, a short time after returning to my Provencale farmhouse hideout, La Petite Pomme, I crowned my notorious career by becoming the wife of Sir Thomas Curtis, Scotland Yard's revered Inspector Emeritus. So now, when I was called to duty—occasional assignments that I accepted reluctantly—I worked for the good guys, on the side of the law.

Some may say I'm lucky—they'd be wrong. I don't believe in luck and I didn't get where I am by wishing it so. I've always believed in cautious, considered, controlled advancement, leaving as little as possible to life's inevitable vagaries. But it was true, I had earned time off for good behavior. Maybe I would lighten up a bit.

I leaned back and watched the beautiful countryside fly by, a slight smile played about my lips. "If you want to know, Thomas, sometimes I do feel as though I've quite swallowed the proverbial canary." I laughed.

What a silly, stupid thing to say.

CHAPTER *2*

Thomas squealed, practically on two wheels, around the corner onto the D-27, the steep curvy road to Les Baux. He couldn't resist revving the big engine of his brand-new Porsche 911 Turbo S Cabriolet and downshifting as loudly as possible as we approached each S-curve and then flooring it so the g's forced us back into the molded seats. (Occasionally, he'd miss the correct gear and shift into one too high or too low, which invariably brought on a whispered epithet. I bit the inside of my lip and didn't say a word.)

Oh, dear, I thought. Here comes trouble. A large convertible appeared ahead. A stately conveyance with the temerity to be going only double the speed limit, instead of three times. Thomas charged up on their tail and gunned the engine impatiently while I silently hoped the offenders weren't going to the Balfours'. But of course they would be. What else would a lovely, shiny, brand new, Meteor blue Bentley Azure—I mean really, there were only a few of them in the world, they were as rare as hen's teeth—be doing on this road at this hour?

Thomas stuck the nose of his car practically beneath the Bentley's rear end and revved again. It was unseemly.

"What shall we do, darling?" I said. "Just go ahead and ram him?"

"Don't be a backseat driver," he snapped.

I looked out the window, trying to keep from laughing.

Thomas was full of contradictions, and that's why I loved him. For instance, he claimed to be retired. It was a ruse. Retired people don't wear pagers or carry BlackBerries, particularly in Provence. In reality, he'd become head of Europe's elite international anticrime task force and had frequent hush-hush conversations and unexpected, unexplained absences. He was a genius, an intellectual snob—brilliant, professorial brain, occasionally absentminded. But, for all his cerebral superiority, he should never be behind the wheel of a high-performance, ridiculously expensive machine like this—the color was sizzling: *Rouge Indiene*—because he was an exceptionally poor driver. He simply didn't pay attention to what he was doing. It takes a certain type of brain—thoughtful and analytical—to be a chief inspector, not the gee-whiz, showboat, zip-zoom, tight leather pants mentality one typically associates with the owner of a machine like a Porsche Turbo.

"Thomas!" I screamed. I couldn't help it.

The two vehicles arrived at the Balfours' drive at the same moment, but theirs stopped just inside the front gate. And when Thomas finally woke up, he had to slam on the brakes and swerve sharply to avoid smashing into them. Gravel sprayed through the air, peppering the side of the expensive convertible like machine gun bullets and making the passengers duck to avoid being pelted by the stones. I even heard one of the ladies cry out. The driver frowned over at Thomas. "Easy. Easy," he patted the air with his hands. His accent was American.

"Sorry, old chap," Thomas called over jovially through my window. "Expected you to go on up to the front." We continued around to the foot of the walk. "Stupid bastard," he muttered once we were well past them.

"Nicely done." I patted his thigh when we rolled to a stop. I untied my scarf and shook the dust away.

"Thanks," Thomas said and patted the dashboard. "This is a great car."

"Hmm," I agreed. In my side mirror I watched the Bentley's owner bend down and run his hand over the mirror-like finish of his $200,000 vehicle, which was no doubt lacquered with one hundred hand-rubbed coats of something very rare. I think I even saw his chin quiver a bit.

Kick!" Flaminia, my Persian-Parisian friend with the world's most exotic appearance and the accent to go with it, ran to greet us. Her coal black hair was pulled into a chignon to which she'd added an enormous shocking pink rose from her garden. She had on slim pumpkin-colored silk slacks, a billowy black silk top, and a torsade of amethysts. "What a gorgeous suit," she said to me. "And I'm so glad you've worn that brooch. One day, if you wake up and find it missing—you'll know where to look."

I glanced down at my lapel—the brooch really was exceptional, part of my jewelry collection that was centered around grapes and wine all basically the same design but with varying stones and precious metals. This particular piece had nine rare golden South Sea pearls—ranging in size from twelve millimeters to eighteen—gathered into a stunning cluster of glistening grapes with garnet pavé leaves. They gleamed from the bronze silk of my jacket—looking luscious and almost edible. The earrings matched, single glowing grapes with garnet leaves and a gold twist of vine.

"Thank you, Flaminia," I said. "I never get tired of looking at it either. Tell me, who all is here this evening?" I slid a slight glance to the glamorous quartet that had emerged from the convertible.

"Oh, you know. Old friends, new friends—summer's last goodbye. Excuse me, will you?" She moved toward the new arrivals and extended her hand while Thomas and I stepped through the gate into her garden where, as Flaminia had said, old and new friends were already well into the swing of the evening.

The sound of the piano could be heard in the background, and white-jacketed waiters moved gracefully among the guests with cocktails in crystal tumblers and flutes of champagne. For some guests, this had been their first residential summer in Provence—such as the now somewhat defensive Americans from the Bentley—and for others, it was where they spent June through the end of September and then returned to their busy lives in Paris or Brussels or New York. Flaminia was considered to be the most gracious hostess in all of St. Rémy, her invitations were certainly the most sought after, and to-night as we gathered around her hilltop pool—a classic art nouveau aquamarine rectangle—the light of the setting sun bathed our faces in its clean, pure light.

Thomas and I were chatting with a small group along the stone wall where the terrain fell away spectacularly, vanishing from sight until it reappeared on the valley floor hundreds of feet below. When I say "Thomas and I were chatting" with them, that's not entirely correct. Thomas was. He was, after all, Scotland Yard's celebrity Inspector Emeritus. I, on the other hand, was looking around for the waiter with the bottle of champagne to come our way for refills, nibbling on a Beluga canapé, and eavesdropping on the "Bentley American" men on the opposite side of the pool. The water magnified the sound of their voices as it ricocheted across.

"I understand from Keesling Fowler that Ballantine's is going to settle rather than have this situation go public," said the man who'd been driving the car. He had on a dark green sport coat and tan linen slacks. "Apparently, Sir Bertram acknowledged that the jewels are fakes—and not even very good ones, at that. Someone changed the stones between when the Fowlers bought the necklace at the auction and received it in registered post."

Sir Bertram. Fake jewels. My skin was instantly cold. Chills ran up my spine and I think I stopped breathing.

The other man, who was bald and wore glasses with heavy black rims, didn't respond.

"You know as well as I do this is the sort of bad publicity that could put an auction house out of business," he continued. "Switching goods on the buyers. Didn't you just join the Ballantine Board, Logan? What the hell's going on?"

"The firm is definitely facing a number of challenges at the moment," Logan shrugged and answered casually. "A lot of it is just business as usual in an auction house. Nothing that can't be handled."

The man in the green jacket studied him for a moment before speaking. "You can't B.S. me, Logan. We've been good friends for too many years. Our kids grew up together. We've vacationed together. We've bailed each other out a few times. I want to know what's happening—you know you can trust me, it will not leave this place. I've got my eye on a couple of pieces at the fall sales but I'm not sure I want to bid on them if there's a chance they or their provenances are false."

Logan nodded again, and absentmindedly rotated his cocktail glass between his hands before answering. "If you want to know the truth, just between us? It's a hell of a mess. Fake jewelry is just one of the issues. The house has had a few irregularities in the paintings department, as well. At the third-quarter Board meeting last week we gave Sir Bertram till the end of the year to get the place cleaned up. He's let Andrew Gardner go—the Director of the Jewelry Department who's always been considered a genius—he's the one who put Ballantine's on the map in the jewelry world."

Fake jewelry? Fake paintings? Andrew Gardner fired? For those in the know in the world of Magnificent Jewelry auctions, Andrew Gardner was considered the ultimate authority worldwide, and to lose him just a matter of weeks before the major autumn auction season opened was suicide.

I'm not the fainting type, but suddenly I was dizzy. I saw lightning and heard thunder—although there wasn't a cloud in the sky—and then the world started to spin. The next thing I knew, I was under water. Bill Balfour had a hold of one of my hands, my champagne glass was still firmly clenched in the other. The serene, secure expression had been washed off my face.